W9-BOA-995

"I like you, Janie."

"You... What?"

Aidan took her by the shoulders and leaned his head toward hers. One hand traveled up and slipped around the back of her neck. He paused for a few tension-filled seconds and she wondered if he was giving her an opportunity to back away. Yet there was no possible way that was happening. She inched closer so that they were chest to chest. She reached up and grasped the collar of his rumpled shirt.

When his lips covered hers, Janie knew she was in serious trouble, even as it occurred to her that this shouldn't be happening for so many reasons. She was too...simple...in direct opposition to her life, which was too complicated. But then again, he wasn't the man for her, either. He was too complicated while his life was too...simple. And yet it felt so...right.

Dear Reader,

After reading *Mountains Apart*, the first book in my Seasons of Alaska series, my oldest sister, Shelly, called me up to tell me how much she loved the book (sisters have to do this—it's a sister requirement). After gushing appropriately and making her little sister feel awesome and talented and loved (also required), she asked me when Janie (the hero's sister) was going to get her own story.

"Janie is a grieving widow," she told me in a particularly heartfelt tone, "all alone and raising four children and suffering from postpartum depression. She *needs* to find someone—she *deserves* to find love!"

As a mother herself, I love how Shelly connected with Janie. Since then I've had more people "suggest" that I give Janie her own love story. I'm so thrilled to be doing just that.

Janie first meets Aidan Hollings in *Mountains Apart*, but it's a brief encounter and she is in no condition to notice, much less appreciate, the brainy, seemingly self-absorbed scientist. Their first (second) meeting in *If Not for a Bee* does in fact involve a bee; although it doesn't exactly set them off on the right foot, either. But the title reveals so much about this story because indeed, if not for a bee, these two would never have that first encounter that leads to many more... Literally, if not for a bee, they'd never get their happy ending.

And they do eventually (I'm talking to you here, Shelly). I promise!

All my best,

Carol

CarolRossAuthor.com

HEARTWARMING

If Not for a Bee

Carol Ross

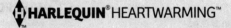

If you purchased this book without a cover you should be aware that this book is stolen property. It was reported as "unsold and destroyed" to the publisher, and neither the author nor the publisher has received any payment for this "stripped book."

Recycling programs
for this product may
not exist in your area.

ISBN-13: 978-0-373-36743-6

If Not for a Bee

Copyright © 2015 by Carol Ross

All rights reserved. Except for use in any review, the reproduction or utilization of this work in whole or in part in any form by any electronic, mechanical or other means, now known or hereinafter invented, including xerography, photocopying and recording, or in any information storage or retrieval system, is forbidden without the written permission of the publisher, Harlequin Enterprises Limited, 225 Duncan Mill Road, Don Mills, Ontario M3B 3K9, Canada.

This is a work of fiction. Names, characters, places and incidents are either the product of the author's imagination or are used fictitiously, and any resemblance to actual persons, living or dead, business establishments, events or locales is entirely coincidental.

This edition published by arrangement with Harlequin Books S.A.

For questions and comments about the quality of this book, please contact us at CustomerService@Harlequin.com.

® and TM are trademarks of Harlequin Enterprises Limited or its corporate affiliates. Trademarks indicated with ® are registered in the United States Patent and Trademark Office, the Canadian Intellectual Property Office and in other countries.

Printed in U.S.A.

Carol Ross lives in the Pacific Northwest with her husband and two dogs. She is a graduate of Washington State University. When not writing, or thinking about writing, she enjoys reading, running, hiking, skiing, traveling and making plans for the next adventure to subject her sometimes reluctant but always fun-loving family to.

Books by Carol Ross

Harlequin Heartwarming

Mountains Apart
A Case for Forgiveness

For my favorite moms—Granny, Shelly and the two Tammys. Thanks so much for your seemingly endless supply of love and support. I'm truly the luckiest daughter, sister and stepmom in the world.

CHAPTER ONE

"Hold still. I'll kill it."

"Wait…"

"Don't move."

"Mom, Mom, Mo-o-om…" Gareth stared with wide-eyed terror at the box he held clutched in his hands. Janie could tell he was on the verge of losing it and she knew the precious cargo inside was the only thing keeping him from succumbing to the panic.

"Honey, please relax. I will get it." Janie reached into her bag for some kind of weapon. "Do you want me to take the box?"

"No, Mom, I've got the box. Just get it… hurry."

"Gareth, please don't drop the box."

"I'm trying not to," he squeaked.

"I know, honey. And I'll get it." She began rolling the newspaper she'd retrieved from her bag.

The door to the bakery jingled as Lilah stepped out. "Janie, is everything okay?"

The monster crawled closer toward Gareth's

hand. He let out a whimper and Janie felt her own pulse of fear.

"We're fine, Lilah. Or we will be soon—a bee landed on the cake box but I'm going to take care of it."

"Take care of it?" a deep voice said from somewhere over her left shoulder. "What do you mean?"

"I mean," she said, "that Mr. Bee is about to go to the great honeypot in the sky."

"But that's a bumblebee."

"Yes, and this is a newspaper." Janie raised the makeshift swatter a little higher. Her hand came down in a lightning-fast swipe, but something nudged her elbow at the last instant.

She missed.

The bee flew up toward Gareth's face. He let out a scream. The box went flying. Lilah grabbed for the container—almost had it—but the waxy cardboard slipped from her hands. Janie winced as the box crashed to the ground.

"Oh, no!" Lilah exclaimed.

"Mom," Gareth cried. "I'm so sorry." Janie looked down at her thirteen-year-old son crouched on the ground, his eyes glued to the box now oozing yellow mush from its seams. Tears glittered on his thick black lashes.

"Sweetie, it's okay."

She turned and glared at the perpetrator, who

had caused this unmitigated disaster. "What is the matter with you? Why did you do that?"

"Oops," the man said. His crooked grin matched his feeble explanation. Sun-streaked blond hair curled around his ears—he looked like a surfer who'd spent too much time chilling on the beach. And he was wearing shorts? It was spring, yes. But springtime in Alaska didn't exactly call for shorts. The temperature was a not-exactly balmy fifty-one degrees.

"I'll buy you another one."

"That would be perfect," Janie said coldly, letting plenty of sarcasm seep into her tone. "Why don't you go do that right now?"

"Okay, great," he said enthusiastically. He looked at Lilah. "You work here, right?"

"Yes, but I'm afraid that's not possible." Lilah twisted her fingers together nervously, her eyes darting from Janie to the doofus surfer and back again.

"Janie, I'm so sorry," she said.

"It's not your fault, Lilah." Janie looked back down at Gareth, her chest squeezing so tightly she could barely breathe. His eyes were still trained on the mess of cake and pudding and chocolate. She could only imagine what he was thinking. His eyes met hers and it was all she could do not to cry at the stricken expression on his face.

"Mom, I'm so sorry. I ruined it. I ruin everything."

"Gareth—"

"Hey, I think we might be overreacting here, huh?" Beach Bum pulled his wallet out of one of the numerous pockets decorating his cargo shorts. "Is it your birthday, sport? I'll buy you any kind of cake you want."

Sport? Who calls a thirteen-year-old sport? Janie looked at him again—really looked this time—and noticed a pair of laughter-filled gray-blue eyes set in a tanned face, a perfect match to his boy-band hair. Tourists, she thought with disgust, were a blessing and a curse. She loved her brother, Bering, and sister-in-law, Emily, for enticing them here, but sometimes she wished out-of-towners would stay away. Today, obviously, was one of those days.

She wanted to tell him to go away and let her clean up the mess he'd made, although she had no idea how she was going to do that... Poor Gareth. And Reagan would be disappointed, too.

"I'd really like to replace the cake. But that bee didn't deserve—"

"Thanks, but no, I've got this."

"No, really I can—"

Janie felt her scalp begin to tingle with anger. She needed him gone, but apparently he needed some encouragement in that direction. She lifted a hand and interrupted. "No, thank you. You have done more than enough—*really*."

But he still didn't move. Just stood there, watching, as if he wasn't sure what to say.

She wasn't normally one to lose her temper, but he'd completely ruined their day—*this* day. This already difficult, excruciatingly painful day... What were they going to do now? How would they get through it without Boston cream pie?

"Why is it impossible to get another cake?" he asked Lilah.

"Oh, um, because it's a special-order dessert."

"Can't you special-make another one?"

"No," Lilah said with a sad shake of her head.

"Why not?" He asked with that same light-hearted tone.

"I don't have any more—"

Janie turned toward him. "Look, I don't want to be rude but I feel like you're kind of forcing me to be, so will you please just go away? You can't fix this."

"But I want to and I think—"

"*I* think you missed your turn a few thousand miles ago—the beach you're looking for is south of here. Take a right at Canada and keep driving until you see a sign that says California. Now go... Skedaddle." She shooed him with a hand and then stooped to put her arm around Gareth.

"Skedaddle?" His eyes widened as he raised his hands in a defensive gesture. But his lips were twitching like they were all taking part in some big funny practical joke. "Maybe we all need to chill out a little, huh? I was only trying to save the bumblebee."

"What?" she snapped. He did *not* just tell her to chill out...

"The bee," he repeated.

Something dawned on Janie. Bees... Shhh-oot, she thought. Today was Thursday... She squeezed her eyes shut for a few seconds. Could this day possibly get any worse? She stood, nudging Gareth to his feet along with her.

She studied the man now and wished with all of her might that this wasn't happening. She didn't know why she still made wishes because she knew very well they didn't come true. But why couldn't she have recognized him sooner?

She sighed and decided to get this over with. "Aidan, right? Dr. Aidan Hollings?"

"Uh, yeah," he said, his brows scooting upward with surprise. His eyes narrowed as they traveled over her. "Do I know you?"

"Sort of." She attempted a smile. She imagined it looked more like a grimace and really didn't care. "We've met. About two years ago. Your sister is married to my brother. I'm Janie Everett—Bering James's sister?"

BERING'S SISTER? AIDAN HOLLINGS stared at the woman and absolutely for the life of him could not reconcile his memory of the hausfrau he'd met two years ago with this attractive yet prickly, helicopter mom standing in front of him. This wasn't Janie. Janie was plain and boring and… quiet. He wanted to laugh out loud, and probably would have if he wasn't so shocked. The hair color seemed right, though—that shade of deep red was rather unforgettable…and maybe the only characteristic about her that he could clearly recall.

"Hey," he said, getting his brain back on track. "Janie, how have you been?"

"Better," she answered tightly.

"What?"

"I've been better." Her tone was dismissive as she flicked her eyes away.

She addressed the baker. "Lilah, I'm so sorry about the mess."

Lilah smiled sadly. "Don't worry about it, Janie. I'll have Isaac clean it up. That's what we hired him for."

Janie checked the watch on her wrist. "We need to go. Thanks so much, Lilah. The cake *was* beautiful."

Gareth looked at Lilah. "I'm sorry about the cake, too."

Lilah reached out a hand and squeezed his shoulder. "It's okay, hon. I'm sorry, too, for you."

Janie glanced in Aidan's general direction but didn't even try for eye contact. "Bye, I'm sure we'll see you around, Aidan."

Aidan thought these people were getting awfully worked up over a dessert. He watched Janie and her forlorn son trudge down the street like they were headed to a funeral...

Odd.

Lilah turned and grasped the door handle.

"Hey, um, Lilah, right?"

She spun back around and scowled at him. "Yes."

"Why can't you make another dessert?" he asked again.

"Because Reagan is lactose intolerant so I made that one with soy milk. Besides, it's too late. I could never have another one done in time." She looked near tears as she turned away and ducked back inside the bakery.

Aidan shivered lightly as a cool breeze swirled around his legs. He stood on the street wishing he would have packed some pants in his carry-on bag and wondering if he'd somehow landed on another planet instead of the remote little town of Rankins, Alaska.

JANIE DID HER best to salvage the evening. She and Gareth swung by the grocery store and picked up a package of festively decorated, dairy-free cupcakes. At least her two-year-old twins would be happy. Gabe had this adorable habit of carefully picking off sprinkles with his tiny fingers one at a time. She mentioned this to Gareth and joked about the mess they would make with the frosting. Her attempts to cheer her oldest son fell disappointingly flat.

Janie let the silence fill the car as she drove them home. She knew she should say something—offer words of wisdom and comfort. She was a mother—weren't these things supposed to come to her effortlessly? In natural, normal-type moments they seemed to, but she felt completely inept when it came to this… Probably because there wasn't anything natural about your husband and the father of your two boys getting killed in the prime of his life while you were pregnant with two more.

A snap of the fingers and she'd gone from a happily married mother of two with twins on the way to a devastated, grief-stricken widow and single mother of four. And then, as if Cal's death hadn't stolen virtually every bit of her joy, a difficult pregnancy had leeched away what little remained. She'd ended up bedridden with pre-eclampsia, the twins had been born premature, and she'd immediately sunk into that cruel pit of despair known as postpartum depression. She could barely think about that nightmarish time without being overwhelmed with guilt or growing cold with the fear that those feelings might somehow return...

She pulled into the driveway of their home—the home she and Cal had so lovingly built the year after they were married. They'd been so excited to purchase the property a mere half mile from her mom's. They'd poured countless hours into constructing the modest Arts-and-Crafts-style house, doing most of the work themselves—with help from family and friends—all the while making plans to fill it with the family they wanted to have. Well, they'd managed to get a good start on the family part before Cal had died. Now it was a struggle to keep up with the care and maintenance the three-bedroom home and the five acres of ground required. She wouldn't be able to do it at all if it wasn't for the help of her family.

She turned toward Gareth to say...something—she knew she needed to say something. But he was already climbing out of the car. Her mom met them at the door. Janie didn't know how she'd survive without her mother—how any of them would survive. Grandma Claire had watched the younger boys while she and Gareth went to town to run a few errands, which included picking up the now-trashed dessert for the birthday celebration her oldest son insisted they have for his deceased father.

Janie wanted to cry.

"Hey," Claire said. "Where's the birthday cake?"

"It's ruined," Gareth said. "I ruined it. I dropped it, Grandma."

"Gareth, *you* didn't ruin it." *No, the bee patrol ruined it,* she wanted to say, as she allowed her anger over the incident to overrule the despair. "It was an accident." She looked at her mom. "There was a bee—"

Claire's face turned white as her eyes darted from Janie to her grandson. "You didn't get stung, did you?" She smiled—or tried to. "Of course you didn't—you wouldn't be here if you'd been stung. You'd be at the hospital."

Reagan walked into the kitchen, where they were now gathered. "Hey, where's the cake?" he asked.

"We didn't get it," Gareth said.

"What? Why?"

Janie answered, "There was an accident."

"What kind of accident? A car accident? Are you guys okay?"

"No, Reagan, honey—an accident where the cake got ruined."

"Oh." His face fell, displaying his disappointment. "How are we going to celebrate now?"

"I think under the circumstances your dad

would understand. We picked up some cupcakes. We'll use those. Come on—let's go sit at the table."

Claire offered, "I'll bring in the cupcakes if you want to round up the little guys."

Finn toddled into the kitchen and let out a happy squeal at the sight of his mother. Janie scooped him up and kissed his velvety soft cheek. The thought flitted through her brain that at least the twins had been spared having to grieve for their father. They'd never known him. She immediately felt guilty—her signature emotion these days, it seemed. Of course it was better that Gareth and Reagan had known Cal for at least those precious early years. He'd been an excellent father, but it had just been so incredibly difficult to watch them suffer after his death—to watch them suffer still.

She secured the twins in their high chairs and took a seat. Claire walked into the room with the cupcakes neatly arranged on a platter. Brightly colored candles poked out of the frosting-covered peak of each cupcake. At least they looked pretty, which was something because Janie was certain the prepackaged, dairy-free treats would taste like cardboard slathered with sugar-infused shortening.

Claire handed Gareth some matches. He began lighting the candles.

Gabe pointed and chirped, "Cup-cup."

Finn slapped his high-chair tray and laughed with delight as if his brother had told a hilarious joke. At two years of age, they already shared some kind of secret twin language.

"Mom, how many birthdays did you and Dad celebrate with Boston cream pie?" Reagan asked.

"Twelve," Janie said and heard her voice crack. She tried to cover the sound with a cough. "I made your dad his first one while we were still in high school."

Gareth turned his head and glanced out the window.

Her mom began singing the birthday song and she, Gareth and Reagan joined in. The twins shouted out their own joyous version of gibberish.

Reagan and Gareth blew out the candles as the twins blew raspberries and clapped with happy, reckless abandon. Gareth placed the cupcakes on small dessert plates and Claire added a generous dollop of "rice cream" next to Reagan's and then dished up ice cream for the rest of them. Janie set a plate before each of the twins.

Janie and Gareth shared a smile as Finn immediately picked off a single sprinkle and examined it before delicately placing the candy bit on his tongue.

Janie swallowed her tears. She needed to be

strong—she had to be strong for the boys. Three years had passed since Cal had been killed and she felt like she'd recovered as much as she possibly could, but the boys...

At times she thought they were doing well, for the most part—except maybe Gareth. He had these rituals—this birthday party for his father being one. He'd devised a ritual of some sort for virtually every holiday. The counselor had told her repeatedly that sometimes the grieving process could take a while. "You can't rush it," she said. "Don't try too hard," she advised. Gareth needed to somehow reach that elusive step of acceptance on his own. Janie wished there was some way of gauging how close he was because sometimes she had the feeling he might be sliding backward...

AFTER THE BAKERY FIASCO, Aidan strolled down the street trying to get a feel for the town that, as of today, he would be calling his home base for a while. His baggage had been left in Anchorage, but was supposed to be arriving on a small charter flight in a of couple hours and he didn't see the sense in calling his sister, Emily, to pick him up until the luggage arrived.

Aidan's purpose in accepting this position as head of the state of Alaska's native-bee-population study was multifaceted. He'd earned his doctorate in botany and had spent the bulk of his career traveling the world studying endangered plant species. As such, he had a particular interest in bees and other pollinators.

He'd spent most of his adult life living in tropical locations and enjoyed the adventures, but lately he'd begun to crave a break from the heat. So when the opportunity to spend the spring and summer in Alaska arose, the change of climate had been enticing.

Aidan worked for various environmental foundations, nature preservation organizations and sometimes corporations or even governments of foreign nations. And for the last several years he and his colleague Blake Tryce had spent every spare moment on a film project highlighting the plight of endangered plant species. After attempting and failing to secure funding, he and Blake had financed the project and persevered. *Seeds* was finally finished. And while their goal in making the film was to inform and educate, *Seeds* had recently become the talk of the scientific community—and beyond.

Blake was ecstatic, Aidan not so much. He was grateful, on one hand, to be successful in spreading their message, but he'd never been thrilled with what came along with his pseudo fame. As a successful, renowned scientist he was continually turning down event invitations, public-speaking engagements and interviews as it was. The few he accepted, he chose very carefully. The added interest from *Seeds* had increased this kind of attention exponentially.

One particularly bad experience a couple years ago had left him especially wary and...beleaguered. He was in no hurry to make the same mistake twice. He needed a break and Alaska felt like the place to take it.

Not only did Emily now call Rankins home, but three months ago she and her husband, Bering, had also welcomed the first addition to their family—a baby girl they'd named Violet. Aidan couldn't wait to meet his new niece.

Hmm, he thought, he and Janie shared a niece. This family connection could conceivably be a little uncomfortable, especially when he already knew from Emily how close the James family was—the entire extended family. Unfortunate, running into each other under those circumstances...

Aidan kept walking partially to keep warm but also because the quaint town intrigued him. Rankins was small, but not too small. Comparatively, his field work as a botanist meant camping in the rain forest for weeks on end with nothing but a couple of tents and maybe another scientist or two for hundreds of miles in any one direction. Those conditions had a way of changing one's view of "civilization." To Aidan, Rankins seemed to have the right amount of everything, including a decided lack of one thing he tried to avoid—people.

Food seemed plentiful, too, he realized happily as his nose alerted him to the fact that someone was serving up a hot meal. He hadn't eaten since very early that morning, when he'd changed planes at LAX.

Ah...the idea of being able to get food whenever he wanted—and not something freeze-dried that became edible only when doused with water. Living in remote locations like he normally did, he couldn't always be choosy about meals, but it sure made him appreciate a good one.

He opened the door to the Cozy Caribou and stood for a few seconds enjoying the delicious aromas assaulting his senses—bacon? Yes. And the yeasty smell of fresh baked bread...

Emily had told him about this place, had mentioned that she thought he would like it. She was right; he hadn't even sat down yet and he liked the cozy feel of the restaurant already—the smells, the sounds, the friendly faces. All of the faces in Rankins had been friendly so far. Well, except for Janie's, and her son's, and Lilah the forlorn baker's.

Aidan found an empty booth and decided it was a good omen that he'd already seen his first bee, even if he'd angered his...? What was she? His sister-in-law? No, but she was Emily's sister-in-law. He thought about the episode again for a moment. He couldn't think of a better way that he could have handled the situation. He hadn't had time to talk her out of it—she'd already made up her mind to go for the kill, but he couldn't very well let her run around town murdering the very creatures he was committed to saving.

LATE THAT SAME evening Gareth stared into the darkness, waiting for the sound of his little brother's sleep. Reagan didn't know it, but he snored—softly. Not enough to keep Gareth awake but enough for him to know when Reagan was asleep and when he was faking.

So annoying that he had to share a room with his little brother at all. His friend Abe didn't have to share with anyone and he had a room easily three times the size of Gareth and Reagan's. Abe had a TV, too, and three different game systems.

Abe also had a dad. Gareth would trade all of that and more to have his dad again…

There it was—the snore. Gareth waited a few more minutes to be sure and then slipped out of bed. That was one nice thing about sharing with Reagan—once he was out, he was out.

He retrieved the flashlight he kept under his bed, directly below the secret stash spot that he'd made in the box springs. It was the perfect hiding place because even when his mom went on one of her cleaning rampages she couldn't see the spot. And when Reagan looked for one of his stupid darts or a Lego guy he couldn't see it, either. Gareth was proud of how well hidden it was.

He crept to the doorway, and paused to listen. He hadn't turned the flashlight on. He didn't need the light yet. His mom's room was right across from theirs and she always left her door cracked open so she could hear if one of them needed her. She was great that way. It seemed like if he or one of his brothers even twitched in their sleep, Mom would be there in less than a second. Reagan had had terrible nightmares after their dad got killed and *bam*—Mom would somehow know as soon as he started to whimper. Sometimes she would be there before Gareth even woke up. This was cool, but it also meant that he had to engage superstealth mode when he got up for these midnight raids.

He passed the twins' room and grinned a little. His baby brothers were so cute. Gareth wasn't sure it was normal to love his little brothers like he did, but he was grateful to them for existing because they had seemed to be the only thing that would get their mom out of bed there for a while. Maybe he should feel bad about that, like hate them instead because he hadn't been able to get her up himself. But he didn't. He had been sad after their dad died, too. He'd understood. It had been hard for him to get up sometimes.

He felt safe once he reached the room—the den. He wondered why it was called a den, because to him a den was where animals slept. But nobody ever slept in there—not anymore. His dad used to fall asleep watching football sometimes, but he'd never stayed there all night.

But the den was where Mom kept the stuff—*her* stash. But she didn't hide it very well. Gareth had first found it a couple months after his dad died. He didn't know what he'd been looking for when he'd found it. He hadn't meant to snoop—not really. He'd just felt so alone—felt that way still—without his dad. He and his dad had been a unit, a team—"simpatico," his Uncle Bering had called it. Gareth had looked up that word and it totally fit him and his dad.

Uncle Bering was cool, too. Uncle Bering had been what had gotten *him* out of bed after his dad died, but now he had a baby of his own and things were changing…

He froze for a second when he heard a sound. He exhaled a whoosh of breath as Crosby strolled into the room and let out one of his half meows. Gareth called it a half meow because Crosby opened his mouth really wide but only about half the sound you expected to hear would come out.

The giant black-and-white cat had taken to "helping" Gareth in his quests. When he'd first started doing this he'd been afraid the sound of Crosby's purr would wake his mom, but it didn't. It didn't even wake their dog, MacGyver, although he really wasn't much of a watchdog anyway. But MacGyver slept with Mom and that was good because Gareth felt that the dog would be at least adequate in alarming him if anyone ever broke in and got to Mom's room. Gareth thought about that kind of stuff because as the man of the house he had to be prepared for anything.

He stroked Crosby's soft fur for a moment. Then he took the key out of his pocket and unlocked the cabinet, still without using the flashlight because he'd gotten good enough at this that he only needed the light when he got to the stuff…

CHAPTER TWO

"WHY DID HE hit your arm again?"

"I guess he was *saving* the stupid bee," Janie told her friend and boss Laurel the next morning as she settled in behind her desk at the *Rankins Press*.

Janie felt herself getting worked up all over again. "I swear if Gareth would have been stung…"

Laurel winced. "Did you tell him Gareth is allergic?"

Janie shook her head. "No, I asked him to go away, but he wouldn't listen. He's not at all what you'd expect a brother of Emily's to be like."

Laurel sat at her desk, clacking away on the keyboard of her computer. "Wait—I thought you've met him?"

"I have—on the cruise two years ago, when Bering went to propose to Emily. I barely remember it, though. I remember thinking he looked a lot like Emily. Then I went to take a fourteen-hour nap in my cabin…" She trailed off with a helpless shrug.

Laurel glanced up long enough to give her a

sympathetic smile. Everyone in Janie's life remembered the dark days of her grief and postpartum.

"Oh, my gosh, you're not going to believe
this…" Laurel's ability to talk, type and listen
at the same time constantly astounded Janie and
the other employees who worked for her at the
Rankins Press.

Janie had begun working at the newspaper
part-time about six years ago, when Gareth and
Reagan were both in school all day. After Cal
died, Laurel had hired her full-time. She'd done
about every job at the paper, and now wrote local
and human interest stories, and contributed articles to the newspaper's regular feature, Insider's
Alaska. Nearly a year ago, she'd started writing
her own weekly column—Domestic Endeavors.

"I don't know," Janie said skeptically. "There's
not much I wouldn't believe at this point the way
my life is going and I—"

Laurel let out a happy yelp. "Sorry—hold that
thought. We got them. We got *all* of them—the
tourism articles. This is fantastic… They accepted
the entire proposal." Laurel beamed a smile in her
direction. "Janie, guess what this means? I need
to call Emily. She's going to freak."

Finally, Janie thought, a bit of good news. Laurel had already told Janie she would be contributing to the series of articles about Alaska if

the proposal Laurel and Emily submitted to the tourism website was accepted. *North America Live* was one of the most popular tourism websites in the entire world and they would now be posting three articles from the *Rankins Press* about Alaska.

"She is," Janie agreed with a smile. She found herself getting caught up in Laurel's excitement. She was happy for her friend. This newspaper was Laurel's life. The regular column Laurel had started several years ago, Insider's Alaska, showcased unique and interesting aspects about their state. The column had been receiving an increasing amount of attention in the last few years, so nobody would be surprised.

"I'll sit down with Emily as soon as we can and plan the series. I'll let you know what you'll be working on. Isn't this exciting? Global exposure, Janie—for the paper and for Rankins…"

Laurel held the phone up to her ear. "Em, hey! It's me—amazing news…"

"AIDAN, PLEASE. I DISCUSSED this with Laurel this morning and she's thrilled with the idea."

Aidan had spent the day catching up with Emily, visiting with Bering and getting to know his baby niece, Violet. Now he stared at his sister and thought, poor Bering. His brother-in-law didn't stand a chance against Emily's charm, not to mention those gray-blue eyes of hers that glowed with such utter sincerity. Add this to Emily's background, when she'd been a corporate executive for Cam-Field Oil & Mineral, and the result equaled unprecedented skills of persuasion. Aidan figured he could very possibly be the only person in the world who had the power to resist being suckered in by her.

"Nope. Won't do it."

"What? Why?

"Emily, you know why—I hate reporters."

"Oh, Aidan." She waved a hand dismissively through the air. "That's a silly thing to say. It's like when people say they hate the dentist. They don't really hate the dentist—they don't like having the work done."

He eyed her skeptically from where he sat relaxing against the cushy softness of Emily's new sofa, his beautiful niece dozing peacefully in his arms. "Yeah, I don't really get the connection..."

"I mean it's not personal."

His distrust of reporters was in fact both professional and personal, but Emily didn't know about the personal part. He'd never told her about Meredith. Emily knew he didn't enjoy being in the spotlight, she knew he'd had a negative experience but she didn't know the entire story. And she'd probably written off much of his hesitancy to his inherent lack of people skills. Of course, Aidan understood the point she was now attempting to make, but he would not cave no matter the circumstances.

"Emily, I came up here in part to avoid this kind of thing. I just want some peace. This bee study is supposed to be sort of a sabbatical for me."

Emily nodded slowly, her face a picture of sympathy and understanding. But Aidan knew his sister well. It wasn't in her nature to easily give in. He braced himself for another pitch.

"I understand that, Aidan. I do. And I'm so thrilled that you chose here to get away from it all and, and...rejuvenate, or whatever it is that you're calling this. But these articles are going to be such an incredible coup for Rankins. All I'm asking is that you let us do an article about you. If we could include you in this series? Imagine—a world-renowned scientist, the cocreator of *Seeds*, working right here in Rankins. Do you know what kind of attention that would bring us?"

"No."

"Aidan!"

"I mean yes, I do. But I'm not doing it."

"I know Laurel will agree to let you have total veto power before the article is published."

"There is no article. Emily, I love you. I am so happy for *you*—that you've found your niche here in Alaska. I never thought the corporate-executive thing was really you anyway. And I'm absolutely thrilled you found a great guy and I could not possibly love this tiny niece of mine any more than I do." Aidan kissed the top of Violet's fuzzy head. She was cuddled against his chest, her perfect baby cheek lying on his shoulder. He'd had such an incredibly long day of travel from Costa Rica the day before he'd like to tip his head back and join her—if only Emily would drop this ridiculous plea.

Emily dipped her chin, clearly gearing up for another angle. "But—"

"No interviews, Emily. No exceptions."

"Aidan, I've heard you say so many times that 'the media is a necessary evil' in your quest to save endangered plant species." She added air quotes but Aidan didn't think he'd ever actually made that statement, although he had alluded to the concept.

He carefully lifted a shoulder, so as not to disturb Violet. "There are plenty of people picking up the slack for me in that area right now. I'm not interested in contributing to the collective rhetoric at this point in time."

"Okay, how about this… What if Bering's sister, Janie, writes the article? She works for Laurel at the *Rankins Press*. You know Janie—you would trust her, right?"

Aidan felt a twinge of discomfort as he thought

about his encounter with Janie the day before. He hadn't mentioned the meeting to either Emily or Bering and he didn't really know why exactly. For some reason the encounter had left him feeling unsettled—like he'd somehow made a huge blunder. But he hadn't…had he? He didn't think so, yet he kept doubting himself.

Janie had been angry, the baker clearly distraught and Janie's son—who seemed way too old for that kind of reaction—had nearly cried over a cake. Something felt…off about the encounter. Too much drama. And Aidan didn't want any drama in his life right now. Who was he kidding? He never wanted drama. And for the immediate future he just wanted to study Alaska's native bees in peace and spend some time with his sister and her family.

"No, I don't know her, Em. I realize she's your sister-in-law, but I don't *know* her. Is she even qualified? Does she have a journalism degree?"

"Well, no… But she has experience—she's learned hands-on from Laurel at the newspaper. Trust me—that's better than any education that money could buy. Laurel has a master's degree in journalism from Columbia and took over the newspaper right out of college. And Janie is one of those people who is good at everything."

"Really?" he retorted skeptically. "Everything?"

"Yes, really."

"*She's* a good reporter?"

"What does that mean?" Emily countered.

Aidan thought. "I don't know. She's so... mommy-ish."

Emily scowled. "Yeah, well, she's exceptional at that, too, Aidan. And I'm not sure what you're trying to imply? I'm a mom, too, in case you haven't noticed."

Violet let out a little cry as if to emphasize her mommy's point. Aidan shifted her from one shoulder to the other.

"Settle down—you're going to upset my niece." He smiled and lightly patted Violet's back. "I'm not implying anything really... Simply making an observation. She seems very... maternal."

"A silly one—why would being a mom preclude her from being a good reporter?"

Aidan sighed. "I didn't say it would, Em. You just don't..."

Emily rolled her eyes. "I don't what?"

Aidan let out a sigh. "I don't think you realize how excruciating this would be for me—that's all. And you have been much more than a mom in *your* life, Emily. You and I—we have *life* experience. Janie has lived here in Rankins her entire life, right? I mean what can she really know about the world?"

JANIE WASN'T EAVESDROPPING on purpose. She'd knocked softly on the back door like she always did in case Violet was sleeping. No one had answered so she'd let herself in, immediately heard voices, headed for the sound and almost walked right into the middle of the conversation. She'd had every intention of making herself known until she'd realized they were talking about her. And as the meaning of the words gradually coalesced in her brain, she'd stood frozen in shock. Eventually, she'd managed to turn around and quietly exit the way she'd come in.

If she didn't have to pick up Gareth and Reagan she would simply get back into her car and drive off. But Bering had picked up the boys after school, which meant they could be anywhere within a ten-mile radius around here.

Uneducated? Fine, so she didn't have a journalism degree. But qualified? Yes! She did have years of experience working for Laurel at the *Rankins Press*. What did *he* have? The answer immediately popped into her head—a doctorate degree, a lifetime spent traveling the world, articles published in prestigious scientific journals, television appearances and an important, soon-to-be-released documentary film… Fine, so he was more educated and accomplished, but that didn't give him the right to mock and belittle her in that way.

And *mommy-ish?* What…?

Janie looked down at her khakis, pink button-down shirt, sensible "comfort" shoes. She reached up and smoothed her hands over the loosely twisted bun situated above the nape of her neck. Her fingers skimmed over the dainty white pearls in her ears…

Well, crap.

She'd obviously made quite an impression on him the day before. A niggle of insecurity crept over her…

She quickly squelched the feeling. Indignant, that's how she should feel, she decided. So she was a mom, so what? Yes, it was a big part of her identity. But she loved being a mom, and raising four children didn't exclude her from being a qualified journalist. And Emily was right, Laurel would never entrust her with an assignment if she didn't think she could handle it.

She grinned as she thought about Emily's defense of her. If she didn't already adore her sister-in-law she certainly would now. But how could such a judgmental, condescending attitude belong to any brother of Emily's?

Janie lightly tapped a fisted hand to her chin and tried to decide what to do. She didn't like confrontation, yet she wasn't afraid of standing up for what she thought was right. And her fighting side was urging her to march back into the house and confront him. To tell Dr. Hollings and his overeducated opinion exactly which cliff he could jump off of...

Suddenly she heard voices coming from the direction of one of Bering's outbuildings. She turned and saw her brother and her two oldest sons waving at her. She lifted a hand in greeting and began walking their way.

"Hey, guys," she said, trying to dampen her anger while infusing some enthusiasm into her tone. "Did you have fun?"

Her brother owned a successful local business—James Guide and Outfitter Service—that offered guide trips for fishing, hunting, wildlife and glacier viewings. People traveled from all over the country, even the world, for Bering's excursions. Gareth and Reagan loved to spend time with their uncle while he was working—and when he wasn't.

"Mom, we went out to the cabin and through the window we spotted a bear with two tiny cubs," Gareth told her. "So cute."

"A bear already?"

"Yep, first cubs of the year," Bering said with a wide, cheerful smile.

Viewing wildlife never seemed to get old to Bering.

"That's great," she returned. "Spring is definitely in the air."

"Mom," Reagan said, "Tag is flying to Anchorage tomorrow and I need a few more things for my science project. I can't wait for you to see it." He fished a folded piece of paper out of his pocket and handed it over. He'd made a list.

"I can't wait, either." And knowing her eleven-year-old genius like she did, she would undoubtedly be blown away by his efforts. Reagan had been working on the project for months, but hadn't yet let her see his progress. He'd commandeered a corner of the garage and kept a tarp over the area when he wasn't working on it.

"What are you guys up to now?"

"Unloading firewood." Bering tipped his head toward the pickup, where most of the wood had already been tossed into a large haphazard pile ready to be split and stacked. "The boys helped me get a load while we were out." He looked at his nephews. "You guys can call it a day. I sure appreciate your hard work, though."

"No problem, Uncle Bering," Gareth said proudly.

Reagan asked, "Mom, is it okay if we go down to the river?"

"Sure."

She and Bering watched the boys head toward the river that bordered Bering's vast property. Bering removed his baseball hat, ran a hand through his dark brown hair and then rearranged the cap back on his head. "Aidan is in the house with Emily and Violet. Have you seen them yet?"

"No, but Gareth and I ran into Aidan yesterday." She hadn't actually *seen* him just now—only heard his insensitive comments.

"You did?"

"Yep, in town. I didn't recognize him at first, and we didn't really have time to visit." She vaguely related the occurrence, not wanting to rehash the finer details of the event.

"Oh…" Bering looked confused. "Aidan didn't mention that he'd seen you guys."

"Yeah, well—it was pretty brief." Not surprising that Aidan hadn't thought their encounter significant enough to mention, Janie thought, considering what she'd heard. That pretty much sealed her belief in her level of importance on Dr. Hollings's scale.

"Do you like him?" Janie asked. She desperately, and yes, selfishly, wanted her brother to say no.

Bering rubbed his chin. "I don't really know him very well, either. I mean—I haven't seen him since the cruise and I was pretty single-minded then. All I really cared to see was Emily."

Janie chuckled. "We were quite a pair, weren't we? You lovesick and me…grief-sick."

Bering grinned. "He seems like a good guy,

though. Emily is crazy about him, so that means I want to be, too. We've talked on the phone here and there, used Skype a bit, but I'm looking forward to spending some time with him to get to know him better. He's already crazy about Violet—of course." Bering paused to widen his grin and then gestured toward the house. "Come on, let's go in and say hi."

"Sure," Janie said quickly, "but why don't I help you with this wood for a few minutes first? Get a jump on that pile."

Janie knew Bering would never pass up her help and she wasn't ready to face Aidan when she was still so angry and…deflated. Touching, she thought cynically, how Dr. Hollings was so intent on saving bees yet had no qualms about killing a person's self-esteem. She felt a fresh spike of anger. Bering handed her a pair of gloves. She slipped them on as she walked over and picked up an ax, now counting on the physical exertion to calm her ire.

Chopping wood always helped ease her anxieties, like some primitive form of therapy. Although, it probably wasn't all that healthy from a psychological point of view to imagine what she began to imagine about Aidan as she gripped the ax, and began chopping the thick circles of wood into wedges small enough to fit into the woodstove.

"SOUNDS LIKE BERING'S chopping wood," Emily said a while later as she and Aidan stepped out the back door. "Come on, we'll go say hi."

As they walked toward one of the outbuildings, Emily pointed here and there and recited what Aidan was sure were some very interesting facts about their property, Bering's business and Alaska in general. But he'd quit listening because he was mesmerized by the sight that had suddenly materialized before his eyes. Bering and a...woman? Who was skillfully chopping wood like some kind of tiny, female Paul Bunyan. Suddenly she stopped and lowered her ax, apparently to laugh at something Bering said. She grabbed ahold of his arm and doubled over. The throaty sound carried all the way over to him and he wondered why Emily wasn't scratching this woman's eyes out for pawing at her husband.

"Oh, good." Emily smiled in their direction. "Janie's here."

Janie? Aidan felt a stab of surprise as they drew closer and he realized that it was indeed the woman he'd encountered the day before. She looked so...different—lively, vibrant and... happy.

But as they approached something shifted in her eyes, like a curtain being drawn or a sheet draped over a surprise. Aidan knew he was likely the cause and he almost cringed at the awkward moment about to unfold. Not that he was a stranger to awkward moments, but for some reason he particularly dreaded this one.

"Aidan, Janie, you guys remember each other, right?"

"Of course," Janie said. "I was just telling Bering about how we ran in to each other in town yesterday."

"You did?" Emily shot a baffled look in Aidan's direction. "Aidan, you didn't mention that you saw Janie?"

"Yeah, um…" he said, feeling tongue-tied. "It wasn't…"

"Gareth and I were in a huge hurry," Janie explained smoothly. "We didn't really have time to chat."

With quick little tugging movements, Janie removed the gloves she was wearing and smoothed the delicate-looking fingertips of one hand across her brow. Aidan stared at those same hands that had only moments ago been grasping an ax and chopping wood like an experienced logger. His eyes traveled over her as he searched for words to explain…

Emily commented on the pile of wood growing against the side of the barn. She and Bering began to discuss how much wood they'd need for the coming winter. The banal exchange slowly drew him back to reality. Winter seemed to provide an unlimited source for conversation around here he'd noticed. Some people he'd met at the Cozy Caribou yesterday had been talking about their winter preparations, too, which he found funny because it was only just spring. He commented on it jokingly.

Janie stared back at him, stone-faced.

Bering grinned.

Emily frowned. "You can't believe how cold it is here in the winter, Aidan. It looks like heaven now, but I can guarantee this is a cold like you've never felt before. I almost froze to death the first winter I arrived."

"Yeah, I've heard those fluffy little snowflakes can be downright deadly," he quipped.

Janie's face twisted with something that looked like disgust, reminding him of the woman he'd encountered the day before.

Emily plopped her hands on her hips, and when she spoke her tone was teasing, but Aidan felt the passion she had acquired for this remote locale that was now her home. "Laugh it up now, buddy, but you would probably last about thirty seconds in one of our snowstorms before hypothermia set in."

Janie did laugh at that, before tossing Aidan a determined look. "Yep, it's all about survival of the fittest up here. You'd be surprised at how many transplants we get from the lower forty-eight who come here in the summertime thinking they've found paradise, and then winter sets in. Only the hardiest manage to last until the spring thaw."

The way her eyes flicked over him had Aidan suddenly feeling the need to defend himself, and to prove he was tough enough for this charming little hole-in-the-wilderness even when it was iced over. Tough people lived in warm climates, too, he wanted to say, but for some reason he felt the need to provide proof.

His brain ran through a quick catalogue of his adventures, trying to settle on the most dramatic example to recount; he had endured a near-deadly snakebite in the Brazilian rain forest, an infected baboon bite in Borneo and a scorpion sting in Africa. He'd been nibbled on by fish even scarier than piranhas in the Amazon, suffered a torturous jellyfish sting off the coast of Queensland and had so many vicious insect bites he'd lost count. He'd experienced heat so intense it had melted the rubber soles of his sandals to his feet. He'd battled malaria, giardia, gangrene and dengue fever. Any one of those things had to be worse than a harmless drift of snow...

"I need to get back to the house," Emily said, before he could decide upon which harrowing ordeal to smoothly weave into the conversation.

She tipped the portable monitoring device she held in her hand. "Our baby girl is beginning to stir."

"I'll go with you," Bering said. "I need to make a couple of phone calls."

The pair walked away hand in hand, and just like that Aidan was left alone with Janie. Not a situation he would have chosen for himself, he thought, as the air seemed to thicken with a fog of silent unease.

CHAPTER THREE

AIDAN RACKED HIS brain for something to say. Janie remained silent, slowly spinning the handle of the ax around in her hands; her expression appeared to be one of disdain mixed with a bit of the same discomfort he was feeling. Maybe he should mention their run-in the day before? Get that out of the way and try to clear the air between them.

"So…about yesterday?"

She stared blankly. "What about it?"

"Um, I hope everything turned out okay for you and your son." Aidan didn't feel compelled to apologize because he felt certain that he'd done the right thing. A lot of people were woefully uninformed about the importance of bees in this world, and he was more than happy to educate them.

"Everything?"

"Your cake… I didn't mean to upset anyone. I was just saving the bee. Bees are really—"

"Well, the cake was ruined. But we really don't need to talk about it, okay? And I think I have a pretty good idea how you feel about your bees. Besides, I couldn't possibly expect you to understand—" Janie squeezed her eyes shut and dipped her head down. She inhaled deeply and then slowly released the breath, like his mom did when she was practicing yoga.

"What couldn't I understand?"

She met his look, her green eyes flat and unreadable. "My life. Can we just drop it? I really don't want to discuss it. Everything is fine."

Good. She clearly didn't want him asking, and quite honestly he didn't want to know.

"You're pretty handy with an ax, huh?"

"Yes, well, Emily is right about our winters. Chopping wood is something that most people do around here."

He glanced at the pile of wood in front of them. Plants he could intelligently discuss, and seemed safe territory.

"What kind of wood is this—do you know?"

UNBELIEVABLE, JANIE THOUGHT. Apparently it wasn't enough for him to ruin their day yesterday and not even bother to apologize, and then insult her behind her back today, now he felt the need to insult her in person, too? Did she *know*? Did he think she needed a botany degree to identify the type of trees she'd been chopping for firewood virtually her entire life?

"Birch."

"Hmm." Aidan reached down and picked up a chunk. He ran a hand over the fresh-cut surface. "Why birch?"

"What do you mean 'why birch'?" Janie's tone held a sharp edge and she didn't care. "It's not endangered, if that's what you're getting at."

Aidan let out a surprised chuckle. "Oh, I know that. I'm wondering about the properties that make it suitable for burning."

She shrugged and informed him confidently, "It's plentiful here, easy to split and when it's properly seasoned it has a very high energy content—somewhere in the range of twenty-three MBtus per chord. It's very efficient."

He didn't bother to mask the surprise on his face. Apparently, the fact that a simpleminded small-town mommy like he'd implied her to be had recited an intelligent fact had left him stunned. She was suddenly grateful for the project that Reagan had done earlier in the year, where he'd studied Alaska's trees and the properties of their wood. She had to admit that her son's genius often came in handy, even though it nearly as often left her bewildered.

Aidan smiled at her, a slow, wide smile, and his eyes danced with what looked like appreciation—completely the opposite of what she'd expect after hearing his harsh words earlier.

"That's amazing."

He was obviously talking about the piece of firewood he held in his hands, but his eyes were fastened on hers. They reminded her of that intense, swirling gray of the sky right before a snowstorm—beautiful and a little unsettling. His mouth was tugging up at the corners like he was fighting a grin.

"What is?" An odd sensation crept over her, along with a warm churning in the pit of her stomach. The combination was something she hadn't felt in a very long time. Not since… Wait…what? Unacceptable—she was too old to be affected by the charms of some overgrown beach bum. So what if he was nice-looking? That didn't impress her. She'd been caught off guard that's all—surprised that he was being so nice to her after the way he'd talked about her earlier. This kind of hypocrisy was only proof, she reminded herself, of his character—or lack thereof.

"Incredible…"

Her thoughts exactly…

His eyes skimmed over her face and seemed to settle on something in the vicinity of her mouth. Why was he doing that? Did she have something really embarrassing going on there? Something in her teeth? Or dried ketchup from the Tater Tots she'd shared with the twins when she'd run home for lunch earlier today? One hand shot up-ward and smoothed over her mouth. She tried to wipe at it as unobtrusively as she could. He kept staring…

"What?" she finally snapped.

"Oh, sorry." He shook his head. "I was think-ing about how, uh… Wood is used for so many different purposes throughout the world."

"Huh?" she said, not quite sure how wood could be a source for such amazed speculation.

"It's incredible how wood is such a truly re-newable resource, don't you think? There are hardwoods—ironwoods they're called actu-ally—that I've seen that are so solid you vir-tually can't cut them without a power saw. Did you know there are some woods so dense they won't even float?"

"Yeah, well, birch floats and you can cut it and chop it. Here—" She raised her arm, offer-ing him the ax.

"What?" He stared down at it like she was handing him a dirty diaper.

"Chop a piece. You can see for yourself."

"Oh, uh," he said, palms up as if in surrender. He shifted uneasily from one foot to the other. "I, um, I don't think… I mean I don't—"

She flashed him a frosty smile. Apparently wood chopping didn't count as "life experi-ence." "I see. Well, chopping wood is a very useful skill here in Rankins, where, *you* might be shocked to learn, there's not a huge call for bug doctors." She punctuated her statement by pivoting around and chopping cleanly through a large round chunk.

"Plants," he corrected her lightly. "I'm actually a botanist not an entomologist. I have an interest in entomology because of bees and other pollinators, but my doctorate is in botany."

She shrugged. "Whatever—bugs, plants, if you can't burn it or eat it, I'm not really all that interested." She put one foot up on the massive circular piece of spruce she'd been using as a chopping block.

Aidan stared back at her for a long silent moment, his eyes drifting again to the ax in her hands. His expression looked almost wary—like he was afraid she might turn it on him next. What in the world was he thinking?

Why did she care what he thought? She didn't...but something dawned on her as she followed his gaze.

She fought the grin tugging at her lips. "You don't know how to chop wood, do you?"

"Uh, guilty," he said with a shrug and a sheepish smile. "I can't say I've ever had the occasion to, which seems strange somehow considering my profession."

"Boy, all those degrees of yours are really going to come in handy up here, aren't they?"

Aidan cocked his head, like he might finally be processing her contempt. "Yes, I believe they will," he answered slowly. "For the work I've signed on for here in Alaska I'm confident that a doctorate is sufficient. I don't have much experience with the flora of this geographical location or even this climate, it's true, but I also don't expect Alaskan plant life to be nearly as diverse and complex as it is in the tropics. I won't go into the details because it's very complicated, but I can tell you…"

Janie stared at him as he rambled on and wondered if he had any idea how condescending he sounded. She held up a hand, palm forward, to interrupt him. "That's not necessary. I'm sure it would be *excruciating* for you."

"What?" His face twisted with genuine confusion.

Yep, genius all right. Apparently, he'd already forgotten the word he'd used to describe his feelings about doing an interview with her.

She decided to remind him. "Look, Dr. Hollings—"

"Aidan," he corrected her with an easy smile.

"Whatever. Listen—"

"Mo-o-om. Mom!" She heard shouts and turned to see Gareth and Reagan jogging in their direction, which was probably best, she thought, because her patience with Aidan Hollings was wearing thin. But this experience with him had been a good lesson, really…enlightening. Because aside from his attempt to put his best foot forward, she had a very good idea about who he really was and what he was all about. And one thing was for certain—even if he had agreed, there was no way in the world she would do that interview.

Yep, fate had done her a favor. It was about time, too. She felt like she deserved a favor…

Her boys politely introduced themselves, calling him Dr. Hollings and making her very proud. He asked the boys to call him Aidan, and Reagan immediately began firing off questions about a variety of sciencey topics. Reagan had been so excited to meet a real scientist and Janie had been looking forward to it on his behalf, had thought it would be good for Reagan to see what life could hold for him someday. Of course, that was before she'd actually met this man. Janie silently prayed that Aidan Hollings wouldn't be unkind to her brilliant but quirky son. Reagan had been blessed with an aptitude for facts and learning, but somehow this seemed to have left him lacking in social skills.

Gareth was well mannered, but predictably standoffish. Her oldest was always slow to warm up to new people and she felt sure yesterday's debacle wasn't going to help any. He had to be feeling a combination of embarrassment and resentment. She did—and she was a grown-up.

Janie felt a sense of relief as she watched Aidan and Reagan chatting like they'd known each other for years. Reagan was like that—always more comfortable with adults than with kids his own age, especially smart adults.

She wondered what her oldest son was thinking. Gareth looked ready to bolt and Janie felt torn between taking him with her to the house and not wanting to leave Reagan on his own. Bering and Emily took the decision out of her hands as they came out the door and walked in their direction, Emily cradling Violet in her arms.

Aidan smiled and tried to pull Gareth into the conversation but he responded with a series of short, though civil, replies. Then he subtly blew him off by looking toward his Uncle Bering and striking up a conversation about wolves—one of Bering's favorite topics.

GARETH WISHED HE was bigger. He watched the man who had ruined their dad's birthday and thought that if he was as big as his dad or his Uncle Bering he could punch the guy out, or somehow keep him from hypnotizing his little brother.

Reagan seriously seemed hypnotized. He'd been so excited to meet Aunt Emily's scientist brother—a "real" scientist. Gareth had to admit he'd been kind of excited, too—at first, before he'd actually met him. Before he'd ruined the Boston cream pie and Dad's birthday had been totally trashed.

Now he was listening to Aidan tell Reagan something boring and stupid about arctic bumblebees. Gareth hated bees. He'd been stung twice in his life and had almost died the second time. He could still remember that terrifying feeling as his throat closed in, slowly choking off his air supply until he could no longer breathe... Then the world had gone black. Luckily his cousin Tag had been there at the picnic that day to cut a hole in his neck and save his life.

Or maybe not...

Because if Tag hadn't been there Gareth might be with his dad in heaven right now. If there was a heaven—he wasn't entirely convinced.

Reagan's comment drew him back into the moment. "It seems like it would be too cold for a bee out on the tundra."

"Well, one of the exceptional things about bumblebees is that they can regulate their internal body temperature—"

"Thermoregulation," Reagan interrupted excitedly. "I've read about that."

"That's exactly right." Aidan sounded impressed. "That fuzzy coat helps, too, and they also shiver their flight muscles."

Gareth quit listening again. Aidan was clearly impressed with Reagan—everyone was impressed with Reagan...adults anyway. Not so much some of the kids at school. Even Gareth was impressed by his brother, though he didn't understand him sometimes, and he drove him crazy a lot. But he did love his brother, despite the fact that the workings of Reagan's brain were sometimes a complete mystery to Gareth.

He'd tried to explain to Reagan what had happened with Aidan and the cake but Reagan didn't get it. Instead, he'd seemed to relate to Aidan's reasoning, telling Gareth all about what important pollinators bumblebees are. Reagan was like literally a genius but he could also be completely clueless about certain things, which meant that the responsibility of taking care of the family fell entirely on him.

Gareth wished he could be better at it. He wished his dad was still alive to help him and tell him what to do. But that was dumb because if his dad was still alive he wouldn't have to constantly try to figure out what to do...

JANIE TURNED TOWARD the house as she heard the sound of a car traveling up the long driveway.

Bering looked, too. "It's Tag."

A vehicle came into sight and she recognized her cousin Tag's midnight blue one-ton pickup. He parked and hopped out, holding a basketball in his hands.

Tag smiled and tossed the ball into the air. "Hey, who wants to shoot some hoops?"

Janie grinned. That was a no-brainer where her boys were concerned, especially Gareth.

They gathered on the concrete pad Bering had poured solely for the purpose of playing basketball. They briefly discussed how to divide the teams.

"I'm warning you guys," Emily called from where she now sat in a lawn chair off to one side of the homemade regulation-sized half-court. Violet rested peacefully in her arms. "Aidan is really good."

Janie tried not to roll her eyes; she was highly skeptical of Emily's assertion. She loved her sister-in-law dearly but athletics weren't exactly Emily's forte. Bering was a good basketball player. Tag was exceptional—he'd been all-state two years in a row as well as MVP his senior year. His sister, Shay—Janie's cousin and best friend—was also an amazing player. Janie was no slouch herself. Janie doubted Aidan could hold a candle to any of them.

They finally agreed on Janie, Tag and Reagan versus Bering, Aidan and Gareth. But after only a short time Janie begrudgingly admitted to herself that Aidan did seem pretty comfortable with a basketball in his hands. The game was shaping up to be a good one. She passed the ball to Tag and he tossed it up from way outside, sinking another three-point shot as Reagan hooted with glee.

Aidan passed the ball to Bering and he answered with a jumper of his own. Gareth threw a fist in the air. She smiled; this game seemed to be exactly what Gareth needed to snap him out of the funk he'd been in for the last few days.

The score was now tied, so Janie put her head back in the game. She moved toward Aidan to guard him. He dribbled the ball behind his back, switching from one hand to the other. She scoffed at his showboating, and reached out to swat the ball.

He laughed as he dribbled the ball backward between his legs and out of her reach. Next, he pulled some kind of Harlem Globetrotters move, bringing the ball up and spinning it on one finger. He quickly shifted it to the other hand and somehow passed the ball to Gareth while it was still spinning.

Janie found herself gawking.

Reagan shouted, "Awesome," Tag belted out a laugh, Bering whistled and even Gareth cracked a smile.

"You've been holding out on us, Hollings," Tag remarked.

"Nah, just scoping out my competition."

Gareth took an outside shot, which fell short.

The game continued and Gareth missed three more baskets. Janie could see his frustration building. He was a very composed kid, good at hiding his feelings, so she felt confident that she was the only one who could see it. But he was always so hard on himself.

Janie took the ball out for her team. Aidan intercepted her pass to Tag. She quickly got into position to guard him. He dribbled the ball and moved like he was going to shoot. Janie jumped to block his shot, the ball went flying and Aidan let out a yelp.

"Foul!" Aidan yelled.

"What?" she cried. "I didn't even touch you."

"I saw it, Mom. You fouled him."

"Yeah, own up to it at least," Aidan teased.

She gaped at her son. "Reagan—we're on the same team."

"I know, but you hit him right here." Reagan pointed at his own arm.

Aidan rubbed his elbow and winced with ex-aggeration. "It's probably going to bruise."

Emily called from the sidelines. "Aidan, did you do something sneaky to draw that foul? He does that, Janie—you can't trust him."

Bering and Tag laughed. Gareth nearly smiled.

They'd been doing free throws on obvious fouls—often called or corroborated by Emily—to give Gareth and Reagan some extra practice. Now Aidan stepped up to the free-throw line. He bounced the ball a couple of times. The first shot went through the net with a quiet swish. He winked at Janie, an amused grin playing at his lips.

She ignored him. He motioned to Gareth and they walked toward one another. Aidan bent and whispered something in his ear. Gareth nodded, and then moved over behind his mother, who was positioned on the lane line near the basket.

Aidan missed the shot but the ball somehow ricocheted off the rim over Janie and into Gar-eth's waiting hands. He put it up for two to win the game. Gareth was clearly ecstatic. He and Reagan high-fived, then Reagan wrapped an arm around Gareth's shoulder. Janie felt a flood of joy—she loved when her boys exhibited this kind of brotherly affection.

Janie narrowed her eyes at Aidan in question. He shrugged a shoulder as if to say "I have no idea how that happened." But Janie knew very well what he'd done for her son. She just didn't know how he'd done it, why he'd done it or exactly how she felt about it.

CHAPTER FOUR

THE NEXT MORNING Aidan found himself traveling along a stunning stretch of coastline in Bering's pickup with Bering, Emily and Violet headed toward Bering's favorite clamming beach. Thick forest bordered the road on one side while intermittent slices of craggy ocean shoreline flashed in and out of view on the other.

After several miles, Bering slowed and turned off onto a narrow gravel road. They inched along the bumpy drive until it finally ended at a wide sandy beach. Bering turned the pickup around and backed onto a section of gravel. The tide was definitely going out. Aidan quickly took in their surroundings, noticing where the surf had receded to reveal rocks, seaweed and other ocean detritus.

They unloaded buckets, shovels and supplies and even though the sun shone bright in the sky a brisk chill permeated right through Aidan's jacket and seemed to seep into his bones. He added a windbreaker over the thick fleece.

Aidan heard the sound of another vehicle and

soon a metallic gray SUV pulled alongside Bering's pickup. Janie barely had the car turned off before Gareth and Reagan bailed out. Reagan greeted him enthusiastically while Tag and an older woman exited the vehicle. Bering introduced her as his and Janie's mom, Claire. Aidan noticed immediately that Janie had inherited her mom's hazel-green eyes and bright smile. They chatted for a few minutes before Bering got down to business.

"Let's get digging. I'll take the boys with me and try to get our limits as quickly as possible. Mom can limit out, too, and then she can watch Violet while I take Emily out to get hers. Janie, can you give Aidan a crash course?"

"Sure," Janie said, but Aidan didn't think she looked too enthused by the prospect.

"Janie is not just an expert clammer—she's an expert clamming instructor," Bering added.

Emily was nodding. "It's true, Aidan. Janie taught me. Bering gets impatient, forgets he's supposed to be helping, because he wants to get his clams."

"I have a problem," Bering confessed with an easy shrug. "Clam fever."

Aidan grinned. "I understand—there are certain mushrooms back home in Oregon that I get wild-eyed about."

Emily added, "Pay attention to Janie, Aidan. You do need to be kind of careful."

Bering agreed. "She's right. The surf can be sneaky here."

"Got it," Aidan said.

Bering, Claire, Gareth and Reagan gathered their buckets and shovels and headed down the beach.

Tag was busy pulling on his waders—the kind that fit like coveralls and reach up to the chest. Aidan slipped on the tall rubber boots Bering had packed for him.

"I feel like we're getting outfitted to go on a safari hunt after a wildebeest or an alligator or something. This is a major undertaking."

Tag laughed. "We do take our clamming very seriously. There are few things in this life as delicious as a fried razor clam."

Janie watched them with a kind of half frown on her face.

Aidan suspected she was trying not to show her displeasure at being stuck with tutoring him, reminding Aidan again of how dramatically they'd gotten off on the wrong foot.

She picked up a shovel and a bucket and started walking toward the ocean. After traveling several feet she stopped and turned around. Her voice held a tinge of impatience. "Let's get going there, Safari Boy. The tide waits for no man."

"Oh. Right," Aidan said.

Janie raised her brows and gave her head a little shake. "Yes, so that means we need to get going." She turned and headed once more toward the surf.

Aidan grinned at Tag, picked up his gear and jogged after her.

Maybe it was an Alaska thing, Aidan thought as he followed Janie toward the water—taking normal activities to a level of seriousness that didn't seem quite warranted. It was a *clam*—a simple bivalve. How tough could this be?

JANIE KNEW WHAT Aidan was thinking—or she imagined she did. The esteemed scientist was going to easily master this task, slay some clams and probably teach her a few things in the process. Well, she'd let him try. Was she hoping to exact a little revenge for the comments she'd overheard? Maybe. Initially. But at least part of what happened next he deserved, because she did try to warn him.

Janie quickly explained the basics of razor clam digging.

"See these holes?" She pointed out some indentations in the sand. "That's where a clam is showing. The back of the clam will be toward the ocean. So you put your shovel about this far from the hole." She placed the tip of her shovel in the sand. "Dig down with a couple quick strokes. If you're good—or lucky—you'll get close to the shell, almost grazing it, as you remove enough sand to stick your hand in and pull out a clam."

She smoothly demonstrated her instructions and held up a clam.

"Looks simple enough. Wow. They're bigger than I expected." He took the clam from her and examined it.

"They're also fast. So—"

"I've got it," he interrupted with easy confidence.

Numerous attempts later and he still definitely had not "got it." Janie glanced in his bucket and counted four clams. They would be here all day at this rate and the tide definitely would not wait that long—and neither would she.

"I don't feel it. Where in the world is it?"

"Probably about halfway to China, I'd guess," Janie responded as he mucked around in another hole.

Aidan chuckled but kept scrounging around in the sand, his arm buried nearly to his shoulder.

"No, seriously—give it up. They can dig like nine inches in a minute—probably faster here. Even though it's cold, this sand is pretty soft. That clam is long gone. Here, watch me again."

His voice held a note of disbelief. "Nine inches per minute? That would be—"

Janie talked as she dug and tried not to let the exasperation seep into her voice. "Yes, that means they could dig several feet in no time flat. I'm not making these numbers up. You've met my son, right? He finds these kinds of facts extremely interesting and recites them nonstop."

Aidan flashed her a quick grin. "I can relate. But, wow, that seems awfully quick…"

She leveled another look at him, daring him to dispute her as she placed three more clams in her bucket.

He held up a hand. "Okay, I'm trying again."

"Don't dig quite so much sand this time. You don't need a hole that big—you're not burying a body."

Untold minutes later he was on his hands and knees with his arm elbow-deep in yet another still too-large hole, feeling around for a clam she knew was long gone.

Janie glanced toward the ocean and saw it coming. She called quickly, "Wait, Aidan, you need to move—"

"I'm getting this one."

"Aidan—"

"Hold on a sec…"

Picking up Aidan's bucket as well as her own,

she backed up the beach a ways to watch the action unfold.

Seconds later the incoming wave doused him, surging right over his back, which was unadvisedly turned toward the ocean.

He yelped and popped to his feet, water whooshing out the tops of his boots.

Janie smothered a laugh in the crook of her arm, before looking up again. Aidan stood there, holding a clam, dripping and silent, gaping at her in that breath-stealing, cold-water-plunge kind of way. It reminded her of when the boys surfaced after jumping into the river on a really warm day.

"Hey, good job! You got it." She snorted out a laugh—it was too funny not to.

He finally found his voice. "You could have warned me."

"I did."

"You said not to turn my back on the ocean."

"Exactly." She gestured toward the water because that's precisely what he'd done.

"I thought you were being overly cautious. I was envisioning a tsunami. I figured the odds of that were slim and that I'd have plenty of time."

Janie shrugged and chuckled again. "I tried to warn you that the wave was coming, but you shushed me. Do you want to go back to the pickup so you can warm up? Bering usually has extra clothes in his vehicles." She hoped he'd say yes.

"No, I don't have my limit yet."

"Um, I doubt that you're going to get—"

"I will get my limit."

"Or hypothermia," she quipped.

Aidan grinned and ran a hand through his wet hair. Then he leaned on his shovel. She had to give him credit for being a good sport. But suddenly the intensity on his face had her bracing herself for an uncomfortable question.

"Why do I get the feeling you don't like me?"

Really? she wanted to ask. Instead she said, "I have no idea."

"Is this still about the bee?"

She sighed. "No, it's not about the bee."

"Then what? I, uh, I'm not the best at reading people. Sometimes I need things spelled out."

"Well, do you think you've done—or *said*— something to earn my dislike?"

He looked perplexed. "No, of course not, or else I wouldn't be asking." He sounded like he thought she wasn't very bright, which was true—he did think that.

She couldn't take this anymore. She knew how he felt about her and he needed to know that she knew… "Maybe it's my incompetence that's the problem or my lack of education? I know how *excruciating* this must be for you—spending time with a simple mom like me."

In an instant his features seemed to sharpen—eyes narrowed, lips thinned, jaw tightened, even his cheekbones seemed to jut more dramatically than they normally did. Satisfaction seeped into her because she'd managed to rile him. She was gratified to see something other than the laid-back, happy-go-lucky facade that normally seemed to emanate from him like an obnoxious Hawaiian shirt.

His voice was coldly disapproving when he spoke. "You were eavesdropping?"

"Not on purpose," she returned. "You've got a very…loud voice."

He stared at her for a long moment and his gray eyes felt almost menacing. Janie had no idea what he was thinking but she suspected it wasn't good. In fact, she expected him to blow up at her, or at the very least let loose with a resounding reproach; even an apology would have surprised her less than his reaction. His face broke into a smile and laughter began spilling from his lips.

First he judges and insults her in that unfair manner and now laughs about it? Unbelievable. She wanted to let him know precisely what he could do with both his educated babble-talk and the interview she didn't want to do anyway.

"Listen—"

He interrupted, "I never said I thought you were incompetent. I asked if you were qualified."

"I don't have a degree."

"I didn't say you needed one."

Janie huffed. "You implied it, but I'm not going to play these silly semantics games with you. That's what you meant."

His sigh sounded gruff, aggravated. "I did. You're right. But there's a good reason why—"

"I don't care about your reasons."

She glanced around the beach and realized they were the only ones still digging. She could see Bering and Tag sitting on the tailgate, probably sipping coffee and snacking on the cookies she'd made. And that was where she was going to be soon…

She tapped her shovel and quickly scooped out a few piles of sand, stuck her hand in and nabbed a clam. She put it into her bucket and repeated the process. "You can stuff your reasons. There are no good reasons to speak about someone the way you spoke about me—all judge-y and imperious. You don't even know me."

She looked up to see frustration dance across his face. "Okay, fine. Maybe you're right."

"I am right." She dug another clam, and then several more.

He stood watching her for a few moments before he gestured at the sand. "That's astounding—how good you are at this."

She dug some more and dropped the clams in her bucket. "It is shocking, isn't it? That someone as unworldly as I am could be good at this? Now, I have my limit and I've taught you all I can, so I'll see you back at the pickup."

"Wait a minute."

"Nope."

"But I want to tell you something."

"I don't want to hear it." She slipped her shovel over her shoulder, picked up her clam bucket and turned to walk away.

He reached out and snagged the handle of her bucket. "Yes, you do."

She tugged. "No, I don't."

He held tight, looking puzzled by her words. "Why not?"

"Why in the world should I? You didn't say those things *to* me. You said them *about* me, never dreaming I would hear. There's no need to apologize for your opinion, but don't pretend like you think better of me than you do. I am a simple person—that's true. A *mom*." She gestured at herself in her blue jeans, ponytail and Rankins Rebels hoodie. "What you see is what you get. And I'm fine with that. No, I'm happy with that. But don't insult me and then patronize me by trying to be fake-nice."

His face transformed with what looked like genuine surprise. No doubt he wasn't used to people calling him on his bad behavior.

"What? I don't think… I mean you're… What I mean to say is, I'd really like to explain—"

"No, thank you. That's not necessary. Let go." She yanked hard on the bucket, but he held firm. She felt like one of her kids playing tug-of-war with MacGyver and she was suddenly afraid that he would let go and she'd tumble backward onto the sand. So she released her hold, intending to leave the bucket, even as she wondered what he'd been going to say about her.

"Can you please wait a second? I want to tell you why I said those things—some of those things."

She stopped, turned and glared as his words sunk in. "You want to explain *part* of it now?"

"Yes."

He seemed determined and not at all fazed by his odd comment. Janie suspected he wouldn't leave this alone until she heard him out— or heard whatever part he deemed important enough for her mommy brain to hear. "Okay."

"Okay?" he repeated.

"Yep," she answered along with a one-shoul-dered shrug. "Let's hear it."

He seemed momentarily taken aback by her acquiescence.

"Um, all right... So, there was a woman a while back—a reporter—who wasn't really a reporter..." He set the bucket down, then lifted his hand to the back of his neck and squeezed, looking up toward the sky as if searching for the right words to explain away his behavior. Finally he let out a whoosh of breath. "Long story short—she wrote an article about me and... It was unfair and dishonest."

Janie watched him, silently waiting for him to add more. But he just stared back, all serious and sincere and...wet.

She felt a prickle of annoyance and finally asked, "That's it?"

"Yes."

"You're sure?"

"What do you mean?"

"You don't want to add anything else? That's your big explanation?"

"Yes, it was a very bad experience. It caused problems for me and..."

"I'm sure it did," she said somberly.

He nodded like she was actually being sympathetic now and not sarcastic.

So much like Reagan, she thought, and wondered why supersmart people were often so literal. Reagan she felt sorry for—this man, not so much.

"You poor thing—how did you survive it?

Someone said some unfair things about you, which you knew to be inaccurate and untrue? That's just awful. I bet you were really angry, huh?"

His face evolved into a frustrated scowl. "Oh," he said, "I get it."

She shook her head. "I doubt very much that you do."

"You're a very stubborn and unforgiving woman, aren't you?"

"No, I'm actually really, really not. Normally I'm way too forgiving and I let things go that I shouldn't. I hate confrontation and I avoid it as much as I can. But you..." She stopped herself from adding an insult, barely.

"O-kay," he muttered.

He was obviously not sure what to do with that statement and she couldn't blame him. It was probably a bit of an overshare on her part, but talking to him was so frustrating...

And apparently he wasn't finished. "So I can see you're not ready to forgive me."

She tipped her head like she did when one her boys was feeding her a line of nonsense. Not ready to forgive him? Was he really not aware of the fact that in the course of this conversation he hadn't ever apologized? Only "explained"? But she wasn't really expecting an apology and she knew this conversation wasn't going to get her anywhere. It wasn't going to resolve anything. And she was being truthful when she'd said she didn't want him apologizing when he really didn't mean it anyway.

She sighed. "Let's just forget about it, hmm?"

"I don't—"

She silenced him with a look. "That's your only option at this point. Either give it up or I walk."

He muttered something under his breath, then said, "All right, fine. For now."

"Forever," she countered.

He grinned. "Let's dig some clams. I feel like if I go back to that pickup without my limit, Bering might leave me here."

That actually made her laugh because Bering wouldn't, but he would want to. "He might," she teasingly agreed.

Janie had to give Aidan credit for improving; he managed to get half a bucket, but after a few methodical, yet unsuccessful, attempts in a row, Janie could see they were running out of tide… and time.

"You need to be a little faster," she advised after he failed to get yet another.

He nodded. "I can do faster."

He looked around determinedly until he found a dimple in the sand. He began scooping furiously, but she could see that the blade was too close.

"Aidan, hold on—you need to make sure you keep enough distance—"

But he was *too* fast this time, and Janie winced as she heard the telltale crack of the clam's glass-like shell. She didn't realize that he didn't recognize the sound himself until it was too late.

He'd already dropped to his knees and pushed his hand into the hole.

"Wait, wait—"

"Ouch!" he yelped.

Janie squeezed her eyes shut.

"Crikey… That hurts."

Janie cringed when she looked down and saw the bloody ends of his fingers. The water was cold—if he was bleeding that much already this really wasn't going to be good.

Janie turned toward the surf, shielding her eyes from the glare of the sun as she looked for Tag.

"Is this why they're called razor clams?" Aidan's voice was perfectly calm as he studied his injured hand. "Because the shell is literally as sharp as a razor?"

"I don't know about that, but this is why it's nice to have a cousin who is a paramedic."

AIDAN SAT ON the tailgate of the pickup and watched Tag clean the wound. He examined the cuts.

"You're definitely going to need stitches. The tip of this finger is almost sliced clear through."

Aidan repeated his earlier observation. "I can see why they're called razor clams."

Tag chuckled and applied some disinfectant. "Maybe—I've heard different accounts on that. On the east coast they're longer and skinnier—more like a straight razor. They also call them jackknife clams back there. Our Pacific razors are a lot more oval-shaped, and bigger—fatter and meatier. Tastier, too, I think. Anyway, a lot people claim the shape is where the name comes from."

Aidan shook his head. "Not as far as I'm concerned."

Tag laughed. "I'll drive you to the hospital."

"My fingers, they're going to be—"

"Don't worry. Dr. Grady is on today and he's great. I've never seen a doctor who can sew better. It'll barely even scar."

Aidan watched as Tag wrapped his fingers in a length of soft white gauze. The blood seeped through and Tag kept wrapping. Aidan thought about the repercussions of an injured hand, but scars were the least of his concerns.

Emily examined Tag's handiwork. "Aidan, what will you do? How are you going to work?"

"I'll manage. They're just lacerations, Em—

they'll heal." Leave it to Emily to voice his concerns.

"But your boxes are arriving tomorrow, right?"

"That's right," Bering said as he began transferring clams into a cooler. "Your stuff. Don't worry, we'll help."

Bering turned to address Janie, who had been hanging back silently. Aidan wondered what she was thinking. "Can I borrow the boys in the morning? To give Aidan a hand?"

"Yes, of course."

Tag closed his first-aid kit and stood. "Hop in my pickup, Aidan. We need to get you to the hospital."

CHAPTER FIVE

"Janie, the response to your ugly-Christmas-sweater column has been unbelievable. Mayor Cummings is talking about having an ugly-Christmas-sweater contest at this year's Festival of Trees in December. People are asking if you'll teach a class. We could print a summary in the paper the day after each one, so people who have taken your earlier classes can follow along in the paper. What do you think?"

Janie handed a plate of scrambled eggs over to Laurel, who had stopped by to discuss the matter since it was Sunday—the only day the paper was closed, although Laurel worked every day.

"But I don't get it," Claire said as she rinsed her plate in the sink. She and the boys had already eaten so she could drive Gareth and Reagan into town for the work party at Aidan's. "Your sweaters aren't ugly—they're beautiful."

Laurel tried to explain and Janie let her. She had been over this with her mom too many times to count. "That's kind of the point, Claire. The silly design versus the quality of the knitting and the beauty of the yarn… That's the appeal and no one does these better than Janie."

Claire shook her head in confusion. "That's what Janie says, too, Laurel. But I still don't understand why you have to call them ugly."

Janie and Laurel exchanged grins, as her mom continued her argument.

Janie had held basic knitting classes in the past, always with a great turnout. Students would complete the class with knowledge of basic stitches and a scarf or the start of a throw blanket. A sweater would entail much more detailed teaching, but knitting was her passion and she enjoyed teaching the skill hands-on.

"I would be happy to do a class."

"Awesome." Laurel beamed. "I'll get it set up."

Claire put on her coat. "We're leaving now. Bering is bringing the boys home, right?"

"Yes, thanks, Mom." Janie explained to Laurel, "Bering, Tag, Gareth and Reagan are helping Aidan Hollings move a bunch of his stuff in today."

The boys appeared with their plates and stowed them in the dishwasher. They said their goodbyes and filed out the door. Janie poured herself and Laurel cups of coffee.

"Which reminds me," Laurel said. "Emily said Aidan was really resistant to the idea of an interview, so I called his agent. He thinks Aidan will do an interview when he hears what the Insider's Alaska column is all about…and we settle on terms."

"Terms?"

"That's actually pretty standard procedure with celebrity types. They'll let you know right off the top what topics or questions are off-limits—most of the time they'll even want a list of questions beforehand."

Janie scoffed. "Celebrity types? Are you kidding me? Some guest shots on *Here's the Dirt* and *Flower Power* make him a celebrity? I played Eliza Doolittle in *My Fair Lady* back in high school—maybe I should get an agent?"

Laurel chuckled. "And you were excellent. Did you know *Here's the Dirt* is the most popular gardening show on cable television? And don't forget about that film on endangered plant species. He cowrote, produced and directed that, you know? It's already being considered a pretty important piece of work in the scientific community and it hasn't even been released yet. The film is going to be shown in IMAX theaters all over the world. And they are having like a real film premiere later this summer. A bunch of movie stars and business people and politicians are attending. I was thinking our articles could coincide with that."

Janie took a bite of toast. "Sounds great."

"I know, and I want you to do the interview. Emily is right about this and you would be perfect—"

"Laurel, I'm sorry, but can you give this one to someone else? I don't want to do it."

"Of course you do. Don't be nervous—you'll be great. It's a human interest story—you're great at those."

"I'm not nervous. It's not that." This wasn't actually true—the thought of doing the interview made her stomach knot like the ball of yarn Crosby had gotten ahold of last night. The yarn had been hopelessly shredded and tangled, so she'd had to toss the expensive wad of mohair in the garbage. "I don't want to interview *him*— Aidan Hollings."

"What? But why?"

"I… We didn't really click."

Laurel peered at her intently. "You don't like him?"

The words flew out of her mouth before she could stop them. "Not particularly."

"Really? Why not? Everyone seems crazy about him."

Everyone hadn't heard him talking to Emily about *everyone*.

Laurel stared at her expectantly, waiting for more information. Janie should have known Laurel would push the subject and she knew better than to try and lie to her friend.

"He's… We're very different."

"How?"

"How?" Janie repeated the word and heard the sharpness in her tone. She inhaled a breath, searching for calm.

"Yes, in what ways are you so different? What's he like?"

"Not what I expected."

"I have this impression of him as this nice, easygoing, laid-back kind of guy… Plus, he's Emily's brother."

The implication being that he must have some redeeming qualities as Emily's relation. That had been Janie's assumption, too.

"Half brother—they have different mothers, you know? They weren't even raised together."

She looked at Laurel and silently willed her not to push the subject. But this was Laurel—Rankins's very own Lois Lane. Laurel would never pass up the opportunity for a story and Janie felt certain Laurel would never understand how Janie could.

"I see… But not liking someone doesn't necessarily disqualify you from interviewing them. Reporters interview people they don't like all the time."

"I know, and it's not that necessarily," she lied.

"I'd just prefer not to do this one. It's an important article and I feel like I would need to give it all my attention, but I've got so much on my plate right now..." They both knew very well that Janie always had an overflowing plate, so this wasn't much of a stretch. Janie had never used her crazy, single-mom schedule as an excuse to get out of an assignment, but she shamelessly found herself doing so now. "Reagan has his science project coming up, Gareth is playing club basketball and now with this knitting class..."

Laurel eyed her carefully. "You're sure about this?"

"I am. I understand what an opportunity this would be, Laurel. And I really appreciate you offering it to me."

Laurel looked surprised, and slightly suspicious. And Janie really couldn't blame her, it would seem odd to her, too, if she was in Laurel's place.

She added another layer to her excuse. "Tag flew to Anchorage yesterday and he was going to pick up some things Reagan needs for his science project—he had a Barbie doll on the list. The informational meeting is this week to go over the rules for the national program the science club is participating in this year. I can't wait to see what he has planned."

Laurel laughed and Janie was relieved when

she allowed the subject to change. "A Barbie, huh? At least it's not battery acid. I thought Principal Dundee was going to call the cops last year when he saw those bones in the bottom of that bucket."

Janie grinned and shook her head. "I know."

Last year Reagan's experiment had tested the corrosive properties of different types of acids. The high point had involved actual moose skeletons, which his Uncle Bering had procured for him. A series of large, high-resolution photos showed how Reagan had managed to melt the bones down until they fit into a five-gallon bucket, the contents of which he'd proudly displayed in his booth—along with another bleached moose skeleton of similar original dimensions that he'd arranged on a table for size comparison. The line to get a glimpse had formed all the way out the door and around the side of the VFW hall.

"That kid…" Laurel chuckled. "What did he think of Aidan? I know how excited he was to meet a real-life scientist."

"Already thick as thieves. Reagan is ecstatic to have him here." Something made her add, "He was actually pretty nice to Gareth, too."

Laurel tapped her fingertips together thoughtfully. "Well, that says *something* about the guy, right? That he was a hit with your boys?"

"Yeah, I suppose," Janie said, acquiescing. She thought about how he'd gotten the ball to Gareth so he could score the winning basket. He didn't have to do that, and yet she'd also heard what she'd heard. And he never did apologize for ruining the cake…

Laurel sat frozen in her thoughtful-reporter pose, palms together, fingers tilted in Janie's direction.

Janie racked her brain for something that might derail Laurel's train of thought.

"I'm meeting Shay at the bakery later to sample wedding cake…"

ONE PROBLEM SOLVED, Aidan thought as he directed Bering, Tag, Gareth and Reagan as to where to put the boxes. The plane had arrived at seven as scheduled, and the entire shipment fit in the back of one of Bering's full-size pickups. By nine thirty they were unloading the boxes and stacking them in Aidan's rented building. Emily had found the vacant building on the edge of downtown before he'd arrived and Aidan could not be happier with her choice. His sister was truly a wonder of efficiency.

The brick structure consisted of one large, rectangular-shaped room with worn hardwood floors, and a kitchen area was situated along the far wall complete with a small refrigerator. There was a bathroom on one side of the room adjacent to a walk-in storage area with floor-to-ceiling shelves. Lucky for him, Rankins had no restrictions on what the space could be used for—yet another reason to like this little town, because he intended to both live and work in the space.

Aidan already had a cot set up in one corner of the room to sleep on. He'd purchased it, along with a sleeping bag, for a surprisingly reasonable price at Bradbury's, the hardware/sporting-goods store that was also a computer repair shop that Bering had recommended in town. Aidan had mentioned Bering's name while shopping and he suspected it had helped in determining the final discounted sale amount.

Somewhere during the building's history a second sink had been installed along the wall opposite the bathroom. With the addition of a few tables and some lighting, that area would serve as his lab. Emily had already found him a desk for his computer and a comfy secondhand office chair. She and Bering had recently bought new furniture so Bering had hauled over their two gently used recliners for him to use as well.

Aidan opened a carefully packed crate and found his favorite microscope intact. In another box he discovered that his video camera also looked fine. He plugged in the battery pack with the intention of testing the camera out later, but he realized he was going to need help setting up some of his equipment.

Bering came through the door again, followed by Gareth and Reagan, each holding boxes that they added to the pile.

"This is the last of them, Aidan."

"I can't thank you guys enough. How about if I buy everyone breakfast at the Cozy Caribou?"

That suggestion was met with enthusiastic agreement. Reagan walked over and inspected the microscope. "Wow, awesome microscope. What's the magnification?"

As Aidan discussed microscopes with Reagan something occurred to him. "Do you boys think you could spare a few more hours after breakfast? I could use some help getting unpacked."

"Yes," Reagan said excitedly.

"No, sorry, I can't," Gareth answered politely.

Bering glanced down at the watch on his wrist. "Gareth is playing basketball. I'm supposed to drop him off in an hour. But Reagan can stay if he wants. Emily or I can swing by and pick him up this afternoon. I'll call Janie and let her know. I'm sure she won't mind."

Aidan wasn't nearly as sure, but he was desperate enough for help that he put that thought aside. Surely the misunderstanding between him and Janie wouldn't extend to her children.

THAT SAME AFTERNOON Aidan strolled down the main street in Rankins admiring some of the old buildings and the homey feel of the town. The sun had disappeared behind a patch of clouds, which seemed to instantly lower the temperature. The chilly air began creeping into his open jacket and he wondered how long it would take him to acclimate to the cooler weather. He reached for the zipper, felt his stitched-together fingers throb painfully and switched hands, reminding him again of his predicament—and a possible solution.

Reagan had been a world of help to him, which had prompted him to ask if he'd like to assist him on a regular basis—at least until his hand healed.

He felt his phone buzz in his pocket, pulled it out and checked the display—his agent, Drummond Baker. He'd already let three of Drum's calls go to voice mail today. He always enjoyed being able to use the excuse of spotty cell service in remote locales like Rankins to not answer calls. But he also knew Drum would never quit calling until he picked up.

"Hey, Drum, what's up?"

"Aidan! So glad I reached you finally. How's the Alaskan netherworld? Never mind—I don't really care. Because I have great news! You know how I thought you were going to mold and rot in that little town up there? And everyone would forget who you are?"

"That's kind of the point, Drum."

"Oh, you… Stop with the modesty."

Drum couldn't imagine that anyone could truly not want to be "famous." Blake had turned out to be the exact opposite of him and Aidan was more than happy to hand the promotion for their film project off to him. Aidan thought their partnership was perfect—Aidan focusing on the research and Blake on the business. But Drum wanted Aidan to take a more active role in publicity. He thought the combination of Aidan and Blake as some kind of lovable "odd couple" was "endearing" and "highly marketable."

Drum kept accusing Aidan of false modesty. "Drum, I'm not—"

"Yes, sabbatical. I know. But before you start with that speech, I've arranged for you to speak with a reporter—"

"No." Aidan felt a twinge of irritation mix with amusement and alarm.

"Please, hear me out."

"No. Drum, I wouldn't even agree to an interview for my sister, there's no way I will—"

"You didn't even let me finish." Drum had this way of pitching his voice that always reminded Aidan of a sulky teenage girl. He thought Drum must be the only grown man who could pull off such an effective pout—and over the phone, no less.

"Drum, I don't need you to finish. I know you. 'Speaking with a reporter' is an interview no matter how you word it."

Drum sighed dramatically. "Can I explain?"

"You can if you want to waste your time."

Drum opted to take that as a yes. Aidan listened to him drone on and thought about his last disastrous experience with the media—with Meredith. He'd been blindsided—personally as well as professionally. He hadn't done an interview since, nor had he had a date for that matter. But he'd learned a lesson, one that he'd already known but the experience had confirmed. *Reporter* was a very loose word in this internet age—reporters were not to be trusted, and with his not-quite-seamless people skills he was better off to avoid personal relationships anyway.

Aidan stopped to admire an old fishing boat and a rusty anchor that had been tucked in between two buildings as part of the town's push to incorporate its history into the landscaping—an idea Emily had actively expounded on since she'd taken over as head of Rankins's tourism bureau. He thought the tactic was extremely effective; the diverse history of the remote town was so compelling, what with fishing, mining, logging, fur trading... He smiled as he thought of Emily's not-so-subtle attempt to guilt him into an interview.

He began walking again and forced himself to tune back into Drum's speech. "...and the owner of the paper there—Laurel Davidson is her name—she is a go-getter I tell you what. I don't think you can pass on this opportunity, Aidan. And they're giving you free rein. You can talk—or not talk—about anything you want. Imagine the exposure this would be for *Seeds*? This could be an opportunity to generate some funding for your next project."

Aidan hated that they were forced to mold their projects around funding. It made him feel like a politician. Although he had to admit financing for their next project would be nice. After one rejection had followed another, he and Blake had funded *Seeds* themselves. Their shoestring budget had made for painful stops and starts and much added difficulty to the process, but they'd done it.

Aidan stopped and carefully shifted the phone to his other hand. He glimpsed a familiar figure emerge from a doorway on the next block. Janie? Yes, he knew for sure when she paused and flipped that curtain of red hair over her shoulder. In spite of the challenges and the cut fingers, he'd enjoyed their morning of clam digging. There was so much about her that had been so…unexpected. He wondered again how he could have been so far off in his assessment of her when they'd met two years ago.

Emily had been right to chastise him for his comments; his first impression had been almost entirely inaccurate. And she may have been having an overly maternal moment that day in front of the bakery, but her boys were great kids.

He had hit it off with Reagan immediately, which was no surprise. He reminded Aidan a lot of himself—too much perhaps, because Aidan knew very well the challenges he faced, which was why he couldn't say no when Reagan invited him over to check out his science project.

Gareth was exceedingly polite almost to the point of being aloof. But Aidan figured that was probably understandable after their initial meeting. He had the makings of an excellent basketball player and Aidan wondered if that might ultimately be the key to connecting with him.

He felt drawn to Janie and to her boys and he wasn't quite sure why. Empathy maybe? Aidan had lost his father at a young age as well, so maybe that had something to do with it.

Plus, these people were important to his sister— they were Emily's family now. So, it was safe to say that no matter what, they were also a part of Aidan's life in some respect. So it only stood to reason that he should try to develop an amicable relationship, right?

Yes. He needed to fix this situation with Janie. Even as he realized that doing so might pose a bit of a challenge. She clearly wasn't all that keen on him. Aidan grinned as he realized that he kind of liked that—that she didn't seem intimidated by him.

He tried to think of an interesting conversation starter—maybe he'd go with the jellyfish sting. He watched as she fished around in her bag for a moment, pulled out a phone and began tapping on the screen.

And suddenly it occurred to him that there was one very obvious way to get to know her better—and to let her get to know him.

"Drum, stop, okay? Stop talking. I'll do it. I'll do the interview. I'll go talk to Laurel Davidson right now. On one condition…"

He filled in Drum on his impulsive plan as he kept his gaze glued on Janie. He ended the conversation with Drum by promising to call back after he'd met with Laurel.

Suddenly Janie dropped the phone into her bag, looked both ways and hustled across the street. A twinge of disappointment nicked at him as he watched her head away from him down the sidewalk in the opposite direction—right past the bakery.

The bakery…

Another idea occurred to him, reinforced with something his nana had always told him—it was bad manners to show up as a guest at someone's home empty-handed.

CHAPTER SIX

Tonya and Lilah should make an air freshener that smelled exactly like the Donut Den. Janie decided this as she stepped through the door of the bakery only to be plunged into the most heavenly mix of scents: yeast, vanilla, cinnamon, chocolate, coffee—and today she could also smell…maple. They'd make a million dollars.

"Oh, Lilah, is that maple? Please tell me you've made Emily's?" Emily's were a new addition to the Donut Den—maple-glazed and custard-filled delights that Lilah had started baking at Emily's request. They were so popular Lilah and Tonya had decided to name the pastry after her, which was only fitting as she was one of their best customers.

Lilah giggled. "That nose of yours is unbelievable, Janie. Yes, I just finished frosting a batch."

Janie glanced at her cousin Shay. The bride-to-be's face was contorted with a scowl as she stared down at a tray containing a vast array of cake bits tucked into paper muffin cups and

labeled with tiny toothpick-and-paper signs—
vanilla bean, toasted coconut, salted caramel,
German chocolate… None of these delicious flavors were even remotely scowl-worthy.

Her cousin Hannah—Shay's younger sister—
was standing next to her.

"They all look delicious. How's it going?"

Shay's eyes met hers and Janie felt her heart
lurch. Something was wrong. As Shay's cousin,
best friend and maid of honor Janie's job was to
fix it—whatever it was.

"Shay, what's the matter?"

"Jonah booked our honeymoon." Shay said
these words like she was informing Janie that
her fiancé had kicked a puppy into a street full
of busy traffic.

"Oh… Well, that sounds like good news."

"No-o-o," she drawled. "He booked it without asking me."

"But that sounds romantic."

"Thaff's what I said," Hannah chimed in as
tiny cake crumbs flew out along with the words.
She covered her mouth with a napkin."Oofhs,
sorfy." She held up a finger, made a show of
swallowing. "I told her the same thing, Janie."

"A Caribbean honeymoon sounds romantic?"

"Uh-oh." Janie grimaced. Shay didn't like
tropical weather; she particularly disliked humidity. She didn't sunbathe and she didn't like

to play in the ocean unless fishing in it counted.
Shay was a doer, a go-getter—hiking, fishing,
seeing sights, yes. Everyone knew that. Everyone
except her lost but recently rediscovered high
school/college love turned fiancé Jonah, apparently…

"You should have seen him when he told me—
all proud of himself and so confident I would
love it. The brochure has a picture of a ham-
mock and a sunset on it. When I told him to surprise me I assumed he would surprise me with
someplace that I would like. I never should have
agreed to let him take on this task."

"What did you tell him?" Janie asked carefully.

"I told him I'm not going to the Caribbean for
my honeymoon. What do people even do there?
Sit around and sweat? Fry their skin in the sun
all day? No, thank you. Plus—I don't even like
the taste of rum."

Hannah howled with laughter as Janie let out a
snicker. She said, "Shay, I don't think that sounds
so bad. Cal and I didn't even go on a honeymoon.
I would be happy going anywhere."

Shay's eyes went wide as shock and hor-
ror transformed her features. "Oh, no… Janie,
you're right. I am a horrible person. Jonah is
trying so hard and I'm being picky and snippy

and ungrateful." She let out a gasp. "I'm—I'm…
bridezilla."

"Shay—no, you're not. You're not bridezilla.
You're just stressed. You always do this. You
take too much on yourself. Delegating isn't only
about asking someone else to do a task—it's
about letting go of it enough to not worry about
how it turns out. Trusting in another person."

"What? Really?" Shay looked distressed by
the notion. She wasn't exactly known for her
ability to relinquish control of any situation.

Janie chuckled and shrugged. "I don't know,
but it sounds good. You're letting Hannah and
me choose the bridesmaid dresses. And I'm putting on your shower. You haven't even asked me
about it."

Shay nibbled on a piece of cake. "That's because I know you and Hannah will choose cor-
rectly and that the shower will be beautiful and
perfect."

Hannah chimed in enthusiastically, "Yeah, and
that reminds me, Janie—this is funny. Jonah suggested we wear those skimpy French maid out-
fits in lieu of the traditional bridesmaid dresses
since the wedding is going to be at the inn. You
know—in keeping with the hotel theme?"

Janie and Hannah shared a laugh.

Shay scowled. "See what I mean? He's not
taking this seriously."

"Shay, one of the things you love about Jonah is his sense of humor. I don't think you've quite entered the bridezilla zone, but you might need to lighten up a bit."

Hannah nodded her agreement as she chewed. "Mmm." She pointed at the sign marked vanilla bean and lifted up a thumb. She added, "Janie's right, Shay, this is supposed to be the happiest time in your life."

Janie tried a bite of carrot-and-cream. "Oh, my goodness," she drawled.

Shay nodded. "I know. Try the toasted coconut. Now *there's* something positive about the Caribbean—it's supposed to be full of coconuts, right?"

Janie chuckled and tried a piece, which seemed to melt in her mouth before she could truly appreciate the flavor. She picked up another bite—same effect.

"Lilah, you are a genius. How many flavors do we have to decide on?"

Shay said, "I'm thinking four—each tier a different flavor."

Lilah suggested, "You could always add another flavor or two with a cupcake tower."

A half hour later they'd successfully narrowed down the choices. Shay had, thankfully, already chosen the design for the cake. They talked frosting colors and discussed other details with Lilah.

When they were finished Shay and Hannah stepped outside, talking about the music for the wedding while Janie lingered to purchase a box of doughnuts. She thought it would be a nice treat for the kids, and admittedly a few pastries would give her something to look forward to that evening.

Looking forward to eating a doughnut, and knitting while watching her favorite television show—was that sad and pathetic? She thought about Aidan's "mommy" description of her. Whatever, she didn't care—this was her life and she'd take these little nuggets of happiness wherever she could get them.

Lilah handed over the bright pink box with one of her quirky smiles. Her voice was soft, but intense. "I feel so bad about the Boston cream pie the other day, Janie."

"Not your fault, Lilah. It was just one of those things. It was a rough day."

Lilah stared at her intently, her dark brown eyes reminding Janie of the fresh-brewed espresso she served. "It's nice when life offers us another chance at something, though, don't you think?"

Janie wasn't sure if Lilah was trying to tell her something important and profound about her spiritual well-being or commenting on Shay and Jonah's second chance at love. Lilah was prone

to these moments of philosophical inquiry. Janie
wasn't sure she agreed, but she loved Lilah and
knew her intentions were good.

"Yep, it sure is, Lilah."

It wouldn't be until later that Janie would realize Lilah wasn't talking about either one of those
things—and that in this particular case she most
certainly would not agree. Because sometimes
a second chance just meant another opportunity
to make a mistake.

THE NEXT EVENING Janie scooped up her sobbing
two-year-old from the kitchen floor and cradled
him in her arms.

"Gareth?" she called. "What's wrong with
Finn?"

"He fell." Gareth stepped into the kitchen and
relayed the details of the incident. "He didn't fall
very hard, and I gave him his buddy bear, but
he still wouldn't stop crying. I think he might
be getting a cold."

"Thanks for trying, honey. You may be right
about him being sick." She propped Finn on her
shoulder and began bouncing lightly around the
kitchen as she put away the groceries she had
brought in from the car. Gareth jumped in to help
and by the time they were finished the baby was
snoozing peacefully in her arms.

"Mom!" Reagan hustled into the kitchen, his

red hair askew and his green eyes shining with excitement.

"Hey, Reagan—how was your day?"

"Good, but listen, I have something important to tell you. I took a sample of Finn's mucus, looked at it under my microscope, and I—"

"Of what?" Janie blinked slowly.

Gareth filled a glass with milk. "Snot, Mom, he was looking at snot."

Reagan stared at his brother, aghast. "Shut up, Gareth. That makes it sound gross."

"It *is* gross."

Reagan's voice shifted into lecture mode, which sometimes brought out the worst in Gareth. "You think that you would know by now that it's a perfectly natural occurrence. There are certain bodily functions that are common in all Homo sapiens and mucus in the nasal passage is one—"

Gareth laughed. "I can think of a couple you—"

"Stop!" Janie put up a hand to ward off a squabble or a verbal exchange of "natural" bodily functions, neither of which she was up to dealing with right now, although she wasn't quite sure how to respond to Reagan's comment.

"Listen, you guys—no fighting. But, Reagan, you have to admit it is kind of gross." The deflated look on his face had her adding a quick placation. "For us nonscience people—even though it is, in fact, as you pointed out, natural." All correct, it was just that he was constantly regaling them with these rather unconventional— okay, and kind of gross—truths.

Janie watched Reagan roll his eyes, no doubt wondering how he could possibly be saddled with such ignorant relations.

"I was careful, Mom. I didn't touch it. But have you ever noticed how our own bodily excretions don't gross us out nearly as much as other people's do?"

Janie opened her mouth to respond but apparently he didn't really expect an answer.

"I'm guessing it has a lot to do with pheromones because why else wouldn't a mother vomit every time she changed her baby's diaper?"

"Reagan—"

"I know. I'm getting off point. Mom, I used a swab and I was wearing gloves. You know how important it is not to contaminate a sample. Finn has—"

"Hi, sweetheart." Claire walked into the kitchen. "You're home early."

"Hi, Mom. I am. I finished my column for next week, which has me looking forward to planting my own garden." Janie laid a hand on

Reagan's shoulder. "Reagan, you were saying? You think Finn has…"

"A respiratory infection—I think Finn is getting an upper respiratory tract infection. You can't see the virus with my microscope, I'd need an electron for that, but—"

Gareth let out a laugh. "You needed to magnify his boogers to figure out that he's getting a cold? How about the coughing and the sneezing—wasn't that kind of a giveaway?"

They all laughed at that, Reagan included, and Janie was glad the situation had so easily been defused.

"Mom, is it okay if I invited someone over tonight to help with my science project?"

"Sounds like a great idea, Reagan."

Janie was thrilled; she secretly dreaded the science expo. She should enjoy helping the boys with their projects, and she did most of the time, but at eleven years of age Reagan already seemed to be smarter than she was—smarter than most everyone she knew. His project had something to do with electricity, and quite frankly the whole notion scared her to death.

"What do you guys want for dinner? Spaghetti or chili dogs?"

"Are there meatballs?" Reagan asked.

"Yep, I've got some in the freezer."

"Spaghetti," they answered in unison, and

Janie smiled with satisfaction. It would be a rare and coveted night where everyone would eat the same meal without complaint.

Her mother took a now-sleeping Finn from her arms. Janie was elbow-deep in chopped lettuce for a salad when the doorbell rang. She wiped her hands on a dish towel as she headed for the entryway, assuming it was Reagan's friend Elena. But when she opened the door she found Aidan Hollings standing on her porch, once again reminding her more of a hippie surfer than a doctor of anything in his rumpled khakis, faded T-shirt and worn Converse tennis shoes. His streaked blond curls were tucked behind his ears and caramel-colored whiskers graced his smiling face.

"Hi," he said.

She forced a smile through her surprise. "Hi, um, what are you doing here?"

"Didn't Reagan tell you?"

"Tell me what?"

"Yesterday when we were unloading my boxes, he invited me over to take a look at his science project."

This was so Reagan. Aidan was the "friend" he'd invited. She knew better than to be irritated with her son because details he considered pertinent were not always the same as hers.

"Sorry, come in. He did mention that he invited someone, but he wasn't specific."

"Oh, well…" Aidan held up the bag along with an easy smile, his bright, white-bandaged hand somehow a reminder of his humanity, and a cue for her to be civil. "Peace offering?"

"Aidan, really—that isn't necessary."

"I know. I wanted to. But I'm pretty sure you're going to like this. I think you'll all like it. Also, there's something I want to talk to you about."

Reagan stepped into the entryway. "Aidan, hi! I've got my third section working perfectly, but I'm still having serious problems with the voltage on my Van de Graaff generator. Can you stay for dinner? We're having spaghetti. My mom makes killer meatballs—they're like this big." He shaped his fingers into a large circle.

Aidan Hollings eating dinner at her table and electrocuting who-knows-what with her son? No, it was too…much. He paused and Janie felt relieved because she thought that meant he was going to decline and save her from having to make an excuse for him.

"Sure. Dinner sounds great. Spaghetti is one of my favorites."

Reagan grinned. "Mine, too. Mom, how long until dinner?"

Janie realized they were both now looking at her. "Um, about an hour?"

"Okay, Aidan, come on. I'm all set up in the garage." Reagan took off down the hall toward the back door.

What choice did she have here? She motioned at the bag he held. "Do you want me to take that?"

"I'll wait until after dinner. Can I just set it out of the way somewhere?"

"Yes, sure, in the kitchen would be best to keep the kids out of it. What did you want to talk to me about?"

"I have some good news for you."

"Oh?" Janie couldn't possibly begin to imagine.

"I've decided to do the interview."

Janie wondered why this was good news for *her*?

He shrugged, his face sporting a lazy half grin. "I, uh, I wanted to do something to try and make things up to you, so I told Laurel I'd do the interview. Emily is really excited. My agent is thrilled, too. So, yeah, congratulations."

Janie tried not to gape. Too? Like *she* was supposed to be grateful and excited in addition to Laurel, Emily, his agent and whoever else because he'd bestowed this honor upon her? Like some kind of prestigious award? She stared at him and tried to decide what to say. She wished she could scoot him right back out the door and pretend this wasn't happening. She glanced over at Reagan, who had doubled back and now stood waiting patiently in the hall.

Lucky for her she did have an out.

"Well, that's great for Laurel and Emily and… whoever. And I appreciate the gesture, but I've already told Laurel to assign someone else to the interview if you, um, decided to…agree. I thought we would both be more comfortable with that under the circumstances."

"Circumstances?"

"Yes—"

"You know what?" Aidan held up a hand toward her like he was trying to stop traffic. "We can talk about this later." The self-assurance in his voice made her bristle.

She infused her tone with a heavy dose of fake sweetness. "No, that's okay, we don't need to do that—to talk about it. I've made it very clear to Laurel that I'm fine with not doing the interview."

He nodded. "We'll talk." He said it like a man used to getting both the last word and his way, but he was in for a surprise. He could last-word her until he was blue in the face, but he would not get his way.

His attention was now focused on Reagan,

who was saying something about the composition of Barbie hair. Janie didn't even want to think about what that meant.

"Sounds very cool. Let's go take a look at that generator." Aidan flashed another proud-of-himself grin before following Reagan down the hall.

Janie moved back into the kitchen to find the sauce boiling and splattering all over the stove top. She silently and irrationally blamed Aidan as she turned down the temperature and mopped up the mess.

She set about defrosting the meatballs. A peace offering? And agreeing to do the article like she was some kind of charity case? He obviously felt guilty, and how mortifying. She wanted to forget everything that had happened between them and just…pretend like everything was fine. *This* was the opposite of forgetting—coming over here with his "good news" and a "peace offering."

She was mangling some garlic cloves and mumbling to herself when her mother came strolling into the kitchen with a fussy Finn cradled in her arms.

"Look who woke up already. Why don't you take him and let me finish that?"

"That would be great, Mom." She took Finn in her arms. Her poor little guy—he was definitely coming down with a cold, or worse. "He sounds so congested. I'll give him a dose of medicine after dinner."

She exited the kitchen when another knock sounded on the door.

This time it was followed immediately by a voice—Shay's voice. "Hey, it's just me. Yum, something smells delicious."

Janie met her in the hallway.

"Shay, hi! What are you doing here?"

"Jonah is playing poker with Caleb and Doc, so I thought I'd pop over—I hope that's okay?"

Janie grinned, knowing very well that Jonah's poker matches with his grandfather Caleb and his friends could last for hours. "Better than okay—can you stay for dinner?"

"Are you kidding? Love to."

Janie breathed a sigh of relief. "Thank you."

"You're thanking me for you offering *me* dinner? How very like you, Jane Elizabeth."

Janie lowered her voice. "Aidan Hollings is here."

Shay shook her head and looked confused. "What does that—"

Janie whispered, "I'll explain later."

Thankfully, Shay ran with it. "Okay," she whispered in return, before switching to her normal tone. "Do you want me to set the table?"

The addition of Shay at dinner was a godsend to Janie. Aidan spent most of the meal talking to her mother and Reagan. Gareth and the twins adored Shay and vied for her attention so Janie didn't feel compelled to make small talk.

After dinner was over, Shay helped Claire with the dishes while Finn fell asleep in Janie's arms. The boys headed for the family room, and Janie tried to ignore the pang in her heart at the sight of Gabe giggling in Aidan's arms.

Finn finally dozed off so she put him down. She made tea for her mom, Shay and herself and they discussed Shay's upcoming wedding, the PTO fund-raiser, and how great the newly constructed community center was turning out to be.

Soon Claire said her goodbyes, kissed and hugged the boys and headed out the door. Gabe toddled into the room and crawled up into Shay's lap and promptly fell asleep. Janie felt a wave of relief as she realized the end of the evening—meaning Aidan's departure—was imminent.

Janie and Shay were still seated at the dining room table when Aidan came in with the boys.

Shay stood with Gabe. "I'm going to go put this little man down."

Janie smiled at her. "Thanks, Shay."

Janie calculated that Aidan should take that cue and start heading for the door.

Instead he lifted his hands and said brightly, "I

almost forgot about my surprise. I brought dessert." He disappeared into the kitchen.

When he stepped back into the room with the familiar-looking bright pink box Janie felt a stab of unease, which amplified dramatically as Lilah's parting question from yesterday about second chances came roaring back to her.

She should have insisted on taking the bag when Aidan arrived and peeked inside. If she would have seen the box she would have figured it out and she could have…

Reagan said, "Oh, yum—it's from the Donut Den."

Janie's eyes darted toward Gareth, expecting him to look wary as well. But he didn't. He looked excited about the prospect of dessert. And suddenly the scene seemed to be unfolding in one of those slow-motion-type nightmares, leaving Janie frozen with panic and yet powerless to stop the impending disaster.

CHAPTER SEVEN

FOR THE SECOND time that evening Aidan stood in front of her wearing the same self-satisfied smile. But the problem this time was that his actions weren't just going to affect her—he was about to hurt her children. Like the wave at the beach, she could see it coming, but now it was vital that she stopped it before it doused them all.

She blurted, "Aidan, can I talk to you in the kitchen for a minute?"

He looked at her and smiled. "Sure, hold on a sec."

She pierced him with a look she was sure would stop a normal person in their tracks. But, of course, she wasn't dealing with a normal person—she was stuck with some kind of…socially bereft genius.

She tried again. "Aidan—"

But it was too late. He was already opening the box. He proudly placed the dessert on the table. "I felt really bad about the other day so I placed my own special order. Boston cream pie—dairy-free, made with almond milk."

Gareth's face fell along with Janie's stomach.

Janie had no idea how to handle this extraordinarily uncomfortable situation. She certainly didn't want to explain. Would not explain, in fact, because she felt doing so would be like a betrayal of Gareth or Cal or…all of them. She really, really wished this wasn't happening.

A wellspring of anger rose within her. Why couldn't he have dropped it like she'd asked him to? There were things in this world that just happened and there were things in this world that couldn't be fixed. She'd accepted that. To say she'd learned this lesson the hard way was the understatement of the century. She assumed that by adulthood most people had. But somehow in all his years of formal education and world travels and "life experience," Aidan Hollings had not learned this?

Janie put her head down and massaged her temples.

The timing for this little stunt could not be worse. Gareth had seemed to be rebounding after his dad's birthday fiasco a few days before, and Janie had been happy that she had a respite for a couple months before the Father's Day pancake breakfast rolled around.

Shay entered the room. "Hey, did someone say…" Her voice trailed off as she glanced down at the table where they were all staring at the Boston cream pie. "Dessert? Oh, no…"

Gareth kept his eyes glued to the cake as he stood up. He backed away from the table. "May I be excused, Mom?"

"Absolutely," Janie said.

He walked from the room with more dignity than Janie would have thought possible, certainly more than she would have had herself.

Janie could see the mix of pain and confusion on Reagan's face as he looked at Aidan. Then his gaze flickered toward the doorway where Gareth had just exited. Janie imagined him being torn between following his brother and trying to make Aidan feel better.

"Um, Mom, is it okay if I'm excused, too? I'm really full from dinner."

Janie nodded, secretly pleased by his choice, by this show of brotherly support.

He politely addressed Aidan. "Thank you for the, uh, cake, Aidan. And thanks so much for the help with my science project." He paused for a second and the earnest yet uncomfortable expression on his face made Janie want to cry. "Can you talk to my mom about me helping in your lab? I really want to."

"Of course, buddy."

Janie repeated the words in her head—*helping in his lab*? What? No! Her entire body tensed.

Why would he ask her eleven-year-old to work with him before clearing it with her first? Shay reached out and took hold of her wrist. She squeezed and that prompted Janie to inhale a deep breath—and another—as she tried to decide what to do, what to say...

Aidan seemed uncomfortable, too, and a bit baffled, and under different circumstances Janie might have felt sorry for him. But she felt too sorry for her boys, and for herself, to let any other *sorry* seep in.

"I've messed this up somehow, haven't I?" Aidan shifted his weight from one foot to the other for a few long seconds. "Is someone going to tell me what in the world is going on?"

At that moment Finn's squeal lit up the baby monitor and Janie had never felt so grateful for a child's cry in her entire life. She bolted from the room and when she returned several minutes later Aidan and the Boston cream pie were both, thankfully, gone.

Janie found Shay in the living room with Mac-Gyver snoozing at her feet. She plopped down beside her cousin on the kid-worn, cat-scratched, oversize sofa.

Shay pulled up a knee and shifted so she was facing Janie. Her face held a mixture of worry and concern. "Do you want to tell *me* what's going on? I'm assuming it's not a coincidence that Aidan showed up here with Cal's birthday cake? And why is Aidan Hollings showing up here at all—without Emily or Bering?"

Janie grimaced. "Where is it—the cake?"

"After I escorted Aidan out, I stuffed it in a brown paper bag and put it in the garbage can in the garage."

"Thank you."

"What choice did I have? You were all staring at it like he was trying to serve us up a piece of roadkill."

Janie snuffled out a laugh in spite of the situation.

"Janie, when Jonah came back to town I could barely think straight—so many emotions were bouncing around inside of me. You are my best friend, and you never proved it more than then— except maybe when I had the miscarriage. But my point is that you are always there for me— you are my comfort and my voice of reason. Let me be that for you. Tell me what's going on."

Janie stared at Shay. "Okay, first of all, please don't compare this situation to you and Jonah. You guys are a love story. This…" She gestured as if Aidan was standing right in front of them. "This is a comedy of errors."

GARETH WATCHED AS Crosby turned his funny cat circles and finally curled into a ball for a nap on his chest. He winced as he thought about the look on his mom's face when she'd seen the Boston cream pie. For someone as smart as Aidan Hollings was supposed to be, bringing that dessert seemed like a pretty clueless move. Although Reagan had a point when he said that likely Aidan didn't know what the Boston cream pie meant to their mom—or to them.

Obviously Reagan was crazy about Aidan, so naturally he would stick up for him. Talk about simpatico—Reagan seemed to have met his soul mate there. And that was good because Reagan needed someone...

Gareth stuck up for him at school but sometimes he couldn't help it and he found himself wishing his brother wasn't quite so...odd. Even being odd was okay, if he wouldn't *show* it so much. For starters, he needed to quit talking about snot and boogers and other disgusting stuff in public. Harmon Vetcher hated Gareth and had it in for Reagan, and Gareth was afraid that one of these days he wouldn't be there to protect his brother.

Gareth had his quirks, too, but he was wise enough to keep them to himself. Like his midnight raids.

He would be making one tonight. He sort of didn't feel like he had a choice—sometimes it was the only thing that made him feel better.

He didn't know why. He couldn't explain it, this compulsion of his. He wondered if it was an addiction. He reminded himself to do an internet search tomorrow about addiction. He knew from this TV show he watched sometimes that people could get addicted to some really weird stuff.

But this wasn't that weird, was it?

Gareth couldn't talk to his mom about it because he knew it would upset her. She had certain expectations of him, and he was trying his hardest to live up to them. His mom, his brothers and his dad—even though his dad wasn't here, Gareth knew he would want him to act like a man—were all counting on him and he didn't want to let them down.

SHAY'S EYES WERE wide when Janie finished the accounting of all of her dealings with Aidan Hollings to date. Janie actually chuckled as she watched her cousin trying to find words—finding words was Shay's strong suit.

"So… He… That's why he has the bandage on his hand? Clam digging?"

"Yep, he now has eight stitches in the fingers of his left hand, for which I feel slightly responsible. And Reagan just now confirmed with me that Aidan asked him to help him in his lab because he can't use his hand. How am I supposed to say no to that? But who asks an eleven-year-old to work with him without consulting his mother? It's bad enough that Reagan worships the ground he walks on—something I encouraged before he actually came to town and we met him and I heard him…" Janie's voice trailed off with a shake of her head.

"Um, first of all—what are you going to do about the interview?"

"Nothing, thank goodness. I already told Laurel I don't want to do it."

Shay nodded, pondering. "I'm so glad Gareth didn't get stung. I don't like that 'mommy' comment—like it's an insult to be a mom? Or that it means that's all you can do? Your column is awesome *and* you're the best mom I've ever seen."

Janie laid back her head against the sofa cushion and stared at the shelf above the television, where there was an assortment of photos and knickknacks. She noticed a cobweb stretching between a photo of Gareth, Reagan and Cal hamming for the camera on the bow of one of Uncle Ben's boats, to a vase that Gareth had made for her in second grade. How long had it been since she'd dusted? She couldn't even keep up with her children, much less the housework. Her boys all looked so happy in that photo. How long had it been since they looked that happy? How long had it been since they'd been that happy?

She blinked back tears and turned her head

toward Shay. She lowered her voice even though she knew the boys were in their bedroom with the door shut.

"I don't know anymore, Shay. As the boys get older I feel like they are having all these thoughts and feelings that I'm not privy to, which of course they are. But I feel like I'm out of touch with them, like I can't relate, like I don't know what to say anymore." This time the tears spilled over and she wiped at them with her fingertips.

This was difficult to admit, but she needed to get it off her chest. "And I feel like maybe Gareth is still having some issues. It's been three years—he should have come to terms with his dad's death by now, shouldn't he?"

Shay turned and reached behind her. She plucked some tissues out of the box on the end table and handed one to Janie and used another to dab at her own eyes.

"I don't know, Janie. I lost a baby more than a decade ago and only recently do I really feel… acceptance or something that finally allows me to talk about it? Grief is so…difficult."

Janie knew this to be true, although Shay's situation had a lot to do with forgiving Jonah and accepting her inability to have children as well as dealing with the miscarriage.

"The counselor said to try not to push him through the stages of grief, but I think we may need to readdress some things. And I…" Janie felt a sob well up within her. "I dread that, Shay. It's so painful. I don't want to dredge up those feelings if I don't need to. And I know this is going to sound weird but somehow, something about Aidan seems to be doing that—stirring things up."

AIDAN HADN'T INTENDED to stir anything. Quite the opposite—he'd been hoping to smooth things over. While talking to Drum about the interview, he'd seen Janie walking toward the bakery…and ordering the replacement Boston cream pie had seemed like a stroke of genius.

He'd even kicked himself for not thinking of the idea sooner. Now he wished he'd never thought of it at all. Obviously he was missing something vitally important where that cake was concerned. But apparently he wasn't going to get the answer from Janie—or her guard dog of a cousin, who had escorted him out as if she'd suspected him of trying to steal the candlesticks.

It was almost comical the way he kept messing up with her, not that a social misstep was unusual for him, but this situation with Janie seemed extreme even for him.

Aidan had worked so hard in his youth to become socially proficient—to be liked. He'd desperately wanted to be liked, and even though he accomplished that much more easily now as an adult, it still wasn't effortless. He avoided crowds and certain social situations and he liked that his job ensured that he spent a minimum amount of time with people. Of course, he also didn't much care anymore what people thought of him, which he supposed was rather ironic, especially since he suddenly found himself caring again—very much so—about what Janie thought.

His phone rang and he looked at the display— Laurel Davidson from the *Rankins Press*. No doubt calling him about the interview—at least in that he felt confident that he'd finally done something right where Janie was concerned.

"Hey, Laurel, what's up?"

CHAPTER EIGHT

JANIE HURRIED INTO the Rankins high school, took a right and jogged down the length of the hall. She exhaled a sigh of relief as the clock above the library door showed her to be right on time. She'd thought she was going to be late because MacGyver had somehow gotten ahold of a bottle of cold medicine for babies and she'd had to rush him to the vet, not knowing how much he'd managed to ingest.

Thankfully Emily had been able to bring Reagan to this science club meeting. Emily and Reagan were science buddies anyway, sharing a love for the subject and for trivia in general, as well as a mutual admiration for, and an unaccountably broad knowledge of, the former president that Reagan's father had named him after.

Janie walked through the door to find more parents and kids in attendance than she'd ever seen at a meeting for any club or activity, with the exception of athletics. Most people were already seated at tables but a few were still milling around. The turnout was undoubtedly due to the incredible prize and scholarship opportunities up for grabs this year. Ms. Treyborn had only been a teacher in Rankins for two years, but her passion for science was already renowned.

Janie saw Reagan waving to her from a table off to one side of the room in front of the periodical section. Confusion and surprise mingled uncomfortably within her when she saw that it wasn't Emily seated next to Regan. Janie did her best to keep the smile glued to her face as she approached the table where her son was happily chatting away with Aidan Hollings.

"Hey, guys."

"Hi, Mom."

"Um, what's up? Where's Emily?"

Aidan had this slow way of smiling, she'd noticed, as if he had tons of time and not a care in the world. Janie knew this shouldn't bother her but she couldn't help it—it did. It somehow served to emphasize how many problems she *did* have, and how little time to deal with them all.

His eyes seemed to assess her. "Emily isn't feeling well, so I volunteered to bring Reagan. I hope that's okay?"

Janie eyed him speculatively. She felt torn between appreciating this generous action toward Reagan and Emily, and selfishly wishing him gone. She'd had a long day—selfishness won out.

"Sure, thanks so much for bringing him. But

since I'm here now, you can go ahead and take off and that would be fine. You probably have other things you'd like to do."

Aidan shrugged a shoulder and glanced at a neighboring table. Janie followed his gaze to where the evil spawn Harmon Vetcher was seated with his father, Marv. "If you don't mind, I'd like to stay."

Reagan looked so excited by the prospect that Janie couldn't force herself to object. She slid into a seat beside Reagan as Ms. Treyborn began to speak in her curiously perky way.

"Well, I'm superexcited to see so many students and parents here tonight. We're going to go over some of the requirements for the science expo—dos and don'ts, if you will. But first—for those of you who haven't heard—I have some very exciting news."

Jacinda Treyborn was a transplant from the lower forty-eight who had admittedly come to Alaska after seeing one of those reality shows about Alaskan men "looking for love." Janie was surprised she hadn't found it; she was young, pretty and enthusiastic about teaching. Reagan adored her and assured Janie that Ms. Treyborn was "wicked smart."

"This year, thanks to a generous donation by Cam-Field Oil & Mineral Corporation, we are participating in the acclaimed Science Is Our

Future Organization's national competition. Our participation in SOFO means winning entries will be eligible to go on to the state competition for a chance to win more scholarships and prizes. If any entries place in the top three at state, they will proceed to nationals."

Janie didn't think it was her imagination that Ms. Treyborn looked hopefully in Reagan's direction while relaying this information.

She went on to explain that in order to compete, students had to strictly follow the guidelines set out by the national program to the letter. A high school student began passing around a handout of the extensive rules and regulations.

Reagan's eyes were wide with excitement—clearly his brain was already set on the task. Janie imagined she could hear all that gray matter humming with possibilities.

"An exciting twist this year will also be the addition of the oral presentation. Along with the normal booth displays, students are required to do a ten-minute presentation of their project to a panel of judges—which will include two national representatives from SOFO—as well as to the audience."

As if she didn't already have enough anxiety in her life, now she had to worry about her socially awkward son demonstrating his project to a roomful of people? Perfect.

Janie picked a handout off the stack and passed the pile to the next table. Ms. Treyborn finished up her speech by reminding everyone that their proposals were due in one week. She would approve their ideas, and students had six weeks after that to complete work on their projects. The science expo would take place on the second to last day of school at the VFW hall.

"Don't forget there are cookies and punch on the back table there." Jacinda patted her tummy and mimed a long drink from an invisible cup. "And I will be available for questions along with last year's high school winner, Hunter Keif." She gestured at the student now standing beside her.

Reagan immediately began chattering to Aidan. He didn't seem concerned about the demonstration, so that was good. But then again Reagan didn't really grasp the extent of his own social shortcomings, which could also be good sometimes, although nearly as often it seemed to make matters worse.

Janie rose to her feet. People were already mingling and talking excitedly about the competition. She made her way over to the refreshments, smiling and greeting people. She snagged a few snickerdoodles and two cups of sweet but surprisingly tasty fruit punch.

She headed back toward the table to find Aidan and Reagan in discussion with Ms. Treyborn. Well, Aidan appeared to be listening while Jacinda chattered excitedly.

Janie handed Reagan a cup and a cookie, watched Jacinda tug on the neckline of her blouse and thought, *Okay, Jacinda, not in front of my eleven-year-old...*

"Janie, you didn't tell me you knew Dr. Hollings. You've been holding out on me." She squeezed Janie's arm like she'd failed to inform her that a gigantic meteorite was hurtling toward the earth.

"Oh, sorry, Jacinda—I didn't realize it was big news. And I don't really know Dr. Hollings all that well."

"But you're related somehow, right?" Janie surmised that Jacinda desperately wanted the answer to be yes.

"No, not really. Dr. Hollings is Emily's brother— so that makes him my brother Bering's brother-in-law. That's kind of a mouthful, isn't it?"

"And, that's practically related, right?" A pair of hopeful baby blues latched on to Aidan. "Um, so, Aidan, like I was saying, if you need anything at all while you're here you come and see me. I will be your science go-to girl." She curled a talon-like grasp around Aidan's forearm. Janie couldn't help but think of the eagles that flocked to the salmon spawning grounds each year and latched on to the fish, trying desperately to fly off with a lot more than they could handle.

Janie lifted her cup for a sip, mostly to hide her snicker.

Aidan glanced down at Jacinda's hand. "Thank you so much, uh…Jacinda, right? I'll keep that in mind."

"Is there any chance you would be willing to speak to my science classes? Or perhaps to the entire school?"

Janie might have missed the subtle tension emanating from Aidan if she hadn't been watching, if she didn't have experience with this herself via her son.

Aidan smiled tightly. "Send me an email with the details of what you have in mind, and we'll see."

"Excellent." Jacinda beamed as she patted Reagan's shoulder. "Reagan, no pressure, but I'm counting on you to give the sixth grade a good showing this year."

Aidan watched her walk away, a smile playing on his lips. Was he embarrassed, or flattered, or perhaps even interested? Janie couldn't tell for sure.

But then he turned a different smile on Janie, a wider smile. His eyes met hers and he added a little head shake, like they were sharing some kind of private joke. Her pulse accelerated and she felt her cheeks warm. She immediately reminded herself that she wasn't interested in sharing jokes or anything else with him, for that matter.

Janie cleared her throat. "Reagan, we should really get going. Thank you so much, Aidan, for bringing Reagan here tonight. Reagan, did you thank Aidan?"

"Yes, I did. But, Mom, we actually need to give Aidan a ride home—to Uncle Bering's."

Janie blinked. "What? Why?"

Aidan explained, "Bering dropped us off on his drive over to Bradbury's. He needed to pick up some supplies so he suggested that you bring us back to their house. He said you had to get Gareth anyway. And it would give us a chance to talk about Reagan helping me out with my work. I'd appreciate it if he could start as soon as possible. I'm pretty worthless with this hand right now." He held it aloft, as if Janie needed a reminder.

Janie had no excuse; she couldn't decline to give him a ride home after he'd brought her son here. She hadn't figured out how to break it to either of them that Reagan wasn't going to be helping him out. Probably because she hadn't been able to come up with a good reason—she couldn't very well tell him that she just didn't like how…intrusive he'd become.

"Absolutely."

Reagan and Aidan chatted most of the trip about the science expo and Aidan's bee study. Janie had to admit that the study Aidan was taking part in did seem kind of interesting.

She asked, "Will you be studying honeybees, too? Or just bumblebees? That honeybee colony collapse disorder is pretty scary, right?"

Aidan glanced at her, surprise evident on his face.

"Yes, even a mom like me has heard of colony collapse," she remarked dryly.

"No, no—it's not that... And no, we're not studying the European honeybee—it isn't native. This study is focusing on Alaska's native bee species, which are thought to be in decline. Other states are heading up similar studies to assess the health of their native bee populations as well. The data will all be compiled and a conclusion issued at the study's completion."

"European honeybees are the *only* pollinator of almonds, did you know that, Mom?"

"I believe you've mentioned it, Reagan."

"There's a researcher who has linked CCD to a certain class of pesticides. It's possible he may have figured out the cause, but some of the chemical companies are doing their best to muddy the waters. And, of course, there are a multitude of other opinions and theories..."

Janie pulled up to Bering and Emily's house. Reagan immediately chimed from the backseat, "Mom, Emily made pies today. Is it okay if I go in and have a piece?"

"Sure, hon."

Reagan bolted out of the car while she gathered her bag.

Aidan sat in the passenger seat watching her and making no move to get out of the car. She was suddenly struck with the feeling that he wasn't quite as laid-back as he appeared.

He asked, "Could we talk?"

A jolt of nervous tension zipped through her. "Um, sure, I guess. What about?"

"About Reagan."

"What about him?" Janie could hear the defensive tone in her voice even as she wondered what Reagan had said or done. He didn't have the best social filter.

"Your son is brilliant."

Janie smiled tightly. "Yes, I know."

"Does he have trouble at school?"

Where was this going? "Only in art—he doesn't like art class. He thinks the grading is too subjective. But his grades are perfect."

"No, I mean socially."

Janie wanted to laugh out loud. Reagan had exactly one close friend his age, almost his age. Elena Stanton—and she was a year ahead of him in seventh grade. Janie lived in fear of the day when those typical boy-girl differences would take over and Elena would leave Reagan in the dust. But why would any of this be Aidan's concern?

Janie eyed him warily. "Why are you asking?"

AIDAN COULDN'T STOP himself from asking. He knew this wasn't any of his business. But that wasn't really true; because he felt like any kid being bullied was, and would always be, his business. He'd never wanted to hurt a child in his entire adult life—until he'd overheard Harmon Vetcher tormenting Reagan. Janie needed to be made aware of the problem. Hell, so did the school's administrator and perhaps local law enforcement.

"I assume you know this Harmon Vetcher kid?"

Aidan watched Janie's mossy green eyes light with fear. "Yes."

"That kid is a snake in the grass."

"Yes, I'm aware of that as well. What happened?"

"He didn't know that I was with Reagan. And Regan doesn't know I heard, but I did. He threatened Reagan. He told him he would pee in the toilet and shove his head in it if Reagan beat him in this project. He also said, and I quote,

'Your big brother won't be around next year to protect you and I can't tell you how much I look forward to that.'

"I looked around to say something—do something—but I didn't know exactly how to proceed. I wanted to grab the little creep by the neck, but I didn't want to make more trouble for Reagan. I didn't want to embarrass him by letting him know that I heard."

Janie dipped her head and placed a hand over her forehead. She didn't seem surprised, which confirmed his suspicion that the problem was a chronic one. Aidan could see the tension radiating off of her. He couldn't imagine what that would feel like, someone threatening your child. Aidan knew very well what it was like to be on the receiving end of those threats, however. He had learned to cope eventually but school had been a long and difficult road for him.

"That kid is a monster. I can see it. I…"

"Believe me—I know. You what?"

"I have some experience with this kind of thing. What are you going to do?"

Janie gripped the steering wheel. "I've talked to the administration. I've talked to his parents. I don't know what else I can do."

Plenty, Aidan wanted to say. Instead, he asked, "What do they say? The principal? His parents?"

"The administration has talked to Harmon

and Riley—Riley Shriver is one of Harmon's minions—and their parents. There's nothing else I can do unless they actually follow through on one of their threats. And Harmon's dad is a police officer here in town. He's a piece of work and a bully in his own right. His favorite line is, and I quote, 'Boys will be boys.'"

"Has he ever acted on any of these threats?"

Janie nodded. "Yes, once—that I know about. Gareth intervened. He actually…" She shook her head. "Harmon is scared of Gareth, and Riley follows Harmon's lead, so Reagan has been relatively safe—physically at least. But I am worried about next year—they will be in different buildings at the school with different lunches and break times. And Reagan's one friend, Elena— she always sticks up for him and kids listen to her. She's very bright too, but much better than Reagan at socializing. Though she's also in an older kids' class, so she won't be there to help, either."

Flashbacks from his harrowing nightmarish days of middle school flickered through Aidan's brain. Cruel, horrific words and embarrassing taunts, duct tape in his hair, dish soap in his lunch, a firecracker in his locker… Before he'd grown, before he'd learned how to handle this problem and before he'd figured out that his brain could be an asset instead of a liability. He hadn't had a dad to help him, either.

Thankfully, like Janie's boys he'd been left with a loving mother. But more important, Aidan had been blessed with a practical grandfather, who'd helped him in one critical way. The rest Aidan had figured out on his own, but it hadn't been easy.

Someone needed to help Reagan figure it out, too. Aidan had already made the decision—that someone was going to be him.

He watched Janie carefully as he made the suggestion. "Maybe there's something I can do."

JANIE DIDN'T KNOW how to handle this situation. Not the one with Reagan—she'd been dealing with this kind of stuff nearly all of Reagan's life. Aidan's interest in the situation was the problem. She didn't know what to make of it, which was shaping up to be a recurring theme where Aidan was concerned.

"Um, I appreciate your concern, Aidan, I really do. And thank you for coming to the meeting with Reagan. I can see that he really looks up to you. But...you don't need to worry about us—about him, okay? I've got it under control."

Aidan stared at her and Janie tried to imagine what he was thinking—that she was a bad mom because her child was bullied at school, that she was a witch because she told him she didn't want help? But that was a lie because sometimes she did want help—she didn't want *his* help.

"How do you have it under control? What are you going to do about it?"

"Nothing."

"Nothing?" His voice was sharp, full of disapproval.

Now she did feel like a bad mom. She squeezed her eyes shut for a few seconds and reminded herself that he didn't understand. He couldn't possibly understand.

She looked at him and said with as much firmness as she could muster, "Look, Reagan is a target and I know that. But he's a target because he's smart. Sure, he's a little quirky but basically he's just smart. He's smarter than the other kids, smarter than their parents, smarter than most of the teachers, smarter than his own mother."

Aidan stared out the windshield for a long moment. When he turned toward her his eyes felt like two gray laser beams zeroing in on hers.

"So…what are you saying? That he's smart enough to keep himself from being bullied? That's not how it works, Janie."

Was that what she was saying? No, but… It didn't matter because she didn't need to explain anything to him. Reagan was her child.

"I'm saying that I can handle it." She could

hear the defensive tone in her voice, but she didn't appreciate the lecture.

His eyebrows swept up, his face covered with his skepticism. "Clearly that is not the case. If that was the case I wouldn't have heard what I heard. I bet there's a good chance this goes a lot deeper than you know. And there's also a good chance that Reagan is keeping a lot of what is going on from you. And Gareth, too, for that matter, is—"

Janie interrupted. "Wait—what are you saying?"

"I'm saying you have a problem and I—"

"You know what?" She struggled for diplomacy, but blurted out, "How dare you?"

"How dare I what? Point out something you probably already know but refuse to acknowledge? And definitely do not have under control?"

She couldn't even remember the last time she'd been this angry, although a tiny part of her appreciated this concern for her children—that was the part that kept her from blowing her top.

She enunciated slowly with the hope that he'd get the message and back off. "I can handle this. I don't need your help. Aidan, you're not even a parent and you can't possibly—"

"Having compassion for children isn't limited to parenthood, especially when I know that I'm right—"

She brought up a hand and stopped him. "Okay. Stop. Please, don't. Okay? Don't *help*. Clearly, you have a difficult time with this concept, and I'm not trying to be rude but you really, *really* need to learn to mind your own business. I appreciate your concern for my kids, but I do not need your help or advice—in parenting or in any other aspect of life."

Janie felt his eyes on her, assessing and critical, and she decided she knew what one of his bees probably felt like.

Finally he nodded once and said, "I can see I've offended you and I apologize for that. When I believe something very strongly or I'm passionate about something, it can be difficult for me to refrain from trying to…help."

He gave her a sheepish grin and Janie knew they were both thinking about their encounter in front of the bakery.

"I hope that you will still consider allowing Reagan to work with me. I really could use his help and I think it would be good for him." He pointed again at his injured hand.

"I'll think about it."

Janie got out of the car and started toward the house. Frustration boiled within her, but was quickly overshadowed by doubt—and concern. Was Aidan right? Was the situation with Reagan more serious than she realized? She wanted to do the right thing for her children. That's all she ever wanted, but how was she supposed to know what that entailed?

Not for the first time Janie wished motherhood came with some kind of handbook or guidelines or something. One wrong move and you could mess up a child's entire life…forever. That's what scared her. But what about not moving? That was a problem, too.

A smiling Emily greeted Janie as she walked into Bering and Emily's kitchen. Reagan sat at the table next to Bering, who held Violet in the crook of one arm while eating a slice of pie with the other hand. The baby looked so tiny, cuddling with her giant of a brother.

"Are you okay?" Emily asked her. "You look kind of funny."

Janie rubbed a hand over her face. "Oh, I'm fine. Tired. Gabe now has Finn's cold and Mac-Gyver has to stay the night at the vet."

"What happened? Is he going to be okay?" Bering asked.

"Dr. Kohl seems to think he will be fine."

Janie looked up in time to see Aidan saunter into the kitchen, looking completely unruffled, like they hadn't had a heated conversation in the car only moments ago.

"What's wrong with him?" Aidan asked as he

took a seat at the table and began dishing out a slice of pie.

"He got into a bottle of ibuprofen. I have no idea how much he ingested."

Aidan's brows flew. "One of your babies swallowed an indeterminate amount of ibuprofen? How did he get ahold of it? That's awful."

"No, Aidan…" Emily started to explain.

Janie jumped in. "The dog got ahold of a bottle of baby medicine and chewed the top off. The twins have colds."

"Oh, I see. That's good." His lips curved down into a thoughtful frown. "I mean I hope the dog is okay, but medication like that shouldn't be left within the reach of a child."

Janie stared at him. Was he serious? The statement was so absurd she found herself sputtering out a laugh. "Thank you for that sound piece of advice—I'll be sure and take the cough syrup out of the toy box."

Emily laughed, too, and everyone soon joined her. Janie looked at Emily. "I'm praying it's not another ear infection. Poor baby's been plagued with them and every time he coughs or sneezes I get all stressed and want to race him to the ER."

Aidan chimed in again. "Unfortunately, ear infections are unbelievably common in babies. It's because of the short length and narrowness of the eustachian tube—makes them very susceptible to infection, especially when they have a cold, or even an allergy. Some kids seem to be unfairly prone to reinfection, almost to the point of a chronic condition..." Aidan's voice trailed off as he glanced around at everyone now staring at him.

"What?" One side of his mouth pulled up to form a lopsided grin. "Too much? Sorry, sometimes I get carried away."

Janie gaped at Aidan and then at Reagan, looked questioningly at Bering and Emily and wondered if they were all thinking the same thing.

Bering spoke first and confirmed her speculation. He pointed his fork from Aidan to Reagan and back again. "Is Reagan channeling him or is he channeling Reagan? How is this working exactly?"

Aidan looked at Reagan and grinned. "Well, that's the best compliment I've received in a long time, how about you?"

Reagan's face erupted with the biggest smile Janie had seen from him in ages. He turned to Aidan and they executed a complicated fist-bump that looked to her like some kind of a gang sign. Her chest constricted so tightly that she could barely inhale a breath.

To see her son bonding with someone in this way—even if it was someone as nosy and pushy as Aidan—nearly did her in. It annihilated the remains of her anger and replaced it with... something else. She swallowed a lump of emotion and admitted to herself that there was definitely a connection between this man and her son. And Aidan really did seem to have Reagan's best interests at heart.

She needed to get over herself and the way he made her feel and put her child first.

She made a decision on the spot. "So, Reagan—Aidan would like you to start helping in his lab right away. You guys can work out a schedule, but you need to keep up with your homework and save some time to work on your science project."

Reagan made a fist and punched the air in victory. "Awesome! Thanks, Mom."

Janie smiled at her son and knew at that moment that she'd made the right decision. She tried to commit the feeling to memory because she felt certain she would need to draw on it in the days ahead. She reminded herself that just because Reagan spent time with Aidan, didn't mean *she* had to. Besides, she'd made it pretty clear that she didn't need his help in parenting her children. She didn't see how it could be possible that he hadn't received the message.

Aidan's earnest blue-gray eyes met hers. He mouthed a thank-you and Janie turned toward the cupboard where she knew the glasses were kept. She removed one and turned on the faucet. Why was her mouth suddenly so dry? She filled a glass and took a deep drink.

Emily said, "I bet you're going to be busy, Reagan."

Aidan agreed. "There is a lot to do and if Gareth is available I could actually use him, too."

Reagan shook his head. "No good, Aidan. Gareth will never go for it. I don't think Mom would even let him—would you, Mom?"

"Absolutely not—out of the question."

"What? Why not?"

Janie crossed her arms over her chest to drop the bombshell. "Gareth is allergic to bees."

But Aidan didn't seem surprised, or even concerned. She'd expected him to look shocked, possibly apologize for his little stunt in front of the bakery last week.

Emily glanced questioningly at Aidan and then opened her mouth to comment, but Aidan asked, "Does he carry an EpiPen?"

"And he wears a medical alert necklace, too."

"Good. But there is really very little danger of him getting stung. There are no bees flying around in the lab. They are all contained—and I only keep them for a very short period of time. Learning about them might be a good way for him to conquer this irrational fear."

"Irrational? His fear is totally valid. He's severely allergic."

Janie watched Aidan's eyes narrow like she'd noticed they did when he was trying to decide what to say. He tipped his head slowly one way and then the other. "That's debatable."

"Debatable? It's a fact. I don't think—"

"Phobias are by their nature irrational, but let's not argue about that." He slipped in a knowing grin. "Shouldn't Gareth get to decide whether he'd like to work for me or not?"

"No! He's only thirteen."

Bering added, "He's almost fourteen."

Aidan leaned back in his chair. "Huh. I was working at the feed store when I was his age."

Bering chimed in, "I started working on one of Uncle Ben's fishing boats when I was only ten."

"Paper route," Emily added. "Twelve. But I was doing odd jobs at Cam-Field even before that."

Janie exchanged a look with Bering, and then with Emily. They were both okay with Gareth working around bees? What was the matter with these people? Janie threw up her arms and let out a huff. "All right, fine. I was sweeping up hair at Meg's Beauty Barn when I was thirteen, but I'm not allergic to hair."

Aidan wiped a smudge of huckleberry pie

from the side of his mouth with a napkin. "So, you don't mind if I ask him?"

She looked at Emily. "You know what he does with these bees and you still believe it would be safe for Gareth?"

"Yes, as safe as anything in life can be, Janie. When he goes out in the field there are bees, of course, like there are when Gareth goes fishing or camping or up to one of the cabins."

Her traitorous brother added, "Or outside playing football or basketball with his buddies. Bees are everywhere, Janie."

Janie felt three pairs of eyes on her and she wanted to say no, but her desire to do the right thing for her child won out. Maybe Gareth should have the option. And, if she was being perfectly honest, a good part of her felt confident about what his answer would be anyway. In this regard at least she knew her son and she believed there was no way he would agree to work with bees.

"Fine. You can ask him, but don't be surprised when he says no."

CHAPTER NINE

JANIE DROPPED OFF the boys at school, knowing that Reagan's euphoric mood had everything to do with her agreeing to allow him to work on Aidan's project. She felt good about that even as she battled with the realization that someone else had given him this happiness.

Janie reminded herself that it didn't matter as long as Reagan was benefitting from the experience. And there was no doubt in her mind that he would. So why did she still wish it wasn't Aidan who was responsible? With his pushiness and his obtrusive...speeches.

She had a few spare minutes before she had to be at work, so she swung by Bradbury's to pick up the heirloom vegetable seeds she'd ordered for her garden. She dialed Shay's number while she waited for the salesgirl to round up her purchase.

"Hey, how are things going?"

"Great. You'll never believe this, but Jonah didn't really book our honeymoon to the Caribbean."

Not sure if this was a good or bad thing Janie went with a neutral response. "Oh."

"Yeah, he was keeping the real destination a surprise so he *pretended* that we were going to the Caribbean."

"And you ruined it by having a little fit—how are you feeling about that?"

Shay snorted out a laugh. "I'd say *fit* is a strong word. He could see I was unhappy with the choice. You know I'm not good at hiding my feelings."

Janie chuckled. "That I do. So, where are you really going?"

"Switzerland."

Switzerland—that fit. *Good for you, Jonah,* she thought. Since high school Janie had believed Shay and Jonah belonged together. Finally they had figured it out, too.

"Switzerland sounds amazing. I'm so happy for you, Shay."

"Thanks, Janie. Me, too. We're hiking in the Alps. It'll be weird hiking somewhere and not worrying about bears."

They chatted for a few more minutes and Janie hung up when she reached the door of the *Rankins Press*. Only Piper greeted her. It was a rare occurrence that she—or anyone else for that matter—arrived at the office before Laurel.

Piper gestured at the ceiling. "Can you believe

this? She was on the phone when I came down and she gave me one of these." Piper placed a finger over her hushed lips.

Piper was Laurel's younger sister and she lived with Laurel in an apartment above the newspaper. Laurel had bought the *Rankins Press* fresh out of college and eventually had purchased the entire building the newspaper's office was housed in. She'd renovated the top floor and her friends often joked about Laurel's penthouse apartment in "downtown" Rankins. It was as close to chic as could be found in Rankins and served as a very convenient meeting place for their group of friends.

Piper placed a palm on the counter between them as if something had just occurred to her. "So…what's going on with you and Aidan Hollings?"

"What do you mean?"

"I mean I heard you were with Dr. Hottie when he cut his hand. I'm not going to lie, Janie, the pickup he borrowed from Bering has been spotted at your house and there has been some speculation."

Only in Rankins could rumors emerge this quickly. And if there were rumors, Piper would be the one to know them.

"Nothing is going on, Piper. Give it up."

Piper snickered. "Come on, Janie. I'm in a dry spell here."

Janie settled in at her desk, checked her email and found several questions regarding Domestic Endeavors in her inbox. This week's column had been about planting a vegetable garden, which could be tricky but also very rewarding in Alaska's unique climate and growing season. The column had focused on raised beds, which Janie preferred herself. She was typing an answer to the last question about the fertilization needs of cauliflower when Laurel appeared.

"Good morning, Laurel. Do you realize in all the years I've worked here this is the first time I've arrived before you? Is everything okay?"

"Actually, the reason I'm late has to do with you. There is something I need to talk to you about."

"Uh-oh, am I getting fired?" Janie clicked the Send button on the email. She'd been joking, but when she looked up Laurel's grave expression stole her smile. "Laurel, what's going on?"

Laurel sank into her own chair and then spun to face Janie. "We have a problem."

"What kind of problem?"

"Aidan Hollings's agent called this morning."

"Oh." What could this possibly have to do with her?

"Well, you know that Aidan has agreed to do the interview."

"Yes, that's great, isn't it?"

"It is—very great. Or it could be…"

Janie felt a surge of nerves, knowing somehow that whatever Laurel was going to say would not be great for her at all.

AIDAN OPENED HIS email to find a lengthy note from Blake. Why Blake insisted on writing him these book-length messages Aidan would never understand. Aidan had once responded to one of his two-page diatribes with this simple line: Get a journal, Blake.

To which Blake had answered: Why should I get a journal, Aidan, when I have you?

Aidan skimmed through the current missive; Blake had hired a media relations specialist to do some marketing for their film, he was thrilled by the reviews *Seeds* was receiving from an advance screening they'd offered, and… What? Aidan reread a paragraph. Blake was thinking about visiting him here in Alaska before the premiere? Aidan wondered what that was about.

He'd love to see his friend, but Blake seemed to be having the time of his life in New York. Aidan couldn't help but wonder what would prompt Blake to leave the city in the midst of all this media buzz he and Drum had created surrounding *Seeds*.

Blake could be such a contradiction. His friend loved the city, yet had chosen a profession where urban life didn't exactly mesh with what they did. Blake was comfortable in the field, too. He might not relish it like Aidan did, but he enjoyed it, making the best out of every experience and often joking about the discomfort and the uneasiness the seclusion caused him, in direct opposition to Aidan, who savored it.

So far working in Alaska was shaping up to be everything Aidan had hoped. It was ruggedly beautiful, relatively undisturbed, remote and isolated...yet accommodating in every way that mattered to him, including the presence of his sister and her family.

It was also interesting and challenging. He grinned as he realized how fitting those descriptors were on both the personal front as well as the professional.

Rankins seemed to promise him a wealth of excitement and...contentment. And, Aidan realized, the perfect mix of those aspects was exactly what he'd been searching for all his life.

JANIE SCOFFED WHEN Laurel told her the news— a too-loud mix of relief and amusement. Laurel looked concerned, like maybe she thought Janie was losing her mind.

"Janie, you do understand what I'm saying here, right? I have to ask you to reconsider. Aidan will *only* do the interview if you're the reporter who does it."

"Laurel, no. I mean yes, of course, I understand. But this is just a misunderstanding. He feels guilty because of everything that has happened. He's trying to patch things up with me or something."

Laurel raised one questioning brow. "Patch things up? You guys have the kind of relationship where things need to be patched? Do you have something you want to share with me?"

Janie felt her cheeks burn for absolutely no reason. "No, no—it's not like that. He's trying to…" Trying to what? How did she explain? She wasn't even sure exactly what he was up to herself. She assumed he felt guilty; just as he'd brought the cake as a peace offering, he'd also agreed to do the interview. Undoubtedly, Laurel had told him that she was assigning someone else so he'd requested her—to ensure that he could fully assuage his guilt.

"Janie, he was very adamant about this."

"I'll talk to him."

After assuring Laurel that she would straighten out the situation with Aidan, she found herself headed to his place. The building wasn't far from the *Rankins Press* office so she chose to walk. In Janie's most recent memory, the space had been a dance studio, a karate dojo and a church hall—nothing ever stuck around in the building for long. She found herself ungraciously hoping this was some kind of an omen where the current tenant was concerned as well. She chastised herself because the opportunity he was giving Reagan was worth more than any discomfiture she had to endure.

The door was open so she walked in to find him sitting in front of his computer.

"Hey, Aidan?"

His eyes snapped up and his gaze latched on hers. His lips tugged up with a slow smile.

"Um, your door is open, so I…" She lifted a thumb and gestured over her shoulder and immediately realized how much she probably resembled a hitchhiker. She lowered her hand and swallowed nervously. Why was she nervous?

"Welcome, welcome."

He stood and came toward her, and Janie found herself wishing he wasn't quite so good-looking. It was distracting.

She glanced around and realized he'd only set up equipment in one relatively small area. "You've got an awful lot of space here."

"I know. I really don't need this much. I'm living over there." He pointed to one corner, and then to what would obviously serve as his lab area. "Working over there and… I have some plans for the rest."

"Oh. Well, *that* explains it."

He chuckled. "I'm really glad you're here. I was going to call you today."

She fidgeted with the charm on her necklace. "Call me?"

"Yes, I figured maybe if I called you on the phone there would be less probability that I'd royally screw things up."

She smiled tightly. "Aidan—"

"Janie, I owe you some apologies. I'm sorry about the Boston cream pie. I didn't know…"

How did he…? "Did Shay tell you—"

"No, no. Oh, no—I thought your lovely cousin was going to drop-kick me off the front porch. She most certainly did not tell me anything. I barely even got a goodbye. I, um, I actually asked Bering and he kind of filled me in on some stuff."

"Oh." Right—a casual question to Bering and he wouldn't think twice about talking to Aidan, his brother-in-law.

"I should have known something was up that day outside the bakery, but for some reason that I can't identify and that I really regret now, I didn't take the time to think past what I could see. That can be a problem for me. That and… I sometimes say things without completely thinking through how it might be interpreted by someone else. If you felt like I was somehow insulting your parenting? Let me assure you that it was not my intention to do so. Your boys are incredible kids and obviously the credit for that is yours.

"Like I said, I have to continually work at diplomacy. As my colleague Blake likes to say, I can be a little clumsy on the social front."

Janie stared, dumbfounded. He was obviously making a reference to their conversation after the science club meeting. She hadn't expected such a…personal explanation. She certainly hadn't expected an apology. It reminded her of Cal. Her late husband had never had a problem apologizing and she'd always loved that about him.

Why was she comparing this situation with Aidan to her marriage with Cal? That was…not okay. She should probably go before this got any weirder. She called herself a coward because an apology didn't change the fact that he'd been acting out of guilt and probably pity as far as the interview was concerned. She didn't need—or want—either. She intended to clear that up right now.

"Thank you for the apology. I appreciate it— more than you probably realize. But my boys and I, we're… It's been three years since their dad was killed, and that might sound like a long time, but grief can be…tricky, and… We're still working some things out."

Aidan began talking quickly. "I can see that now. And I understand—I probably comprehend that more than you realize, definitely more than my behavior has reflected."

Janie found herself at a loss for words.

"Gareth has ritualized some of the important events surrounding his dad?"

Bering had definitely been talking. "Yes, his birthday, Christmas—all the major holidays, plus Veteran's Day for some reason. Cal wasn't even a veteran, although he was very patriotic and made an event of it when he was alive— flags and parades…" Janie took a deep breath. "Anyway, our grief counselor said it was okay for him to hold on to some of these occasions and memorialize them in his own way."

Aidan nodded, but she couldn't quite read his expression. "That makes sense."

Janie was glad it made sense to him because she wasn't really sure how she felt about it. If she was honest she'd kind of like the rituals to go away, although she'd never say that out loud.

But this exchange did have her feeling better about the situation with Aidan—better about him. Amazing how far an apology could go. And for some reason it seemed okay that he knew—

that he understood that they were struggling. It made her feel less…crazy.

She smiled in relief. "So, now that we're… okay—I came over here to let you know that Laurel thinks you won't agree to the interview unless I do it and I—"

"That's correct." He added a pleased grin, once again reminding her of Reagan.

"I want you to know that you don't have to do that. I appreciate the sentiment and I think I understand what you were trying to achieve. But your apology is enough—more than enough for me. You don't have to do any more than that."

He cocked his head. "What do you mean?"

"I mean that you don't have to insist that I do the interview."

"Yes, I do."

"No, you don't. I—"

"I meant it when I said I won't do the interview unless you're the one doing it."

Janie frowned. "Aidan, I just told you that isn't necessary."

"To me it is."

"What? Why? I'm totally fine not doing it. In fact, to be perfectly honest, I don't want to do the interview."

A puzzled expression lit his face. "Why?"

"Do we really need to rehash the conversation I overheard?"

"But I explained that." He sounded truly baffled and under different circumstances she might think he was endearing. But these weren't those circumstances—not even close.

"But it doesn't change the fact that you said what you did, and I believe you meant what you said."

He nodded. "I did at the time, but—"

Janie was shaking her head. "See? You admitted it. This is not going to work."

He crossed his arms over his chest, narrowed his eyes and said, "Fine."

"Fine?"

"Sure."

"Good, then it's settled. No interview." So why didn't she feel more relieved?

He tipped his head very slightly to one side. "Maybe..."

A surge of nervous tension left her flustered. He was still staring, assessing, and the look on his face... "Maybe...what?" she finally managed to ask.

He lifted one shoulder. "I'm more than fine with not doing the interview. I hate interviews. The problem here is that Emily wants the interview. Your boss wants the interview. My agent wants the interview. My business partner wants the interview. The tourism website wants the interview. Heck, from what I hear, the entire community—the state, even—wants the interview. So, if you don't want to do it, you're going to have to tell them all why. If I do the interview—I want you to do it. That's the only way I'll agree."

She felt a fresh stir of irritation at his stubbornness. "This is ridiculous." She debated whether or not to continue because she didn't like to talk when she was upset—she always said something she later regretted. But she decided he needed to hear a few things.

She took a deep breath and vowed she'd keep a check on her emotions. "You know, in addition to not being able to take no for an answer, you also have a problem with accepting when someone tells you—or asks you—not to get involved in their problems. You can't fix everything, Aidan. Sometimes you just need to apologize and move on. Respect their wishes—respect my wishes. I'm giving you the opportunity to do that. I accepted your apology. I absolve you of all guilt. You don't need to do any more than that."

He looked up at the ceiling and let out a chuckle, like he didn't have a care in the world. And that attitude, she thought, was probably a big part of the problem—he didn't have any real cares in this world. Not cares like she had anyway. His cares centered on "saving" plants and bees while her cares were of the more immediate and pressing kind—like feeding and clothing her children and trying to make enough time for each of them every single day so that they didn't end up spending the bulk of their adulthood in therapy or prison…or worse.

He had a different sense of what was important because his world was so much different than hers, resulting in very different priorities, which meant a different emphasis on nearly every aspect of life.

She tried another tack. "You really want me to tell your sister and my brother that I overheard that conversation?"

"Wait a minute—let's back up for a second. Guilt? This isn't about me feeling guilty. What I said about you was inaccurate, but it is true that I believed it at the time. And aside from the fact that I didn't intend for you to hear it, I don't believe it anymore."

"You don't…" She gave her head a frustrated shake. "So, what are you saying? Your opinion changed that quickly?"

"Yes, my opinion…changed as soon as I spent more than two minutes with you. And in conjunction with other factors…" He trailed off, and tried again. "What I'm saying is that we both have a choice to make here. Unfortunately for you, my choice depends on yours. You can either do the interview or not. But I won't agree to the interview unless you're the reporter doing the interviewing. If you decide not to do it, I don't really care which excuse you use when you break the news to my sister. She already knows I said those things—I was talking to her when I said them. She knew I was wrong, and she emphatically told me so."

Janie called on every bit of mom patience she could muster and tried to think this through. She knew there wasn't anything she could tell Emily that would placate her, and there was no way she could ever make it up to Laurel if Aidan didn't end up somehow doing the interview.

Laurel could by all rights fire her if she wanted to—for refusing to agree to the assignment. Laurel wouldn't do that, of course, but Janie supposed she should just agree. What was the point in exhibiting the same childish stubbornness he was? After all, it was only an interview. But this fact made it even more difficult to understand why he was so adamant about her doing it.

She started to clarify that point. "I still don't get why—"

They both turned as Emily burst noisily through the door, pushing Violet in a stroller. "Hey! Janie, I'm so glad you're here." She jogged toward them and stopped. "Wait till you guys hear this." She was grinning and bouncing up and down on her toes, good news dripping off of her like an over-frosted cake.

She clapped her hands together. "Guess who I was just on the phone with? Never mind. Don't guess. You'll never get it, so I'm going to tell you—*Explore Your World*. They've agreed to run two of the *Rankins Press* articles about Alaska as long as one of them is the piece on you, Aidan."

She held up a hand to cut off whatever response he might be about to counter with. "I realize you aren't exactly Alaskan, but you're here right now and studying Alaska and… You get the idea. Isn't this incredible? I can't believe it. And not web only—we're talking print. Janie, imagine having an article you wrote in one of the premier travel magazines in the world. And yes, I said *world*. I'm so excited. Rankins is going to be on the map!"

BACK AT WORK, Janie tapped her fingers on her desktop and pondered the unfairness of this situation. She thought about the satisfied look—the relief—that had transformed Aidan's face while Emily had told them about *Explore Your World* even as she had felt herself falling into a mass of quicksand.

She was stuck, plain and simple. She knew it and he knew it, too, and trying to extricate herself at this point would only make matters worse.

An article in a world-renowned magazine was

an opportunity that any aspiring reporter would be ecstatic about. But Janie was not an aspiring reporter and she most certainly was not ecstatic. She wasn't interested in writing about Aidan or about bees for that matter—unless she happened to be sharing a recipe that included honey.

Janie had never had dreams of a high-powered career. Instead, she'd always been drawn to being a full-time wife and mother, taking care of her home.

Because their own mom had been a widow and a single mother from the time she and Bering were very young, they had both taken on extra chores to make life easier. Janie had naturally gravitated toward the kitchen, partially because she could spend time with her busy mom while they cooked or baked and also because she loved it.

The entire extended family enjoyed good food and family meals. Some of Janie's best memories were of times spent cooking with her mom, her grandmother, her aunts and cousins.

Gradually she'd taken on other tasks like cleaning and gardening, almost always looking at the activities as challenges—although certainly some of the chores were tedious.

Thanks to her mom she'd also learned to sew, which had led to other crafts. When Mrs. Canterbury taught her how to knit Janie had recognized immediately that she'd discovered something special—almost like she'd found her calling.

Janie was grateful to those domestic divas out there who'd made homemaking fashionable and trendy. She enjoyed writing her column because she was able to share her knowledge and experience even though she secretly longed for more time to spend doing these things and not just writing about them.

Janie shook her head. If only Cal hadn't died, then she wouldn't be faced with the myriad problems that she found herself dealing with on a daily basis while trying to be mom and dad and breadwinner.

She'd be able to give their children the attention they needed. She missed Cal. She missed being married and being part of a couple…a team.

Their marriage had been good, but hardly perfect. Whose was? But he had loved her. And they had wanted the same things in life—stability, a family, a home filled with love and laughter—and they'd had them for eight years.

She'd give anything to experience those feelings again for even one more day. Cal had really stepped it up as the boys had aged and he'd taught them so many of the skills that were essential in growing up in such a severe and remote locale.

Too maudlin, Janie, she told herself and realized this trip down memory lane was pointless. She felt another bout of frustration at the situation Aidan had forced upon her. Why was he doing this? She'd made it clear that this wasn't necessary. The man didn't listen, and that fueled her belief in his selfishness. But no, the problem wasn't selfishness exactly, she could see that now. He was actually quite generous… It was just that he was…what? Focused, stubborn, intent on "helping" and getting his way? Were those bad things?

She wasn't sure, but it didn't matter because she was stuck. She might as well get used to the idea and maybe she'd gain some insight into him in the process. She turned toward her computer and began an internet search on Dr. Aidan Hollings.

CHAPTER TEN

FOR SOME REASON Janie wasn't surprised when she pulled into her driveway a few days later and found Aidan shooting baskets with Gareth and Reagan. Aidan had been picking up Reagan after school to work with him and bringing him home in the evenings. No word yet on whether Gareth would be helping out and no indication that he'd asked. Janie had agreed to let Aidan handle it in his own way.

Aidan, she noted, was playing one-handed but the handicap didn't seem to diminish his skill by much. Gareth snagged the ball and they all dutifully stood to one side while Janie tripped the garage door and parked her SUV inside.

She walked into the house to find her mom stirring a pot of soup on the stove. Maybe because her mom had been a widow on her own, raising kids, she often seemed to sense when Janie needed an extra dose of help.

"Oh, Mom, is that dinner? It smells great."

Claire smiled at her daughter. "I had a feeling you could use a break tonight. I hope you don't mind I invited Aidan?"

Janie took a carrot stick off of the veggie platter Claire had arranged. "No, that's fine. It's the least we can do what with him spending all this time with Reagan. I don't know that I've ever seen Reagan happier than he has been this week."

Janie paused with the carrot halfway to her mouth as she realized those words could very well be true.

AIDAN PASSED GARETH the ball and wondered about the best way to get through to him. The more he was around Gareth, the stronger he felt that something was off with the kid. He knew it. He could see the deep, underlying sadness or despair or turmoil or…something.

Gareth attempted to conceal it, but Aidan could spot it—probably because he was good at hiding certain things about himself, too. He couldn't quite put his finger on exactly what Gareth's issues were, but one thing was clear—the poor kid was carrying the weight of the world on his shoulders.

Certainly what he'd witnessed today had to be a contributing factor…

AIDAN NEVER WOULD have seen the incident if he hadn't been a few minutes early to pick up Reagan. Reagan had been helping him every day after school and the situation was working out even better than Aidan had anticipated. He decided to run inside the school because Jacinda had now emailed him twice about the guest appearance in her science classes. The notes had been decidedly lacking in details about what topics she might want him to cover, but he now knew she was originally from Texas and that she played pool at the Cozy Caribou on Wednesday evenings.

He wasn't interested and he wanted the personal revelations to stop, so he needed to remove any reason for further correspondence. But if he was to agree to speak to the students, he'd need time to prepare. After stopping by the office to sign in and ask directions to her classroom he had to travel by the gym.

The gym doors were open and he saw Reagan standing a few feet inside. He started forward to greet him, but something about his stance made Aidan stop and take note; the hunched shoulders, the tension in his posture…

Aidan nearly cringed at the sound of the voice that he heard next. "Eat it, Everett. You like to talk about it so much. So eat it."

Two other boys came into view, both of them laughing.

One of them chimed in, "Yeah, freak. Eat it. This is what freaks like you eat, right?"

Reagan remained frozen—silent and staring straight ahead.

One of the other kids commented. "Maybe his mouth is already stuck shut from eating so much snot and boogers."

"Eat this right now or next time I will feed you worse."

The Vetcher kid stalked forward like he was going to put his hands on Reagan.

Aidan moved quickly on a wave of rage. But before he could reach them, before the kids even saw that he was there, Gareth seemed to fall from the sky. Aidan realized he must have dropped from the bleachers behind the kids.

"Leave my brother alone, Vetcher."

A tall girl with long dark hair appeared next to Reagan. "You touch him and it's assault, you idiot cretin."

Vetcher scoffed. "Why don't you try spending time with somebody your own age, like me, Elena, instead of this weird little dork?"

"Harmon, you're certifiable. Why don't you go check yourself into the mental hospital where you belong?"

Reagan said something Aidan couldn't hear that made Elena laugh.

Harmon's chest puffed out like a cartoon pigeon.

Aidan tensed in case he made a move.

But Gareth took a step forward. "Back off, Vetcher. Do I need to remind you what happened last time you didn't back off?"

Harmon visibly deflated, obviously retreating but trying not to make it too obvious. He raised a hand, palm up. "Relax, man. We were only kidding around. You sure are high-strung sometimes, Everett."

Harmon snorted and Aidan knew there was something seriously wrong with the kid. He also knew from what he'd seen that these boys wouldn't stop. Gareth and the brave girl beside him were only buying Reagan time. Aidan turned and walked back toward the office to wait for Reagan. His efforts to dissuade Jacinda would have to wait.

Aidan made a decision. If Janie wanted to keep her head buried in the sand that was her choice, but Aidan wasn't going to wait around for something to happen to Reagan in the meantime. Her obliviousness wasn't fair to Gareth, either.

Janie might not want his help, but her boys needed it.

PRIOR TO HIS DECISION, Aidan had been waiting for the right moment to talk to Gareth about working for him. He wanted to get to know him a little better first, hoping he could continue to shoot baskets, make small talk and smooth over the

Boston cream pie blunder. And possibly earn the boy's respect in the process.

But after stumbling upon the incident with Vetcher, Aidan now felt a sense of urgency.

Aidan took action when the opportunity to talk to Gareth came up later. On the way over to his lab, he and Reagan stopped by Bering and Emily's so he could look over a map with Bering. Aidan wanted to expand his bee research area and Bering had proved to be an invaluable resource with his knowledge of the geography of the region. While there he learned that Emily had picked up Gareth from school so he could help chop and stack a fresh load of firewood.

While Reagan visited with Emily and Bering, Aidan went outside to find Gareth. He headed toward the outbuilding and Bering's wood-chopping station. Aidan glanced toward the river. He spotted a moose on the opposite side and stopped to watch her for a moment as she foraged knee-deep in the budding green grass. The snow-capped peaks of the mountains seemed to glow in the distance. Alaska held a kind of raw and pristine beauty unlike any other place he'd ever seen—and he'd seen an awful lot of the world.

Aidan noted the wood had been chopped and neatly stacked, but Gareth was nowhere to be seen. Something told Aidan to head toward the water and it didn't take long before he recognized Gareth's dark brown hair. Aidan thought the contrast between Gareth's and Reagan's appearances was as striking as their personalities. He'd seen photos of their father, Cal; Gareth was clearly a mix of his father, his mother and his Uncle Bering. While Reagan seemed pure Janie, from his deep red hair right down to the lichen-green shade of his eyes.

Gareth was sitting on the ground facing the river. Aidan had confidence in his plan, except now that he was presented with the opportunity to have a discussion with Gareth he wasn't quite sure what to say.

Clearly the kid was still grieving for his dad. And as Aidan thought about the loss of his own father, he realized he knew exactly what not to say. He wouldn't say any of the things people had said to him when he was growing up dadless. "He's watching out for you" or "your dad would be so proud of you." Those kinds of statements had always irritated Aidan—no one could possibly know those things for sure. He'd *hoped* they were true, but he didn't *know*.

Nobody knew.

Aidan walked over and lowered himself next to Gareth onto a large flat rock. Gareth glanced at him with a polite half smile, but didn't say a word.

They stared at the river for a long moment,

not talking, but the air was far from silent. The river rushed wildly from the bulging water of the spring thaw and a bird screeched as it flew overhead. They both lifted their gazes skyward and followed the path of a bald eagle. The bird landed in a tree on the opposite side of the river. It rotated its snow-white head repeatedly one way and then the other, casting them a series of suspicious side-eyed glances.

Aidan inhaled a deep breath. He was starting to like how energizing the dry, chilly air felt when it filled his lungs—fresh and clean and so much different than the stifling humidity he had become accustomed to in the tropics.

"My dad liked sandwiches. My mom says he would rather have eaten a sandwich than any other food on the planet. He would eat sandwiches, like, this tall." Aidan held his hands about six inches apart. "I think about him every time I eat a sandwich."

Gareth flashed him a puzzled expression. Aidan almost laughed at how much he resembled Janie when she was annoyed with him and trying not to show it. He looked back toward the river and Aidan imagined Gareth wanted to tell him to go away, but the poor kid was exceedingly polite. He felt a fresh bout of respect for Janie's mothering skills.

"When I was small, I remember him bringing

me bubbles. You know those kinds in the bright containers with the little wand you pull out and blow through the circle?"

Gareth tilted his head in understanding.

"He would blow the bubbles and I would chase them. Then when he would leave I would try so hard to make bubbles like he did, but I never could quite master it…" That memory still caused a rush of emotion. He had precious few memories of his father because he and his mother had never been married, so the time he'd spent with him had been only when he visited.

Gareth's voice was so low that Aidan barely heard him. "My dad liked Boston cream pie."

Aidan felt that one like a punch, but he was happy to get this subject out in the open.

"Yeah, I screwed up there, didn't I? I'm sorry about that."

Gareth remained silent.

"I didn't know about your tradition, Gareth. Your mom tried to tell me, but I was trying too hard to make things better after I ruined the first cake. I can be kind of single-minded some-times—especially when I believe I'm doing the right thing. You'd think I'd learn, but…that's one mistake I'm really good at making."

Aidan thought Gareth nearly smiled at that, but his head swiveled back toward the water.

Aidan joined him in staring at the river and

felt sure he'd lost him. It wasn't going to be easy to proceed with his plan without Gareth's cooperation, but he would. He would help Reagan one way or the other, even if he couldn't reach Gareth. Maybe he could enlist Tag's help. He shifted, getting ready to stand and report that dinner would be ready soon.

Gareth's voice was soft when he spoke. "He liked pancakes. My dad liked pancakes. But he ate only peanut butter on them." Gareth held up his hand with his thumb and index finger a good inch apart. "Like, that much. No syrup. Just peanut butter. I've tried them like that, but I don't like them."

"That's a lot of peanut butter. I'm a butter-and-syrup guy myself," Aidan said.

"Me, too."

Gareth stayed silent.

Aidan picked up a rock and tossed it into the water. It was heavy enough that it made a *kerplunk* sound rather than a decent splash.

Gareth said quietly, "My dad liked movies, too. Any kind of movie—scary, funny, action, romance… My mom says it didn't matter. He would watch anything."

Aidan picked up a smaller rock and threw it, with much greater success. What was it, he wondered, that made throwing rocks into the water so satisfying—and almost addictive?

Gareth picked up a stone and flipped his wrist; the stone sailed through the air, and then gracefully skipped across the water nine times before slipping beneath the surface. Clearly he'd spent some time practicing this skill.

"Wow. You're good at that."

"My dad taught me." Gareth picked up another flat rock. "I like movies, too. I haven't been to the real movies that much, though—a few times when we've gone to Anchorage. We don't have a movie theater here. Aunt Emily turned the gym into a movie theater last summer and everyone is hoping she'll do it again this year." He launched the rock and it skittered even farther than the first one.

Aidan chuckled. "That sounds like something my crazy sister would do."

"She's great. I love Aunt Emily."

"Me, too. She loves you, too, Gareth. She tells me all the time how much she loves you and your brothers."

Gareth nodded.

"It can be difficult, huh? Taking care of your brothers? I'm older than Emily and I've always felt this responsibility for her. It was frustrating for me when we were growing up because we didn't live together so I couldn't always be there for her like I wanted."

"You guys lived in different houses because you have different moms, right?"

"Yep, we have different moms. Same dad. We both lived with our moms. She grew up in California and I grew up in Oregon."

"He's dead, right? Your dad?"

Aidan nodded. "Yes, he died when I was little. Emily was only a baby. It's just been me and my mom ever since."

Gareth looked curious.

"My mom made sure Emily and I saw each other as much as possible. She thought it was really important that we be able to be brother and sister—like a real family."

"I think it's hard being the oldest."

Ah, Aidan thought, finally getting to the crux of the matter. "I do, too. You spend a lot of time sticking up for Reagan, huh?"

A flicker of surprise lit the boy's features before he looked back toward the river. Aidan followed his gaze and watched the eagle swoop close to the water's surface and head back to his tree branch with a squirming fish in his talons.

"My dad would want me to. That's what my mom says."

And this was where he and Janie differed, and he suspected, where he might lose the precious ground he'd gained with Janie. But he had to try. He couldn't sit back and take the chance that something even more serious would happen to Reagan. He knew kids like Harmon all too well, and Harmon was waiting patiently for his chance—exactly like that eagle.

"He would. No doubt about that. But he might want Reagan to learn to help himself, too. That's a lot of pressure to put on you, Gareth—to be your brother's protector."

He shrugged, but kept his eyes pinned on Aidan, and Aidan felt like he might be getting somewhere so he continued. "What happens when you're not there? What happens when that slime Harmon and his sidekick Riley corner Reagan next year and you're not around?"

Gareth's eyes widened and Aidan suspected that he was surprised by this insight. Undoubtedly, Gareth felt very alone in this situation. Aidan felt his chest tighten with emotion. He wanted to put an arm around Gareth's shoulders and tell him everything would be okay. But he certainly wasn't going to say that, either.

"Mom says sometimes people are so smart in some ways that they use all their brains for that smartness and don't have enough left over for other areas."

"That's an interesting way of looking at things. But I'm pretty smart, too—like Reagan. And I manage to help myself. Although, you know what? It wasn't always this way for me, either. I had to work it out."

"What do you mean?"

"I, uh, I had the same problems when I was in school that Reagan does. Worse, actually. And I didn't have a big brother, so I had to learn… I had a lot to learn."

Gareth leaned back and wrapped his hands around one knee. Curiosity lit his face. "Like what did you learn?"

"If you would be willing to come and hang out at the lab with Reagan and me a few days a week, I'll show you. I could really use your help with something, and I think it will help Reagan, too."

CHAPTER ELEVEN

AIDAN'S AGENT EMAILED the list with the topics that were off-limits for the interview. Janie thought the compilation was outrageous and she didn't understand how she was supposed to write an article about him—a human interest story—when she wasn't allowed to ask him anything. And the topics weren't only personal, some of them were downright bizarre. Even Laurel thought it seemed excessive.

Janie had no choice but to ask him about the list.

"It's open," Aidan yelled when she knocked on his door.

Janie found him near the middle of the room with a tape measure and a roll of blue painter's tape. Two strips had been arranged on the floor to form an *L* shape.

He looked surprised to see her. "Janie, hi, what are you doing here?"

"Your agent sent the guidelines for the interview."

"Oh, good, when do you want to get started? Can you hold this?"

Janie set her bag on his desk and reached out for the end of the tape measure. She held the end at a mark on the floor where he indicated as he measured a ways across the room, and then he made another mark on the floor.

"We could get started immediately except according to your list there's very little I can ask you about."

"What do you mean?"

"Aidan, the list is crazy. The things that are on it…" She shook her head while he jotted notes in a spiral-bound tablet. She craned her neck and saw what looked like a drawing of a…pigpen?

She gestured at the creation. "What is this?"

He flashed an enigmatic smile. "A project. I'll fill you in later."

"I'll look forward to it," she responded dryly.

He grinned. "Everything on that list is perfectly reasonable." He jiggled the tape measure that she still held. "You can let go now." He snapped the notebook shut.

She released her end of the tape and stood up. The thin metal strip coiled back into place with a slicing sound.

"I don't see how I'm supposed to interview you when I can't ask you about anything."

His gaze traveled around the large room like he was barely paying attention to what she was saying. With his mussed curls and golden stubble covering his chin, he seemed to epitomize the absentminded-professor stereotype—except she had to admit he was way better-looking than any professor she'd ever seen.

"Sure you can."

"Have you seen the list?"

"Not literally, but it's something that Drum has put together for me over the last couple years so of course I know what's on it."

Janie looked at the ceiling and muttered, "No wonder you have problems with reporters."

That got his attention. His eyes locked on hers and seemed to drill into her.

"I've read about your lack of interest in being interviewed online. I've been doing some research."

"Not having the list is what got me into trouble…before."

"Before what?"

"Before I had the list."

She squelched her irritation and took a shot at conciliation. "Aidan, please let Laurel assign someone else to do this interview. You were right—I'm not qualified for this. I feel like I'm interviewing a reclusive pop star or the head of some secret cult. This—you—are way out of my league. And the fact that it's going to be published in a national magazine really intimidates me."

"Nice try," he said with a flat look. "Have you ever done any acting?"

She felt like stomping her foot; she let out a groan of frustration. "Aidan, I'm not—"

"I've read every one of your columns, Janie. You're very talented."

Her mouth fell open in surprise. "You… What?"

"You didn't think I was demanding you do the article solely because I wanted to get on your good side, did you?"

Janie felt a prickle of discomfort at hearing her assumption voiced aloud. She couldn't help but be flattered by his compliment, although her column wasn't anything like this article.

"Thank you. But in my column I write about things I know about—things I do, things I love…"

"I know. I like that. Your passion comes through in your writing. I like that you enjoy gardening so much—we have that in common, you know?" He added a wink. "And I know that you find canning a bit tedious but also satisfying, and that knitting is your number one, all-time-favorite hobby."

Her mouth fell open. She snapped it shut. Apparently she wasn't the only one doing her research. "Stop trying to distract me with compliments."

He laughed. "I can only see one solution then."

"What's that?" She asked the question hopefully, but somehow she knew she hadn't managed to change his mind so easily.

"I guess you're just going to have to learn to love me, too, huh?"

She knew he was joking but felt her cheeks growing warm. "This is going to be impossible."

He tried to look wounded. "Hey, I know I can come across as a little awkward, a bit eccentric... but I'm not that bad."

"That's not what I meant."

"I know, but it's surprisingly fun to tease you. I have an idea. How about we take a more organic approach and do this interview in bits and pieces. That way you can learn my subtleties— maybe even learn to like me."

"Bits and pieces?" she repeated skeptically.

"Yes, I'm better at conversation when I'm doing something anyway. So let's make a series of, um, dates—for lack of a better word."

Was this his idea of flirting? She repeated the word flatly. "Dates?"

"Engagements?" He tried again. "Rendez-vous-es? I'm not sure how to make that word plural."

"Appointments," she supplied and hated how prudish she sounded. But she needed to stop this...this...whatever he was doing and keep things as professional as possible.

"Fine," he said with a playful huff. "Have it your way."

"If I had my way we wouldn't be doing this at all, remember?"

"Appointments it is," he returned quickly.

Janie had to admit to herself that she'd already learned something about him, and she never would have guessed he possessed this playful and charming side.

AIDAN COULDN'T WAIT to get the stitches out of his hand, although he had to admit it was kind of fun having Janie help him with certain tasks, like washing the pickup. He grinned as he thought about the day before, when she'd "accidentally" squirted him with the water hose after he'd pointed out a spot on the hood she'd missed for the third time.

He was already looking forward to their next "appointment." He especially liked how it seemed to ruffle her that he called them dates.

He dribbled the ball a few times on the community center's outdoor basketball court, executed a perfect right-handed hook shot and reveled in the sound of the quiet swish. As he retrieved the ball he heard his name called. He turned to see Emily walking toward him.

"Em, hey!"

"Aidan, what are you doing here?"

"Waiting for Tag. We're meeting here when he gets off work."

"To play basketball?"

"Yep, afterward we're having dinner at the Cozy Caribou with a few of his friends. I'm going to get fat between Janie's meals and eating at that restaurant all the time."

Emily scowled as she tipped her head toward the court. "Should you be doing that with your hand still healing and all?"

"I'm shooting one-handed, I promise. Nice sweater," he commented partly to distract her, and partly because it was.

"Thank you." She looked down at the chunky knit in shades of red and pink. "Janie made it."

Aidan stared at the beautiful garment. "Of course she did."

Emily chuckled. "I told you she was good at everything. You should see her ugly sweaters."

"Her…ugly…what?" He had yet to see anything ugly where Janie was concerned.

Emily threaded an arm through his. She bobbed her head toward the community center. "Janie is teaching a knitting class. Tonight she's displaying some of the stuff she's made, so I brought a few items she's done for me, Violet and Bering."

She gestured at the red sweater she wore. "Since I'm one of her students, too, I thought

I'd go ahead and model this one. Come with me, dear brother, and I'll show you what real talent is."

OVER THE LAST week Janie and Aidan had looked at plants and bees under his microscope, assembled some shelves he'd had delivered, fixed the chain on Gareth's bicycle and washed Aidan's borrowed pickup. Well, she'd done most of the work while Aidan directed her, teased her and pitched in one-handed.

Janie would never admit it but she found herself looking forward to their interview sessions. She told herself it was because it gave her a break from the office, and not because she found Aidan interesting, entertaining and charming in his quirky kind of way.

"What are we doing today?" Janie asked as she walked toward Aidan's set of comfy recliners and took a seat in one.

"We're making cupcakes."

"Cupcakes? You want me to help you make cupcakes?"

He winced and held up his injured hand. "Well, I don't think I can…"

"You're really getting some mileage out of that little boo-boo, aren't you?"

He gave her a guilty grin.

She chuckled as she popped out of the chair

and headed toward his kitchen. Cupcakes sounded like fun—it was no secret she liked to bake. Janie had also learned that Aidan liked to eat. Yesterday she'd brought him a pan of brownies and watched his eyes light like a little kid's. He claimed he didn't gush over her cooking simply because he spent so much time in the rain forest eating freeze-dried "vittles," but she felt certain that must have something to do with his enthusiasm.

Aidan set about gathering measuring cups and ingredients out of his cupboards and some still-unpacked boxes; odd-looking, unmarked ingredients in baggies and small plastic containers and tins.

Janie washed and dried her hands and then took a quick inventory of the supplies he'd assembled. "Where's the recipe?"

Aidan tapped his temple. "Right here. It's a secret—like the Colonel's."

She rolled her eyes. "If the ingredients are secret how am I supposed to help you make them?"

Aidan let out a playful huff. "Would you just relax? I'll walk you through it."

Janie shook her head as she fetched the stainless steel bowl he requested out of the closet. He handed her a measuring cup and a plastic canister of some unidentifiable herb that looked like dried flower petals.

As she added two cups of the ingredient, she searched her brain for a safe topic. "So, you were raised in Oregon by your mom and Emily was raised in San Diego by her mom and stepdad, right?"

"Yep." Aidan smiled and dumped a cupful of something into the bowl.

"I've met them—Mr. and Mrs. Campbell. They came up to visit after Violet was born. It's hard to believe Emily came from them."

He let out a laugh and Janie felt the warmth behind it. "Indeed. They are a bit rigid, aren't they? Emily always struggled with that. Not the case with my mom. She's the exact opposite— warm and wise and free-spirited. My mom is amazing.

"Here," he said and handed her a bottle. "Three tablespoons of this."

Janie carefully measured the sticky syrup. "I'd love to meet her. Single motherhood is tough—I can attest to that—but she obviously did a great job. She must be so proud of you. What does she do?"

He stopped what he was doing. "Is this for the article?"

Janie let out a surprised chuckle. "I don't know—does it matter?"

Aidan narrowed his eyes in a thoughtful way.

Janie imagined he was trying to figure out how to say yes without aggravating her.

"Aidan, I'm trying to get a conversation started about who you are, where you come from, what makes you tick. You know—what prompted your passion and purpose for plant life?" She smiled at her alliteration.

He lightly grazed his jaw with the back of his bandaged hand. "I can see this is amusing to you, and I understand your perspective. It's just... I'd like to know if a question is being asked for the interview before I give my answer."

She infused some drama into her tone and whispered, "Ohhh... I get it—what your mom does for a living is top secret. Does she work for the CIA or the FBI? Ooh, wait—Interpol?"

"Janie." Her name came out on an impatient sigh.

"Come on, Aidan. Neither your mother nor your formative years are on the do-not-ask list. I'm fishing for something to write about here."

"Herbalist."

"What?"

"My mom is an herbalist."

"Oh...that sounds really cool."

"It is. I come by my love for plants naturally. I used to sit and paw through my mom's plant books for hours on end when I was a kid. I knew the taxonomy of virtually every plant in my neighborhood and pretty much the entire state of Oregon by the time I was seven. Please don't put that in the article."

"Okay, but why not? That's really cute."

"Cute?"

"Yes, I mean that's interesting and actually the kind of thing I'm looking for, for this story."

He looked skeptical. "Really?"

"Yes, the kinds of things that make you relatable to normal people."

"Normal people?" He stepped closer, almost hovering, and the action made her pulse jump. She shifted on her feet and focused on the unusual mixture forming in the bowl.

He reached around her and picked up a plastic canister that looked a lot like oat bran. He handed it to her.

She opened the lid and found the odor sweet, like molasses.

"One half cup of that."

She measured carefully. "You know what I mean—not everyone has brains like you and Reagan. It can be intimidating."

He leaned a hip against the counter. "Not to you."

"Well, no... But I'm used to Reagan."

Aidan nodded. "Yes, but something tells me that wouldn't matter with you. I don't imagine you being easily intimidated. I mean you called me on the carpet for the conversation you overheard. You could have pretended forever that you'd never heard those comments."

"Why would I do that?"

"Because you were intimidated."

"Pfft," Janie said and measured out some gooey liquid that looked like corn syrup. "Intimidated because you made ignorant assumptions about me?"

"That I did," he said softly. "I was very wrong about you."

Something about the tone of his voice made Janie's insides tighten. She looked back down. "What's next?"

"That's it. Now we put the batter in these pans." He pointed at the minimuffin tins. Janie began plopping the mixture spoon by spoon into the pan's divots.

"You are good at that."

"Yeah, well, I've made a few cupcakes in my day—but honestly, Aidan? These look disgusting. Do you plan to eat these? I could give you some recipes."

He laughed. "No, they are for the bees."

She scowled at him. "I just made cupcakes for bees?"

"Yep. It's a bee attractant. I use it in certain instances so I can locate them easier, but it's also natural, good for them, doesn't spoil easy and it transports well. I used to use a liquid nectar but it was such a mess. I would get it all over everything and then I'd have bees in places I really didn't want bees."

That actually made sense and Janie found herself nodding. "That's clever."

"My mom came up with the recipe. She's brilliant with plants in a way that I'm not. She's also a fantastic cook. Not quite your caliber, but you guys would get along great."

Janie shamelessly enjoyed the compliment.

Aidan slipped the tins into the oven, then turned and leaned against the counter so he was facing her.

She swallowed nervously. "What?"

"Now that the cupcakes are almost done— it's my turn."

"What do you mean? Your turn for what?"

"I want to ask you some questions."

"Oh, what? No, I don't think so."

"Why not? It doesn't seem fair that you get to ask me all this stuff and I don't get to find out anything about you."

Janie sighed. "Okay, but I have a list, too, and it's right here." She tapped a finger to her temple. "I can pass on anything I don't want to answer."

"Fair enough." He inhaled deeply and blew it out slowly. "I'm afraid you're probably going to use one of those passes for this first question, but let's give it a shot anyway."

Her mouth went inexplicably dry.

"Why is it that you insist on calling your beautiful Christmas sweaters ugly?"

She let out a relieved giggle. "You've been talking to my mom."

Aidan chuckled. "She has a point, Janie, they are really beautiful. I saw some of your creations at the community center. You weren't there yet, but Emily showed me before your class."

Emily had arrived early and set up the room for her so she could pick up some medication at the pharmacy before it closed and still make it to class on time.

"You are brilliant, do you know that?" The kind words seemed to flow from his tongue.

"Thank you, but it's not difficult."

"Emily said you make your own patterns? That looks difficult to me. And you're so creative."

"Not really. I just—"

"You made my sister a sweater with Christmas elves, and cookies and doughnuts wearing little stocking hats."

"She does like her sugary treats. Did you know the Donut Den has named a pastry after her? It's called the Emily."

"I did hear that," Aidan said with a laugh. "Seriously though, remember when you said that you didn't want to do this interview?"

"Yes…" She answered tentatively, having no idea where this could now be headed.

"That wasn't solely because of me—was it? Because you didn't want to interview me in particular?"

She thought about the question. "Well, that was a lot of it."

"But if you were a normal reporter you would want to do it, no matter what. Normal reporters want to interview anyone who will give them a story—slimy politicians, idiotic celebrities, third-world dictators, serial killers…"

Janie frowned. "Yeah, that's true I suppose. I'll be honest—I don't have that drive."

Aidan stretched and settled against the counter, then asked, "What do you want?"

"What do you mean?"

"What are your goals, aspirations?"

She thought for a moment. Someone as driven as Aidan probably wouldn't understand, but Janie didn't know how to answer the question any way but honestly. "All I've ever wanted is to be a wife and a mother… All the domestic stuff that goes along with that—the stuff I get to write about in my column. I know it probably sounds boring and mundane to you, but that's what I want. That, and to see my boys become happy, productive adults."

"That doesn't sound boring." Aidan studied her for several seconds. "Who did you idolize when you were growing up?"

"When I was a little girl my role models were all domestic divas, gardening experts and great cooks—like my grandma and Mrs. Canterbury."

"Mrs. Canterbury?"

Janie grinned. "She was a friend of my grandma's. She wore these long, colorful flowing skirts that she sewed herself and grew dahlias the size of dinner plates and she taught me how to knit. And when I learned how to knit…" She felt silly saying it, but he had been honest with her and she knew it wasn't easy for him to reveal things about himself. So she went on. "Something clicked into place in my brain. I don't know how to explain it exactly—but it still gets me through the tough times. The feel of the yarn in my hands and making something beautiful…

"Right before Mrs. Canterbury passed away she gave me all of her knitting needles and literally an entire roomful of yarn and patterns that she'd created. She was such an inspiration to me. That's when I started creating my own patterns. It's really special seeing a person wear something that I made just for them. It's… I'll always be grateful to her."

Janie stopped talking and looked at Aidan, expecting to see his teasing grin or even that confused furrow in his brow. But instead he seemed captivated, like he completely understood. So she finished the thought. "Aside from my children and my family, knitting brings me my greatest joy."

CHAPTER TWELVE

"ASK ME ANYTHING."

Janie glanced up at him. "Anything?"

He closed one eye and made a pained face and she couldn't help but laugh. "Let's stick to the rules that Drum sent."

Aidan had let her choose what they were going to do that morning, so she'd turned the tables on him. He was helping her plant lettuce, spinach and peas. Well, he mostly watched and handed her things so he didn't get his bandaged hand dirty.

"Sure, but you do realize that you get to read the article before it's published, right? You can take a red pen and scratch away all you want."

"I know that in theory. But I've learned there are certain things that once they are out there floating around in the ether you can't get them back again."

Janie frowned. "That's true, I suppose."

"Um, yeah it is—have you heard of that big internet warehouse in the sky where all kinds of information is being stored? It's getting a lot of people in trouble."

"Aidan…are you paranoid?"

He shrugged. "Maybe," he joked. "Is technology on the list?"

Janie didn't remember seeing that particular subject, although the list was pretty long and included some peculiar topics like politics, religion, where Aidan lives when he's not traveling, the kind of car he drives, Emily—no details other than the fact that he has a sister and that she's younger—pharmaceuticals and global warming.

"No, not that I recall."

"Hmm. I should have Drum add that."

"Since we're discussing the list, can I ask a couple questions regarding it?"

"Not if it's something on the list."

She huffed out a breath. "I'm not getting paid enough for this."

He chuckled and poured some seeds into his good hand. He held them out for her. "I know the list probably seems random to you, but I promise there is a reason for each and every item on there."

Janie grimaced.

"You don't believe me?"

"Honestly? I suspect you might actually be a little paranoid."

She recalled his excuse for the conversation she'd overheard—the deceitful article someone had printed about him—but she couldn't imagine how all of these things could have been included in one article, or how they could have been so damaging. Plus, he'd said the list had been compiled over the last couple of years. "Interesting…" he said and grimaced as if he were bracing himself for something painful. "Ask me something and I'll prove it to you. All of it off the record?"

Janie nodded. "Deal—let me grab the actual list out of my bag so I can be accurate."

"Good idea."

Janie removed her gloves as she jogged toward the house. She retrieved the folded sheet of paper from her bag and returned to the garden.

She tapped a finger to her lips as she perused the topics. "Hmm… Let's start with global warming. How can you, as an environmental scientist, not discuss this topic? Laurel is dying to ask you about it. And by the way, aren't they calling it climate change now?"

His face erupted with a satisfied grin and she knew she'd somehow walked into a trap.

"Good question, because this topic hits right on the point. I am not an environmental scientist. That is a separate discipline. There is science behind global warming—on both sides of the issue. I don't feel qualified to discuss that science, but inevitably journalists ask me to. I get misquoted, and that can, and does, only lead to controversy. 'Dr. Hollings thinks the earth is warming. Dr. Hollings doesn't believe the earth is warming. Dr. Hollings loves polar bears. Dr. Hollings hates polar bears.' In reality I haven't studied enough of the hard science myself to determine whether the earth is warming or not in any way that would suggest a human cause."

"Huh." Janie thought about how much self-discipline that must entail—to only comment on what you really believed to be scientific fact.

Janie stared, was captivated really, because sometimes his smart talk was fascinating and made him seem even more…attractive. That is, when he wasn't lecturing, or criticizing her parenting skills. She pretended to study the list again, hoping the warmth in her cheeks wasn't noticeable to him.

"What about religion? What's the problem there?"

Aidan reached over and smoothed the dirt over the lettuce seeds he'd meticulously placed one-handed in the trench he'd dug. "I like to explore the local culture when I'm working. I've been photographed in a couple completely innocuous situations that were twisted by journalists to the point that one of them speculated that I might be practicing voodoo. That upset my nana." He patted some dirt into place over the seeds.

Janie had actually seen that story online. She hadn't thought a thing of it, but she could see how it might bother a person. It would bother her if someone printed that about her. Her mom would go through the roof if she read something that bizarre about either of her children.

"Okay, but what about Emily? That seems straightforward and she's interesting, too. Your relationship would be fun to include in the article."

He reached into the basket of seeds on the ground. He chose one and held up the spinach package for her inspection. She nodded.

"Agreed. But you are aware of the fact that she used to work for one of the largest oil and mineral extraction companies in North America?"

Of course. Janie should have seen that one coming. People wouldn't like the fact that Emily's stepfather's company, Cam-Field Oil & Mineral, "destroyed" the very environment Aidan tried to save. Janie was beginning to see his point. A person who valued their privacy and/or their reputation as a serious scientist could get themselves into real trouble.

She studied Aidan for a moment and debated about whether she should apologize for the unfair assumptions she'd made, especially since she'd been furious with Aidan about doing the same with her. She was happy she hadn't voiced hers aloud—although she had made some comments to Shay and Laurel.

She thought about how protective he was of his mother and something occurred to her. "The pharmaceutical industry doesn't really like the naturopathic realm, right?"

He grinned and held out a cupped palm that was full of seeds. "The two schools of thought are often at odds."

Janie believed her life was full of difficulties and complexities—and it was. But, in an entirely different way, so was Aidan's. Life's challenges and complications were all relative, so why had she overlooked this fact where Aidan was concerned?

OVER THE NEXT two weeks the boys spent almost every day after school with Aidan for at least a few hours, giving Janie time to spend with the twins or to tackle an extra task on her perpetual to-do list. She hadn't asked how he'd managed to get Gareth to agree, but he seemed to be enjoying the experience right along with Reagan. On the weekends the boys spent hours with Aidan, so she'd even managed to get extra time knitting.

According to the boys' daily reports, the work varied. They would sometimes scour the countryside for hours searching for bees. Or they would head straight to the lab, where they would be assigned various jobs, the details of which Reagan relayed with the excitement a different kid might describe a new video game.

Aidan would drop off the boys at home unless Janie worked late or happened to be in town for some reason. Occasionally he joined them for dinner. At the end of the evening, often while doing dishes, playing basketball or games with the boys, or entertaining the twins, he would take a few minutes to answer questions for the interview.

Janie felt like she was getting some good material, even as it was coming in bits and pieces.

Now she shuffled the cards for one more game of rummy. She'd put the twins to bed and the older boys had bowed out of the last game of cards to watch the Mariners baseball game.

"So, what's your favorite part about being a botanist?"

Aidan looked thoughtful as he scooped up his cards and carefully filed them into place to form his hand. The way he held them loosely with his bandaged fingers made her smile.

"This is where I'm supposed to say making a difference in the world or discovering a new species?"

Janie looked up from the hand of cards she held. "You've discovered new plant species?"

He smiled. "Yes, although in most of the cases I think that someone surely had stumbled onto the species before me. They just hadn't bothered telling anyone."

"That's amazing."

"It's not that difficult. There are a couple thousand new ones discovered every year. Estimates are that there are still a few million undiscovered species."

"Wow…that means there could be plants out there that hold the solution to countless health problems, right?"

His eyes latched on to hers. "My mom believes the cures to nearly every disease lie in the plant kingdom. It's simply a matter of discovering the right formulas." His lips tugged up into a proud grin.

Janie had noticed this trait before and she liked it, this obvious respect and fondness he held for his mother. "You don't think she's correct?"

He drew a card, slid it into his hand. "My mom is more of an…artist than me—a dreamer. I'm not one to speculate about something without evidence or facts, but I will admit that she's right more than she's wrong." He discarded an eight of hearts.

Janie picked it up. She'd noticed that often he

tended to divulge additional information if she remained silent and let him talk. She wasn't disappointed now.

"Remember I told you about how I don't like reporters?"

"Uh-huh." She flipped a two of spades onto the pile.

"Well, you know my mom is an herbalist. She develops natural remedies—botanicals. A couple years ago she was working on a formula for a sleep aid. There was this woman—Meredith is her name. She was a friend… I thought she was a friend. Anyway, the formula is worth a lot of money—my mom is in the process of selling it right now. But Meredith stole the formula from my mom. I discovered what she'd done before she could do anything, but…"

Janie slowly lowered her cards to rest on the table, outraged on his behalf—on his mother's behalf. "That's…horrible."

"Yep, and at about the same time she published a very unfavorable article about me. She wasn't even a journalist. She was employed in PR for the company who was trying to develop a part of a large rain-forest preserve in Brazil where I was working at the time. I was against the development because of some rare plant species—one of which my mom was using in her sleep aid. Meredith accused me of trying to halt the development in order to line my mom's pockets."

"Aidan, that's outrageous. I'm so sorry."

His gaze dipped down as he drew a card. "I wanted you to know one specific reason why I don't trust reporters."

"That would do it for me, too. What happened? How did it turn out?"

"Like I said, nothing happened with the formula, but the article about me was published online. Luckily this was around the time we hired Drum, our agent. He's a computer whiz and somehow he obliterated the article. It disappeared. I'm sure you could still find the article if you looked hard enough. But the experience left me...wary. And I was already wary to begin with."

Janie thought about that warehouse in the sky he'd mentioned the other day and the significance it could hold for him. "I understand. Thank you, for telling me."

His eyes looked so incredibly gray, like the wintry mist that sometimes crept inland from the ocean. Janie thought about the extremely condensed version of this story he'd relayed a little while ago. She'd blown him off and told him it didn't matter. She felt absolutely terrible about that. Funny how much an opinion could change when you were presented with a bigger picture.

AIDAN HAD BEEN giddy to get the stitches removed from his hand. By the following week he started playing basketball with Bering, Tag and some of their friends either at Bering's or at the community center—and Gareth often participated, too. Janie hoped it wasn't too soon.

Gareth gushed about how well Aidan played, even though he still favored his injured hand. One Wednesday Tag organized a basketball tournament at the community center. The boys had a half day of school and her mom had taken the twins swimming so Janie made arrangements to pick up Gareth there after the tournament.

Janie had spent the morning at the newspaper and was looking forward to an evening with all four of her boys. They were going to make pizza and watch a movie on DVD. The latest superhero adventure had just been released.

When she arrived she immediately noticed a group of women crowded around the edge of the outdoor basketball court. Janie texted her mom to let her know she was there. Thanks to Emily the community center now had wireless internet access, so she took a moment to check her email on her phone.

Janie heard the comments before she could see any of the action. "Oh. Wow. Those abs… He is so…hunky," Lucille Croft whispered loudly and Janie absently wondered whom Lucille had her sights set on these days.

A voice she thought might belong to Tricia Sands added to the mix. "He reminds me of that one actor who runs around all the time in movies with no shirt on? The dishwater blond with the Southern accent?"

"He does! I know who you're talking about— I could watch him stare at the wall if he did it shirtless..."

"That's just...magnificent," Jacinda chimed in reverently and Janie imagined that was exactly how the science teacher would sound if she was ever to witness the phenomenon of cold fusion.

"I've never seen abs like that in real life." That comment came from Shay and made Janie curious. Jonah was a good-looking guy with the lean-muscled build of a long-distance runner so if Shay was admiring someone else he must look pretty good.

"I have." This from Emily and Janie cringed because she knew she was now talking about Bering. No sister liked to hear another woman talk about how hot their brother was—not even if she was married to said brother.

Shay echoed her sentiment aloud. "Ick, Emily. That's my cousin you're referring to."

"How do you think I feel? You guys are ogling my brother!"

Janie's eyes darted onto the court because that meant Bering wasn't the one with no shirt on.

And that also meant… Aidan was.

She spotted him immediately because indeed he was the only shirtless player. She tried not to gape at the way his muscles tensed and rippled as he dribbled the ball down the court. She knew Aidan was fit, that was obvious no matter what he wore, but this was… He looked…incredible as he faked a pass and took a shot, muscles popping out in all the right places. Three points. Perfect swish. No wonder these women were gathered around like groupies at a rock concert.

Spectacle. That's what she should be thinking. He obviously wanted a bunch of grown women to admire him. She caught sight of a group of teenage girls giggling on the other side of the court. How—how tacky! He should be embarrassed at such an obvious display. What kind of man did this? Nobody else had their shirt off.

She caught sight of Gareth as Aidan passed him the ball. He executed a fake Janie had never seen him do before and sank a basket—obviously a move Aidan had taught him. She couldn't help but smile. Gareth was clearly having a blast and looked to be playing well so that dampened her disapproval with Aidan to some degree.

She visited with Shay and Emily and tried not to look at Aidan's bare, sweat-glazed muscles…

But with the sound of his voice and his now-familiar laughter ringing in the air she was aware of him virtually every second—and that made her edgy.

Janie scanned the area for her mom as the game neared its conclusion. Her phone buzzed. She frowned as she read her mom's text. Gabe wasn't feeling well so she'd taken the twins home. She didn't think there was a worse feeling in the world than when one of her kids was sick. She texted her mom a response.

She glanced at the court again in time to see Gareth and Aidan slap a high five. For some irrational reason the fact that Gabe was sick made Aidan's shirtless display even more off-putting.

The game wrapped up and Gareth ran over to her. "We won, Mom. We're the tournament champs!"

"Congratulations, honey."

"Thanks to Aidan—he scored over half our points that last game. I need to grab my math book out of my locker. I'll be back in a couple minutes, okay?"

"Sure."

The crowd was dispersing; the guys gravitating toward their partners—Shay with Jonah, Bering with Emily, teenage boys sidling up to the girls… Jacinda and Lucille and a few other single ladies were circling Aidan, who was nodding and smiling with his hands on his hips but seemed distracted. His eyes darted around until they landed on her. A look of intensity flashed across his face and Janie felt her body betray her with a fresh wave of attraction.

He said something that made his fan club giggle. Then he strode in her direction, all eyes on his retreating form.

"Hey," he said as he stopped in front of her.

"Hi." Janie tried to look anywhere but at his ripped muscles and lightly bronzed skin that still glistened with sweat. He had a body like one of those ultimate fighters—all wiry and hard with virtually flawless skin stretched over lean muscle. He was gorgeous. There, she admitted it, hoping the silent acknowledgment would take some of its power away. She allowed herself another glance, but her pulse jumped in betrayal of this perfectly logical rationale.

Her eyes took another quick sweep, almost as if she couldn't stop them. Oh, for the love of… The way his shorts hung on his hips… Tricia was right, he did look like that movie star. She felt a flash of irritation at herself for falling victim to such a blatant display of vanity. He obviously knew how good he looked. Janie thought about her stretch marks and the smattering of cellulite on the backs of her thighs—they were like battle scars…and worth every minute, of course, because she had her precious boys to show for her flaws.

But still—these were also reminders of how different her life was from that of Aidan's. She could always count on stretch marks and cellulite to straighten out her wayward thoughts.

Aidan shivered lightly. "I still get surprised at how the sun can be so bright here, yet you can still have this chill in the air."

"Well, it would probably help if you weren't running around naked," she blurted.

"Naked?" He let out a surprised chuckle. "What?"

"Half-naked. Whatever. It looks kind of bad, Aidan."

He chuckled. "It looks bad? That's not what, um, Lucille said."

"You know what I mean," she said and heard the disapproval in her tone. She felt like she was talking to one of the boys. "Like you know how good you look and you're showing off."

"I'm sorry if it offends you, but I can assure you I am not trying to show off."

"Obviously," she retorted dryly, looking him up and down and trying desperately not to appreciate the sight. "Don't worry—it had the desired effect. You've got Jacinda's attention and I'm not sure Lucille will ever fully recover, although my friend Ingrid will be grateful because maybe she will no longer pant after her husband, Gary."

His gray eyes zeroed in on her face and he seemed to be pondering her words. Good. Doubtless he was unused to anyone calling him on this kind of juvenile, exhibitionist behavior.

But when he spoke his voice was low and the tone matter-of-fact. "Desired effect? You think I'm playing basketball shirtless to get attention from women?"

He stepped closer, his body radiating tension. A surge of nerves made her light-headed. She shrugged and tried for a nonchalant sigh, hoping to cover up the fact that it bothered her. If she didn't know better she would think she was jealous. She wasn't. But her boys had begun to look up to him and she didn't appreciate this kind of example.

"I don't care why you're doing it, Aidan. I don't mean to sound like a prude or anything—it's just I don't want my boys to think that it's an acceptable way for them to get attention from women—by taking their shirts off and strutting around."

He narrowed his eyes at her but this time his lips began twitching like they were flirting with a smile. "Strutting around? This is really what you think? This is what has been going on in that pretty head of yours? You think I'm some kind of egomaniacal exhibitionist hoping to get attention from women?"

She shrugged and reminded herself that "pretty head" was merely an expression.

"For your information—"

"Hey, Aidan," Bering called as he jogged toward them. He held up a T-shirt. "Emily found one of my shirts in her car." He tossed it over and Aidan caught the gray cotton bundle. He shot Janie a look as if to say "Are you happy now?" and slipped the shirt on over his head.

Bering studied Janie and his brows shot up. "Didn't Aidan tell you about Gabe throwing up all over him before the game?"

Gabe had… Her baby had thrown up on him? That's why he'd removed his shirt? Janie felt herself plummet into the dunk tank of humiliation.

She somehow found enough of her voice to ask, "He…what?"

Bering continued. "Yeah, when Mom dropped Gareth off the twins got all excited when they saw us playing. Gabe ran onto the court and let out this big squeal—you know how much he loves Aidan. The game hadn't started yet, so I picked up Finn and Aidan picked up Gabe and we were playing some ball with them. Aidan was running up and down the court, spinning and doing his tricks, and Gabe was loving every second—doing that belly laugh of his. But all of a sudden the poor little guy was sick—" Bering paused to wince. "All over Aidan."

Janie wanted to claw at the ground beneath her feet and bury herself where she clearly belonged—with her fellow earth scum. She forced herself to look at Aidan, expecting to see anger or disgust or even a gloat. She deserved every one of those and more… Instead his face was a mixture of amusement and concern.

His question made her feel worse. "Have you talked to your mom? Do you know how the little guy is doing?"

Janie knew she should apologize, but in that moment her mortification froze her ability to do the right thing. She swallowed and managed a nod. Her tongue felt thick and heavy in her mouth as she spoke. "Yes, um, Mom said he's not feeling well. Has a little fever…"

Aidan stared back at her with an amused grin on his face, no doubt thrilled by the fact that she was the one who'd messed up this time.

IN SPITE OF Aidan's concern about Gabe and his dismay over the fact that Janie had assumed the worst of him—again—he also felt rather heartened by her reaction. She wasn't worried about him setting a bad example for Gareth, she was jealous.

He grinned, because that meant she found him

appealing. He hadn't cared about a woman thinking he was attractive since he turned eighteen and started receiving attention from the opposite sex. Then he'd almost immediately learned that as far as women were concerned, a pretty body or a pretty face didn't necessarily equal a pretty brain, yet he already knew how much he liked Janie's brain…and the rest of her, too. He just needed to figure out a way to get her to express how much she liked him. So if it took a bit of showing off for her to see that he was more than a brain, then fine.

He should have taken his shirt off weeks ago.

CHAPTER THIRTEEN

GARETH WAS GETTING NERVOUS. As much as he enjoyed working with Aidan, something told him that if his mom found out about what they were also doing after work, she might not be too thrilled. His mom didn't like him and his brother doing "dangerous" stuff. She was even pretty strict about the movies they watched and the video games they were allowed to play.

Reagan wasn't the best at keeping secrets; he didn't tell them on purpose, he was just so… honest. If their mom asked the right question, Aidan had told them not to lie and Gareth knew Reagan would spill the beans.

Gareth may not have been so keen to go along with the plan if he didn't believe that what Aidan was teaching them—especially Reagan—was so awesome. And Tag was helping and seemed completely on board, and that made Gareth feel better, too.

He could only hope that by the time their mom found out, Reagan would have learned enough that it made a difference. He also hoped his mom wouldn't make them quit their jobs with Aidan.

He watched Reagan attempt to copy what Aidan had just taught him and Gareth hoped Aidan knew as much about this as he did about bees.

"Gareth, buddy?" Aidan's voice brought him back down to earth. "It's your turn. Do you want to practice with me or Tag or Reagan?"

BETWEEN THE BOYS working for Aidan, her research and the interview process, Janie couldn't help but be intrigued by Aidan's work. And she had a few questions about it, which was what compelled her to drop by the lab one evening.

Janie knocked but no one answered. She tried the knob and found the door unlocked. She walked in expecting to find her boys hard at work taking samples of bee DNA. She had no idea exactly what that entailed, but she figured she'd find them hunched over microscopes or petri dishes or something equally as sedate. She definitely didn't expect to hear shouting, or to find her children beating each other up.

Gareth and Reagan were dancing around inside a makeshift boxing ring. The boys both wore basketball shorts, T-shirts, bright red boxing gloves on their hands and some kind of padded headgear. Aidan and Tag stood off to one side shouting instructions while the boys circled each other, throwing punches. Aidan seemed to be doing most of the coaching with an encouraging word or two thrown in from Tag here and there.

"Keep your hands up. Up, up, up—that's right. Good. You'll get knocked silly if you don't keep 'em up."

"That's great, now jab. Jab!"

Her boys were bobbing around like they knew exactly what they were doing—too much so. Janie was struck with the notion that the pigpen she'd helped Aidan measure all those weeks ago had been a boxing ring.

"Remember what I showed you. That's excellent, Gareth. Now punch him, Reagan. Good! Again—"

Anger propelled her forward like a bottle rocket. Her voice came out like a roar. "No! Do not punch your brother. What is going on?"

She went up to Aidan. "What are you…teaching my children?"

"Boxing," Aidan replied casually.

She was about to reply, but noticed how Reagan's eyes were wild with excitement. "Aidan's been giving us lessons. And, Mom, I'm getting good." He swiped at the air, all the while bobbing and weaving like a miniature prizefighter. She smiled at Reagan.

She turned an inquiring look toward Gareth. His brows dipped down, a deep furrow of concern forming between them. He could read her much better than Reagan and was probably assuming this wasn't going to end well. Smart boy. But, of course, this wasn't his fault.

Janie squeezed her eyes shut for a millisecond, opened them and formed a special glare just for Aidan. "Obviously it's boxing."

She glanced at her boys and wondered how they'd managed to keep this from her. Reagan, of all people—the kid was virtually incapable of subterfuge. And she knew that's where she'd get the answers to the questions that were racing through her brain.

She forced a smile in his direction. "What do you mean you're getting good, honey? Have you been practicing for a while?"

Out of the corner of her eye, she saw Gareth grimace and Janie knew the answer. Reagan confirmed it. "Yep. We were going to surprise you."

"Well done. I'm definitely surprised."

Reagan happily danced away throwing air punches.

She kept calm and directed her next questions at Aidan. "Can I talk to you for a minute? Outside?"

"Sure. You guys keep practicing."

Janie could hear Tag offering pointers as Aidan followed her out the door. She stopped and he faced her, folding his arms casually over his chest. She could see the cut of muscle beneath his thin T-shirt. Flashes of his shirtless basketball display flitted across her brain, of the muscles he had apparently honed while boxing, but at this moment she wasn't impressed at all.

"Pretty cool, huh?"

"Cool? Teaching my boys how to fight is cool? Not even asking me if you could teach them how to fight—that's cool? This is what you've been doing with my children? I thought you were teaching them about bees and plants and…science stuff."

Aidan's face contorted with confusion. "I have been teaching them science stuff—you know that very well. This is something extra that we've been doing. I never imagined you would have a problem with it."

"Then why didn't you tell me?"

He held out a hand. "Maybe I suspected it might be an issue initially, but I felt confident that you would see that it was the right thing to do. Reagan needs—"

She repeated his statement as something dawned on her. "The right thing to do? You are making decisions about what's right or wrong for my boys now? After I told you I didn't want your *help* parenting my children. This was your response? Taking care of things on your own without consulting me at all? And punching each other out is what you came up with?"

"This isn't some kind of bare-knuckled fight club, Janie, it's boxing. It's a sport. Like basketball."

"Like basketball?" she scoffed. "Aidan, it's not anything like basketball. It's fighting, no matter how you choose to dress it up. I don't want them to think violence is the way to solve problems and I certainly don't want them getting hurt—especially Reagan. He's…" She trailed off as she searched for an accurate description.

"He's turning into a good little fighter is what he's doing."

She spit out the words like a bad taste. "A fighter?"

His face formed a wincing kind of grin. "Oops. It's a boxing term. Fighter, player, boxer, participant… See where I'm going here?"

"Aidan, this is absolutely unacceptable. Once again you have stepped over a line."

"What? How?"

"You should have talked to me first."

"About what?"

Was he serious? "About what? About teaching my kids this vicious sport."

"Vicious?"

"There are sports they can play in school—"

"Reagan isn't interested in team sports and you know it. And how is boxing any more vicious than football? Or wrestling? Gareth plays football."

Admittedly, that had been an ineffective argument on her part—and a good counter on his.

"Janie, your boys need something to be proud of—especially Reagan. And Gareth needs to be proud of Reagan and not so focused on—"

"Reagan is a genius," Janie interrupted. "He can be proud of that. He is proud of that. And Gareth is proud of his brother."

"Janie, listen, please—I know what I'm talking about here. Being smart comes easy to Reagan. He doesn't really have to try all that hard and that's great in a lot of respects. But he needs to learn something. He needs to *earn* something. He needs to practice and *become* good at something. Gareth is a great basketball player. I see you encouraging him to play—to practice. Why can't you see that Reagan needs something like that, too?"

"I... He's..." She almost argued that she encouraged him to do his homework and to excel at his projects. But she knew he would do these things anyway. "I don't know. He's fragile I guess."

"He's not. He doesn't have to be fragile—

that's my point. I know you don't want to hear this, but kids make fun of him. They bully him. He is easy prey for cruel tyrants like Harmon and Riley. And in spite of what you apparently believe, this will not simply go away."

Janie felt a fresh surge of frustration "Gareth protects him. Elena watches out for him. It will get better. Kids will grow up and mature and they will start to appreciate Reagan for who he is."

She saw Aidan's jaw tighten. He looked beyond her shoulder as if he was the one now searching for patience. Then he focused on her. And here she thought she'd seen intensity in his silver-gray gaze after the shirtless basketball game. That had been child's play compared to this. He was clearly angry, but how dare he be angry with her?

"Janie, can you not hear yourself? You can't wish this away and hope it gets better, and you can't protect Reagan all the time—forever. Reagan needs to learn how to take care of himself. Yes, he's going to get hurt sometimes in the process. He's even going to fail, but those stumbles will teach him how to be the most successful man he can be. Being smart doesn't guarantee a person success in life. It doesn't guarantee respect and it certainly doesn't guarantee happiness. In fact, it can actually be a kind of hindrance."

"Hindrance?" she repeated skeptically.

"Yes, high intelligence can make a person socially awkward. People skills are something you have to learn—socializing does not always come easy to people like us. And you can't use his genius as an excuse."

"But Gareth…"

An unsettling revelation halted her words; she'd been about to say that Gareth helps Reagan—helps her protect him. Since Cal had died she'd been operating under the notion that Gareth would always be around to help his brother, when she knew very well that he wouldn't be. He wouldn't even be around next year as the two boys would be in different buildings at school. It wasn't fair of her to put that kind of pressure on Gareth, not to mention her actions were leaving Reagan vulnerable. Janie suddenly felt sick.

Aidan was shaking his head and the look on his face was worse than any pain his brutal observations had yet caused her. His features were awash with pity; he felt sorry for her. Her entire body went hot with embarrassment even as her heart ached. The realization hit her hard that even though she'd been trying, she'd been failing as a mother in this incredibly important way.

She felt a meltdown coming on as tears clouded her vision.

"Can you ask Tag to bring the boys home?"

"I can bring them home."

She wanted to tell him no, that she didn't want him spending time with the boys anymore, but she knew she couldn't be that rash, that small. That would make things even harder on Gareth and Reagan. She had to think past her bruised pride. But she needed a minute—her heart hurt, like it was suddenly being compressed inside of her chest.

"Janie, are you...okay?"

She shook her head. "No, I'm not. I can't talk about this anymore right now, Aidan, but you really have gone too far. You—"

"Yes, you can."

"What?"

"You *can* talk about this. That's your problem, Janie. Where your boys are concerned—you won't hear anything that you don't want to hear. You keep hoping everything will get better on its own."

She couldn't take any more of this. She turned to go. But he reached out and stopped her by placing a hand on her arm.

"Please, don't go. Just listen for a minute. I know you can see how happy Reagan has been while spending time with me, and I've already noticed a change in Gareth, as well, the last few weeks. But your boys have some problems and I think some of them are undoubtedly the result of losing their father, but others stem from different issues and circumstances that you don't seem to fully comprehend or understand—"

"I don't need to hear any more about what a bad mother I am, Aidan."

A look of unbridled surprise appeared on his face. "I never said you were a bad mother. I said your boys have some problems that you don't understand or you're not willing to address—"

"See? I don't 'understand'—those are the kinds of statements that make me feel like a bad mom. Telling me my boys have problems." Even though in her sinking, aching heart she knew he was right, she still didn't want to hear it from him. How could he understand these complex issues when she didn't fully comprehend them herself?

"Everyone has problems, Janie. What would make you a bad mom is if you didn't try something that was right here at your disposal to attempt to fix these issues."

She shook her head and tried to think. He'd basically just confirmed her worst fears. She didn't know what to do anymore. She didn't know how to fix any of this...

"Janie, trust me, I know what I'm doing. I... I

was bullied when I was in school. Horrible, terrible stuff—way worse than anything Reagan has experienced…so far. School was hell for me until I learned how to deal with these things. And that's the point—I've seen kids like these guys in action. I witnessed Harmon harassing Reagan at the school a few weeks ago. It was bad, and I can guarantee you that he's not going to stop."

Janie stared. She couldn't imagine him being bullied. Aidan was so…so cool. And yet he did have a side to him—the awkwardness that most people probably wouldn't notice, but she could see, in part because Reagan shared the same traits; the tendency to tell the truth when diplomacy might serve him better, the observations that made people uncomfortable, the sometimes overinformative lectures that could leave listeners feeling rather inadequate as well as educated.

And her poor Reagan… "I do want to fix this for him. It's just… I've tried so hard to keep him safe…to keep everyone safe. As difficult as this is to admit, Aidan, you're right. Just like with Gareth, I've been telling myself things would get better, hoping the problems would simply go away."

Maybe she did need to do something. But…

But fighting?

She repeated her earlier sentiment. "I don't

want them to think violence is the answer to their problems."

"I understand that, I do. But I'm not going to send Reagan to school and turn him loose on Harmon. That's not the way this works. It's about confidence and having the ability to defend yourself if you need to. Remember that kid when you were in school who nobody messed with, but if you really think about it you can't identify a reason why? And why was that?"

Janie thought for a second. Bering had been like that. Everyone knew he was tough, but she couldn't remember him ever fighting. He exuded this toughness; he had a reputation for it, yet he was really a gentle giant. And being big and athletic had also helped, like it did for Gareth.

Aidan seemed to mirror her thoughts. "Some kids have it naturally—like Gareth. But sometimes kids like me—like Reagan—need some help. I really care about your boys, Janie. I'm confident this will help. My grandfather did this for me—taught me how to box—and it changed my life. Boxing gave me the confidence to play basketball and to try all kinds of things I never would have attempted. And I had to work at it—to practice and improve, which taught me so many important traits. It would have been so easy for me to bury my nose in my books and microscopes and miss out on so much that life has to offer. Let me try this, Janie. Please?"

She blinked back tears and nodded. "Okay."

"Okay?" He repeated the word and she nearly laughed at the shock on his face.

"Yes. Fine. Teach them how to box. I don't know what to do anymore."

"Yes!" He made a fist and his face split into a grin. Janie couldn't help herself—she grinned back. He was excited by the prospect of helping her children. What mom wouldn't be happy about that?

Aidan placed his hands on her shoulders and squeezed gently. His touch was soothing and comforting. His fingers rested lightly on her shoulders and she felt something warm bloom inside of her—something that had iced over three long years ago and had remained frozen ever since.

Janie longed for him to wrap those strong arms around her as his eyes settled on her lips. She wanted him to kiss her. She hadn't felt like this since before Cal had passed away. Aidan's mouth curled upward as his eyes met hers.

The look felt inviting and she felt a tug in her chest, like a magnet trying to pull her forward. She had this urge to touch him, to feel for herself if he was as solid as he looked. She brought her hands up and placed them on his chest as if to push open a door.

His gaze landed briefly on her hands before slipping away. He gave his head a little half-shake as if he was trying to regain his senses. Removing his hands from her shoulders, he took a step back.

Pinpricks of mortification tingled across her skin as he seemed to change his mind. What in the world had she been thinking? He was gorgeous and smart and way too…much for her. Or more likely she was too much for him. Her life was full of boisterous toddlers and challenging adolescents and complications and…baggage. He could probably carry the sum total of his baggage in one single pocket of his rumpled cargo pants. She had to put her boys first, which sounded so simple, but sometimes—like now—she didn't know…

His eyes seemed to be searching her face, but for what she had no clue. "Janie, you won't regret this," he said softly. "I promise."

"I hope you're right about that, Aidan."

She turned and walked back into Aidan's lab/home/"boxing arena" and quickly got her act together. As she neared the boys she caught the look of apprehension in Gareth's expression. She smiled encouragingly and the relief that flashed across his face made her insides clench like she'd just taken a blow.

Aidan was right; she'd put too much pressure on Gareth. He needed time to be a kid, and she had to find a way to help him come to a resolution where his dad was concerned.

And Reagan… She wasn't sure if boxing was the answer but that stuff about him learning something that didn't necessarily come easy to him…maybe there was something to that. This was without a doubt one of her most difficult mom moments ever.

Letting go was definitely one of the most challenging aspects of parenthood. She wasn't about to cut those apron strings, however, but maybe she could loosen the knots a bit.

CHAPTER FOURTEEN

AIDAN TALKED HER in to going out into "the field" with him and the boys one sunny Sunday afternoon. After church, they'd gone to brunch at her mom's house. Most of the family had departed when Aidan asked her if she'd like to join him and the boys for a bee excursion.

Janie probably would have declined, but her mom's encouragement coupled with a longing to enjoy some of the glorious weather had her wanting to accept the invitation.

Claire sealed it by offering to watch the twins and asking, "How can you write this article about Aidan if you don't see him in action?"

Her deadline was only days away and even though the article was pretty much finished, Janie's curiosity got the better of her.

They'd taken off with a meadow of wildflowers up near the Faraway Inn as their destination. After they reached the spot, Gareth and Reagan gathered their day packs, which were filled with supplies. Gareth attached something around his waist and they took off like they knew exactly what they were doing, which she supposed they did.

Grass and low brush dotted the rock-strewn area. The air felt balmy for late spring and Janie peeled off her fleece jacket and tied it around her waist. The smell of flowers tickled her nose and her eyes darted around trying to identify the species.

"So," Aidan said after he'd captured a fluffy bumblebee in a clear plastic capsule about the size of a quart jar. "Do you want to try taking a sample?"

He held up the container and Janie was surprised at how calm the bee seemed. She commented on it and Aidan informed her that bumblebees were docile by nature and so single-minded that as long as they had nectar to focus on they didn't really pay much attention to the fact that they were temporarily trapped.

"That's what this little dropper contains right here. It seems fair to give them a free meal in exchange for a DNA sample."

She peered at it closely. "That's pretty neat. Where do you get something like this? Do you just do an internet search for bee-catcher capsule-container thingy?"

He grinned. "Well, sure, *now* you can."

His gray eyes were dancing with something—pride, maybe? She'd learned over the last few weeks that Aidan wasn't one to brag about himself. He was honest if you asked the right questions, but he didn't offer a lot of extraneous, or personal, information.

"Aidan, did you design this contraption?"

"I did."

"And now you can order them online?"

"Yep."

"No offense, but who would want one?"

He tipped back his head and laughed. "Well, believe it or not, entomologists. You can get these without the nectar dispenser and in various shapes and sizes. You can use them for other insects."

"Awesome," she said dryly. "I'll place my order tonight."

He chuckled again. "So, what do you think? You want to try taking a sample?"

"Um, no, thank you."

"Why not?" He ambled toward her with that slow grin on his face that Janie had come to know wasn't quite as lazy and careless as it appeared. In reality there was a-scary-lot going on inside that pretty head of his.

"I don't want to hurt it."

"Oh, *now* you don't want to hurt the bee?"

Janie felt truly happy for the first time in a long time. She realized that she seemed to always have fun with Aidan, except maybe when he was nosing excessively into her life…

"This is different. The bee isn't doing anything to earn my wrath."

Aidan grinned. "This doesn't hurt them."

Janie eyed him skeptically. "How could you possibly know that?"

"Do you really want to me to answer that?"

"No, never mind." She'd made the mistake of asking similar types of questions in the last few weeks. The explanations she received sometimes made her eyes glaze over. And she'd thought her eleven-year-old genius could be difficult to follow.

"All we do is snip a microscopic sample from the middle leg. The bee goes on to live a long, happy, nectar-filled life—by bumblebee standards, that is. The boys are getting really good at it."

Janie smiled, managing to tamp down the surge of nerves at the thought of Gareth handling bees. "What *are* bumblebee standards?"

"A few weeks, a month, a season if they're lucky. Queens are the only ones who hibernate over the winter, while the males and the female workers die off."

"That's a lot of living to do in a very short period of time. Reagan said you are checking for diseases, too, and not just taking DNA samples?"

"Indeed. And yes—we're looking for mites, viruses, anything out of the ordinary. We're trying to assess the general health of the native bee population. Bumblebees are the focus, but we're gathering information on whatever native species we find."

"The boys are really enjoying this, Aidan, thank you again. I never thought I'd see Gareth voluntarily within a hundred feet of a bee, much less taking a DNA sample."

Aidan took a step closer—too close, she knew, because her pulse started racing whenever he came within a certain radius. Like a Geiger counter or something. Radius measurements and Geiger counters? Clearly science had invaded her life—and a certain scientist in particular had managed to worm his way right into the middle.

"It's good to step outside our comfort zones, though, don't you think? Take risks? Attempt to face our fears?"

"Um, I don't know… I suppose."

"It is. Trust me. That's how we really learn." He set the bee inside of its temporary trap on top of a large rock. The bee was foraging around in the tiny nectar pot and that thought made her smile, because they really did seem like busy little creatures.

Aidan was staring at her, apparently waiting

for a response. She looked at him skeptically. "Learn what?"

He moved again and Janie froze as his lips nearly brushed her ear. Hot zone, she thought, as her pulse shifted into overdrive. She worried he could hear the drumbeat of her heart.

"What we like," he whispered. "It's how we learn exactly what we like. You know what I like?"

"Bees? Plants? Basketball?" she queried and then swallowed nervously. "Boxing…" Good grief, she sounded like her kids playing charades.

He was grinning like he knew he made her nervous. How annoying…

"Yes, I do. I like all of those things. I also like you, Janie."

"You…what?"

"I tried this once before, but I didn't think you were quite ready. But now…" He took her by the shoulders and leaned his head toward hers. One hand traveled up and slipped around the back of her neck. He paused for a few tension-filled seconds with his lips hovering over hers and she wondered if he was giving her an opportunity to back away. And there was no possible way that was happening. She inched closer so that they were chest-to-chest. Her hands reached up and grasped the collar of his rumpled shirt.

When his lips covered hers Janie knew she

was in serious trouble, even as the fact occurred to her that this shouldn't be happening for so many reasons. She was too…simple, in direct opposition to her life, which was too complicated. But then again he wasn't the man for her, either. He was too complicated while his life was too…simple. And yet it felt so…right.

So for once in her life she quit thinking and instead poured every bit of her scared, lonely, damaged, single-mom self into that kiss. And oh, my…could he kiss. His lips were warm and soft and he made a noise deep in his throat that made her think he felt things for her, too. She probably would never have come to her senses if Aidan hadn't stopped.

"Your boys," he said, but kept an arm looped around her waist. He looked around, making sure they were nowhere in sight. Then his lips found her neck.

She inhaled a breath through her teeth as his lips kissed their way back to her mouth. He groaned softly and nibbled on her lips.

This was… She felt like a teenager on a date. And that was the thought that brought her to her senses. She was about as far from a carefree teenager as a woman could be.

She brought her hands up and rested them on his shoulders. "Aidan, we—"

"I know."

He grinned and took a step away, but he kept looking at her with his gray eyes all soft and smoky. "You are so beautiful and so... I've never felt more comfortable with another human being in my life." He muttered something else under his breath, then quickly leaned in and kissed her one more time, harder and hungrier this time, like he couldn't quite get enough of her. Like she was the most desirable woman on the planet and that this was a real first kiss—a romantic start to something special and full of hope and not... this complicated situation that couldn't possibly go anywhere.

A rush of panic flashed through her; she had to stop this before it went any further.

"Aidan—"

Aidan backpedaled a few steps and ran a hand through his hair. He stepped to his left and bent over a patch of wildflowers. He plucked a flower and Janie felt her chest flood with warm anticipation.

If he gave her a flower she would be a goner...

He started toward her.

"Aidan—"

"Shh." He dropped the flower and paused like he was contemplating something. He stepped toward her.

"Remember what happened at the beach when you—" She started to playfully remind him about the last time he'd shushed her. "What are you doing?"

He grimaced like he was in pain. "Janie, I need you to listen to me very carefully. I have to ask you…something very important."

"What…?" she whispered.

"Have you ever given Gareth a shot with his EpiPen?"

Not the question she'd been expecting. "No, I've never had to—Tag has been there both times he's been stung."

"In my backpack, there's an EpiPen."

Janie nodded her head eagerly. "That's good to know. I can't tell you what a relief that is. Gareth says you always have them and I really appreciate—"

"You're terrible at listening sometimes, do you know that?"

"Yes. I do. It happens when I'm nervous. Sorry. I have a difficult time shutting my brain off and it comes out of my mouth…"

He traced a finger over her bottom lip. "I love your mouth, but you need to get an EpiPen out of my backpack. Take the black cap off, then the gray cap." He demonstrated by holding one fist aloft, thumb up. "Hold it like this and—"

"Aidan, I know how to use them. I just haven't had to do it yet."

"Oh, that's good."

He brought a hand up slowly and placed it on his chest. He stood still for a few seconds and then inhaled a raspy breath, like he was struggling to breathe...

Janie felt her stomach do the broken-elevator plummet as the circumstances finally dawned on her.

"Aidan?"

He looked down at his arm. Janie followed his gaze to where she could see a red patch that was already swelling up high on his biceps.

"It wasn't a bee. It was awfully aggressive. Maybe a wasp? I wasn't paying attention because you...and I'm—"

"Allergic," she said, finishing for him. "Where's your EpiPen?"

He leaned over and placed his hands on the large rock beside them. He picked up the bumblebee still encapsulated in plastic, flipped the latch on the container and released it. What kind of man would think about a bee at a time like this? He turned his back to the rock and lowered himself to the ground. He draped his arm across his knee and she could see it already turning an angrier, deeper shade of red.

She tried to quell the panic creeping over her.

"You need to go get the EpiPen and give me the shot... In a few minutes I won't be able to do it...myself." He swallowed and Janie wondered if it was her imagination that the action seemed difficult.

Her voice was sharp. "Aidan, where? Where is it?"

"In the pickup. Inside my backpack. Gareth has—"

Janie didn't stick around to listen to the rest. She took off running toward the vehicle. She felt a wave of heat rush through her followed by a bout of nausea, but somehow she reached the vehicle, tore open the back door, where she remembered Aidan leaving his pack.

It was there—the faded, green-and-brown camo-printed canvas pack. She snatched it up and ran back toward him. Why hadn't he had the pack with him? Why didn't he carry the epinephrine with him at all times? How long did she have? What if she was too late? By the time she returned Aidan's breathing was labored and his arm seemed to be about five hundred times more swollen than before she'd left. The redness and swelling appeared to be creeping up his neck as well.

Gareth and Reagan suddenly appeared by her side.

"Aidan?" Gareth asked calmly. "Did you get stung?"

Reagan's voice took on a harried tone. "Mom, has Aidan been stung? He's allergic, too."

"Yes, I'm looking for an EpiPen." She rummaged through the pack but felt as if she was sifting through a thick pot of oatmeal. "Where is it? I don't see it."

"I got it, Mom." Gareth was already calmly reaching under his own shirt. He peeled off a black neoprene belt. Where had he gotten that? She heard the tear of Velcro and suddenly he was holding a plastic tube. He removed a vial from inside that she recognized as an EpiPen. He pulled the black cap off of one end, the gray cap from the other and then efficiently injected the life-saving epinephrine into Aidan's outer thigh.

Janie and the boys managed to assist Aidan to the pickup. Later, she would take the time to be amazed at how strong her boys had become, but in the moment all she could think about was getting Aidan to the hospital.

Somehow both of the boys knew to lay Aidan in the backseat and to elevate his legs. Gareth sat with him and placed Aidan's legs across his lap. He informed her that this would help prevent Aidan from going into shock. Knowing Aidan he'd probably had a conversation about this very action in case it was ever necessary for him or Gareth.

As she passed the Faraway Inn, where she knew she had a cell signal, she handed her phone to Reagan and told him to call Emily and have her meet them at the hospital.

"HOLY COW, AIDAN. You look like… I'm not going to sugarcoat this, buddy, you're hideous. Whatever you do—don't look in the mirror."

Janie gaped at her cousin. "Tag, stop. That's not funny."

He let out a loud belly laugh and pointed. "Yes, it is. Look at him."

"How old are you? I swear my eleven-year-old is more mature than you. Get out of here." She pointed at the door.

Aidan smiled. "Janie, it's fine. I'm fine. This is nothing. You should have seen me when I got stung by fire ants."

Janie stared at his swollen arm, chest, neck—his skin was red and mottled. He looked… She didn't even want to think about it.

"Barely."

"Barely what?"

"You're barely fine." She felt an aftershock of fear wash over her as the incident replayed in her mind. She squelched the feeling by reassuring herself that he was going to be fine. Yet she had to stop herself from crawling onto the bed with him and wrapping her arms around him… What was the matter with her? What had happened between them? Why was she thinking about that while he was lying in a hospital bed?

"Please, stop worrying. You guys got me here in plenty of time. Reagan told me he's never seen you drive so fast. They were really impressed."

Impressed? "Aidan, you were practically unconscious when we got here and now you look like…"

"Like?"

She frowned. "I can't think of anything that doesn't sound really bad."

Tag laughed again. Janie glared. Bering and Emily walked into the hospital room.

Bering's eyes went wide. He said, "Wow, Aidan—are you sure you're all right? You look miserable."

Tag busted out another round of guffaws. Bering and Aidan joined in. When Tag finally caught his breath, he wiped his eyes and said, "I gotta get to work. But I hope you're feeling better for playing basketball on Wednesday."

Aidan raised his hand and Tag grabbed it.

"Thanks for stopping by, Tag."

"Bering, I was just lecturing Tag about not making Aidan feel worse than he already does."

Bering blew out a loud breath as his eyes passed over Aidan's swollen body. "I doubt that's possible."

Emily scowled at her husband and then at Tag. "You guys are awful."

"Oh, honey, insults are our way of showing affection."

Emily gave him the requisite fake-irritated yet full-of-love glare. "Yeah, well, don't try that on me—ever."

Bering chuckled. "Never." He turned to Aidan. "Seriously, you scared us there, dude. We're really glad you're okay."

"Thanks to your sister and your nephews, I'm fine."

They talked about what had happened and then chatted for a while. Bering announced that he needed to get back to his shop because he had to repair a boat. He patted Aidan on his good shoulder, gave Janie a peck on the cheek and Emily left to walk him out.

Janie peered at Aidan and asked the question that had been foremost on her mind since she realized he was going to be well. "Why didn't you tell me you were allergic?"

One side of his mouth tugged up into a smile. "It didn't seem relevant."

"Really? It wasn't because you were afraid I wouldn't let the boys work with you if I knew? Kind of like the boxing? Where you thought it would work better for you to ask for forgiveness rather than for permission?"

His brows dipped down like she'd asked him a really tough question. "No, I did consider that it would distract you from the bigger picture, but I didn't... I don't think it matters. The chances of me getting stung were remote. The rewards outweigh the risks."

Janie scoffed. "Clearly we have different methods of assessing risk."

He looked troubled by her statement. "You can't really live if you don't ever take risks, Janie."

"Yeah? Well, you won't live to take any risks if you don't think about your safety, Aidan."

He grinned and she couldn't help but smile in return. Why wasn't she more upset about this? Probably because she was too relieved and so incredibly grateful that he was going to be okay. What kind of man studies something that could so easily take his life? A brave one was the answer that immediately popped into her head, but... Brave or reckless? She didn't know—she wasn't even sure of the difference.

She sighed, and grudgingly acknowledged, "You seem to have taught the boys how to stay calm in case of an emergency. They were more levelheaded than I was. So, thanks for that."

"They are wonderful kids. And yes, we reviewed several times what to do in case of an emergency. But for the record I'd like it noted

that I got stung because I wasn't paying attention—not because of the work I'm doing."

"What do you mean you weren't paying attention?"

"I was distracted with trying to pick you a
flower. I was distracted by you. I wanted to…"

Her heart seemed to stop as she waited for him
to finish his thought.

Janie's eyes were still on Aidan when someone walked through the door. His smiling mouth
tightened to form a thin line and his warm gray
gaze seemed to ice over. Janie noted the stunning raven-haired woman give Aidan a searching look.

She stepped around Janie, leaned over and
kissed Aidan on the cheek.

"Aidan, I'm so glad you're going to be okay."
Her tone was part relief and part affection, and
Janie knew immediately that the two of them
were something more than friends. She felt a
knot form in her chest as the woman reached out
a hand and trailed it affectionately over Aidan's
swollen arm.

Aidan seemed utterly nonplussed. "Meredith,
what are you doing here?"

CHAPTER FIFTEEN

MEREDITH? THE FAKE REPORTER? Aidan hadn't mentioned that she was still a part of his life.

Emily walked back into the room and reached out a hand toward the woman. "Hi, I'm Aidan's sister, Emily James. You look familiar, have we met?"

She turned friendly brown eyes on Emily and extended a hand. "We have. It's nice to see you again, Emily. I'm Meredith Montoyo—we met when you were at Cam-Field. I worked PR on a Littleton Oil project you were involved with. Years ago, before Aidan and I were engaged…"

Engaged?

"What are you doing here?" Aidan repeated when Emily and Meredith were through catching up.

Aidan had never mentioned that he'd been engaged to Meredith—Meredith, who had betrayed him. Suddenly Janie was struck with the feeling of how little she actually knew about him. She'd spent weeks conducting an interview, yet she didn't even know that he'd nearly been married.

Now that she thought about it, she didn't know anything about his past relationships.

And here she'd been arguing her case that she was genuinely qualified to write an article about him.

Aside from the obvious, she knew he liked meatballs and huckleberry pie, and drank copious amounts of black coffee. He enjoyed playing gin rummy and watching television shows about restoring old homes. She had thought she was getting to know him. And she'd believed she was chipping away at that shell of privacy he wore like a plate of armor. A lightning bolt of clarification struck her as she realized she'd really only discovered as much as he'd wanted her to see.

"Didn't Blake tell you?" asked Meredith.

"Tell me what?" Aidan replied.

"That I was coming here? He hired me and—"

"Blake told me *he* was coming to see me—but he didn't mention it would be today and he didn't mention that you were coming, too."

A stocky man with a red beard a few shades lighter than his hair barged through the door carrying a cup of coffee bearing the Donut Den's logo. He stretched his arms out wide. "Aidan! Stung again, huh? You would think those fire ants would have been enough for you." He emitted a loud belly laugh as he stepped closer to the bed.

Aidan's smile looked genuine when he reached out and shook the man's hand. "That fire-ant fiasco was your fault and you know it. I wasn't expecting you for a while, Blake."

"I heard you were having some problems. Emily just told me something about cutting your hand on a mollusk shell? Why didn't you mention it?" Another chuckle boomed from his thick barrel chest—he reminded Janie of a Shakespearean stage actor. She was struck with the thought that everything this man did was likely executed with this degree of drama.

"It was nothing—got my stitches out ages ago." Aidan flipped his hand over to reveal where the thin red lines of his healing lacerations were still very much evident.

"That's good. It's always something with you, isn't it, Hollings?"

Blake introduced himself and then Aidan quickly explained who everyone was. Janie couldn't help but notice how Meredith graced her with a warm smile even as she subtly shifted closer to Aidan. She leaned over and whispered something in his ear as Bering and Emily chatted with Blake.

Janie strangely felt very alone. And she realized she hadn't felt this way in weeks, not since before Aidan had stormed his way into the middle of her life, her boys' lives—right into their hearts. He'd made her boys fall in love with him with his basketball and boxing and…bees. Even the twins adored him—Finn shared his normally jealously guarded buddy bear with him, and nearly every time Gabe dozed off in Aidan's arms, he would sleep the whole night through. And, Janie now realized, he'd made her feel alive and hopeful, in a way that she hadn't in so very long. She'd found herself hoping that her life— that the boys' lives—could finally reach a level of contentment that she'd begun to fear would never be possible.

She slipped quietly from the room and exited the hospital, feeling like everything that had happened that day had been some kind of surreal and cruel, foggy dream—except for the viselike ache that gripped her heart.

That she could definitely feel.

GARETH WAS RELIEVED that Aidan was going to be okay. The experience had been scary. Gareth thought Aidan was pretty cool—someone who was allergic to bees but still chose to work with them was really brave. Aidan might be the bravest person Gareth had ever met. Gareth wanted to be like him—to face his fears head-on like Aidan had done with bees.

Aidan had told him and Reagan about how he had been bullied, too, when he was a kid and about how he'd been scared of things in his life and had to learn to overcome his fears. And now he was helping Reagan overcome his, too.

Gareth never would have guessed his little brother would be good at boxing. But somehow he'd taken to it the same way he did chess—"if I do this, then he'll do that…" Strategy—that was something Reagan was good at and it was definitely translating in the boxing ring. And he was fast with his hands—superfast. Faster than Gareth and for the first time in his life Gareth felt like there was the possibility that Reagan might stand a chance if—or rather, when—Harmon got ahold of him. That was a relief. So, the pressure was off of him a little where Reagan was concerned and that was great, but he also felt a little guilty because of the relief. And there was also a piece of him that felt bad about his brother maybe not needing him quite so much.

Even Mom seemed to be doing better. She liked Aidan—Gareth could tell. It had been hard since his dad died knowing how much his mom relied on him. Now he found himself thinking that it was both a relief and a concern to think that she might *not* need him so much, either.

And what about the part of him that felt like he might disappear right along with the memories of his dad? Gareth hadn't gotten into his stash in a week. And he'd been too tired to go on any raids—between working for Aidan, doing his regular chores and homework and playing basketball he was wiped out every night. He should feel freed or something from not needing that since he'd been falling asleep and staying that way the whole night through and he guessed he did in a way. But that made him feel guilty, too.

It was all so…much.

He was starting to think he wasn't ever going to get better—that he wasn't ever going to feel normal again. He was tired. He was really tired of feeling this way. He needed to figure some things out, face his own fears like Aidan had when he'd been bullied, like Aidan did every day when he went out to hunt bees.

But Gareth had already faced one fear, in a way, when Aidan had been stung. Gareth was pretty proud of how he'd managed to give Aidan the shot with the EpiPen. He hadn't been nervous or scared. He remembered what Aidan had said, and that it would be easy if the time ever came because he would be prepared. That had felt good.

Gareth decided to do something he never did unless it was the pitch-dark of night. He crossed his bedroom and locked the door, hurried back to his bed and removed the fabric piece and the cardboard covering his stash spot. He pulled down his treasure box. He tucked what he needed between the mattress and box spring and put everything back in place. He unlocked his bedroom door—he knew his mom would get suspicious if she walked by and found that he'd locked himself inside.

He found a notebook in his desk drawer, propped up some pillows behind him on the bed so he could claim he was doing homework if Mom popped her head in. Crosby jumped up beside him and began to purr.

How did this cat always know when he was feeling down when the people in his life couldn't even see it? Gareth took a few minutes to scratch his fat cheeks the way he liked. Gareth smiled as he let out one of his half meows and curled up on the raccoon-shaped pillow beside him. The love he felt for this big cat sometimes made his eyes well up with tears, not like he was going to cry, but like emotion wanted to ooze out of him. It was weird.

Then Gareth took a deep breath and a feeling of peace like he hadn't experienced in a long time descended over him. He put his pen to the paper and settled in to write one final letter.

"WHAT IS SHE doing here, Blake?" Aidan unlocked the door to his current home. He'd really started to love this place. He'd already acquired so many fond memories—most involving Janie and her boys. He held the door for Blake before following him inside.

Blake spun a half circle, one direction and then the other. "What an outrageous place. I'm always amazed at your ability to settle in somewhere, Hollings. Looks like you've lived here for years and not just a few months. No matter what I promise myself going in, I inevitably end up living out of my suitcase like I'm on a vacation that's lasted too long. Can't tell which clothes are dirty, which are clean…"

Aidan smiled. This was true. Blake always looked put-together, but he was a slob. This was only one of the many ways the two friends were direct opposites.

Blake ambled toward the makeshift boxing ring. Aidan had quit assembling and disassembling the fenced-in area after their practices since Janie now knew the boys were boxing.

"Nice setup. I'd say we should go a couple rounds, but I know you'd knock me silly."

"I might do that anyway, Blake."

Blake snorted out a laugh. "Meredith came to me a couple of months ago really distraught, Aidan. She genuinely feels bad about what happened between the two of you. We talked—went out for dinner and…"

Aidan felt an uncomfortable wad of tightness in the pit of his stomach as if he'd swallowed a rotten apple—whole.

"So...what? You guys are dating now?"

Blake winced. "Uh, no. Jeez, Aidan, you're my best friend and my business partner. Besides, I'm not a masochist."

"Blake—"

"Aidan, I realize that things didn't work out between the two of you. But you're being kind of hard on her. I know there was a huge misunderstanding where the two of you are concerned. I do believe she's changed, Aidan."

Aidan stared at his friend and wondered how someone as brilliant as Blake could be so dense. But this was Meredith they were talking about here. He'd been stupid once, too, where Meredith was concerned. She had made it easy to be stupid. But he'd learned his lesson and he'd thought Blake had learned it right along with him.

Apparently not.

"A misunderstanding? Is that what she called it? She tried to steal from my mom and when I caught her she published an article about me that could have destroyed my career and nearly landed me in jail. I realize you were in Australia when this all went down, but you know this happened, Blake. You've seen the article. She accused me of trying to interfere in the Cocodrilo

Reserve so my mom would have a steady supply of plants. So, which part did I misunderstand?"

"She says your mom shared the formula with her."

"Blake, seriously? That formula is going to make my mom and her partners a lot of money, not to mention there's the importance of the discovery itself. Why would she share it with anyone else, much less Meredith, before the deal was done?"

"Meredith said she didn't realize the implications of what she was doing. She wanted to—"

Aidan lifted his hands, palms up, in a show of frustration. "Blake! Come on…"

"Well, she told me she wants to apologize. She hopes that what happened can all be water under the bridge."

Aidan raked a hand through his hair and all he could wonder was what Janie was thinking right now. Meredith had strolled in, taken one look at the situation and immediately flaunted their engagement around like his nana did one of her lace hankies. Meredith had to have seen Janie's expression—she'd done her best, he guessed, to mask her confusion and…disappointment? But Meredith was sharp when it came to reading people. There wasn't a lot that she missed.

This was the last thing he needed; things were already one step forward, two steps back where

Janie was concerned. This day had been more like a giant leap forward, but then he'd seen the look on her face when Meredith appeared and he'd felt the progress he'd made crumbling. Why hadn't he just told Janie about Meredith? It would have been so simple.

He didn't really know why he hadn't said anything. Yes, he did. He had gotten used to not discussing his private life. He was so careful—and in this case maybe he'd been too careful. Regret and pragmatism raged a frustrating battle within him.

Aidan felt a spike of irritation. He lifted his hands up, gesturing as if she was standing right beside him. "Blake, what is she doing here? She said you hired her."

Blake picked up a plastic vial sitting on Aidan's counter. "I did. She's our media consultant."

"You… She's what?"

"I told you I hired someone to help with PR."

Aidan frowned at Blake; he wanted to be angry. But he had agreed to allow Blake to increase publicity before *Seeds* was released. He'd also told him he didn't care who he hired as long as he kept Aidan out of it.

"You failed to mention who you hired."

"No, I didn't. I sent you an email."

"Really?" Aidan squeaked out the question, afraid he already knew the answer.

Blake laughed. "*Really.* Do you read my emails at all?"

"Yes, of course—I skim them. And I read the important stuff—the personal stuff and the interesting stuff."

"This is important, Aidan. In spite of how you feel about her, Meredith is one of the best media consultants in the business. She is doing great things for us, Aidan, maximizing our exposure in ways I wouldn't even have imagined. And I know you don't like to talk about subjects as indelicate as money, but she may have found funding for our next project. Imagine having money for our next project before we even begin. Not to mention that I'm beginning to believe *Seeds* is actually going to make us some money, too."

Blake bent over to examine a slide that Aidan had left in the microscope. Aidan waited for him to continue.

Blake stood upright again and faced him. "Aidan, Meredith wants to try for a *Seeds* television special—or maybe even a miniseries on one of the nature channels after the film's release. We'll have to do some editing, but a deal like that could mean a lot of money."

Aidan felt a rush of excitement and immediately tempered the feeling. This kind of success was what he and Blake fantasized about. For Aidan that meant freedom to continue projects on preserving endangered and native species. They'd talked about it since college... Meredith knew this—she knew how much this would mean to Blake and Aidan, and that told him that it was probably too good to be true.

Aidan didn't trust Meredith. What was she really after?

Blake looked at Aidan. "You do realize what this means, right?"

Aidan peered questioningly at his friend. "What?"

"You have to play nice, Aidan."

Aidan blew out a breath. "I'll try."

"Well, you're going to have to try hard and very quickly."

"What do you mean?"

"You remember Kyle Wesley? You met him in the Cocodrilo?"

"Sure, of course." Aidan and Kyle had hit it off immediately when they'd met in Brazil. Wesley and his environmental conservation group had been part of the team trying to save the Cocodrilo Reserve. It was only later that Aidan had learned of his personal wealth and commercial success. At the time he'd known him as simply Kyle Wesley, nice guy with a conscience, not Kyle Wesley, billionaire owner of Below Zero Software Engineering.

"Well, he's on his way here to Rankins."

"He's…what?"

Blake grinned. "It seems you made quite an impression on him in Brazil. He's the one considering financing our next project. He wants to meet with you. He wanted me to get you to New York, but I told him you were in the middle of a job and wouldn't be able to get there. He said he respected that kind of work ethic, so he decided to come here."

Aidan's thoughts began to spin. *Seeds* provided an overview about the challenges and threats facing endangered plant species. He and Blake hoped to narrow the focus with their next films. But the list of possibilities was extensive—soil, water, pollination, insects, even animals… They hadn't even decided on a topic yet or exactly how they wanted to proceed.

"Jeez, Blake. But… Do we need to put a proposal together? When will he be here?"

"Aidan, don't freak out. I know how you like to be prepared, but there's no time for that. He'll be here the day after tomorrow. All you have to do is be your charming self—hang out, show the guy around a little. Meredith is taking care of the details. She's talking to Emily about some activities to do while he's here."

"But…why? This seems…odd."

Blake shrugged. "It's kind of a funny story. Wesley is a bit eccentric this way apparently—

and spontaneous. His assistant told me he once traveled to Tibet on fifteen minutes' notice. Anyway, I told him you were here. He said he's never been to Alaska, but a friend of his has been here. And by here, I mean Rankins—on a guide trip. Wesley said his friend couldn't quit talking about it, so he felt like it was karma or something. He decided to come up and do some sightseeing and discuss our future plans."

ONE DAY. IF ONLY Aidan's colleagues had shown up one day earlier, then Janie wouldn't be experiencing these sickening emotions of embarrassment, humiliation...and yes, heartache. The appearance of Aidan's colleagues—one of whom was apparently his ex-fiancée—was a good thing, Janie told herself; a perfect reminder at the perfect time that she and Aidan were from worlds that were very far apart, worlds that could not mesh. She needed this reminder because she could not let herself fall any further. Yes, that was it, she'd only fallen a little.

She could recover from a little, couldn't she?

Janie stared at the screen and told herself this was research, even though it felt like self-inflicted torture. Janie hadn't spoken to Aidan since she'd left the hospital the day before.

He'd sent her a text that read simply: Can we talk?

Janie had agreed although she didn't see the

point. They had no more appointments and her article was nearly complete. A clean break would be the best way to end something before it had really had a chance to begin.

Thanks to Laurel's connections, a production assistant at *Here's the Dirt* had sent a DVD of the episodes Aidan had appeared in. And now Janie felt compelled to watch them. She told herself she needed to do so in order to feel like she'd thoroughly completed her research. So far the sum total of what she'd learned was that he looked just as good on television as he did in person. His responses were thoughtful and eloquent without sounding patronizing. His demeanor was charming and magnetic—every gesture picture-perfect. No wonder his agent and Blake wanted him to take a more active role in the publicity for their film.

Janie never would have seen the additional footage if Finn hadn't decided to take a dip in MacGyver's water dish. She heard the telltale squeal and splash.

"Finn, no!"

She bolted from the sofa, where she'd been watching the episodes on her computer. She found Finn elbow-deep in the dog dish; this was a recurring problem and she was fairly certain her two-year-old believed he was a dog. She tugged his wet shirt over his head, mopped up the mess and refilled the dish for a suddenly parched MacGyver. Finn looked suitably chagrined and toddled out to the living room to join his brother.

She dumped out a bin of large plastic blocks the twins hadn't played with in a while. Janie laughed as they squealed with delight and dove into the mix like it was Christmas morning. By the time she returned to her computer the show had ended. Janie was about to restart the footage when an image popped up on the screen.

Outtakes? Not exactly, more like extra footage that hadn't been taped over? Janie hadn't expected this. The camera had obviously been running before Aidan ever knew he was onscreen. Janie watched, mesmerized, and if she didn't already know him, if she didn't know Reagan, she wouldn't recognize the nervous, uncomfortable stance or its significance. She watched his lips silently moving—like he was rehearsing, which she realized, was exactly what he was doing.

And in that moment Janie knew just how good Aidan was at hiding things—and how well he had learned to adapt.

CHAPTER SIXTEEN

AIDAN STARED AT MEREDITH, hoping they could get this over with as quickly as possible. She re-hashed the events that had led to her betrayal, spun them as nicely as she could manage and followed up with another apology.

"Aidan, I swear I wasn't going to sell your mom's formula. I know how it looked and why you thought that, but think about it—if I was going to sell it, I had plenty of time to do so. Anyway, I really am sorry about everything that happened. I've grown up a lot in two years. I lost my job over the whole…episode. I've struggled to get my media consulting business off the ground. Ultimately, it turned out to be a positive experience for me. But I can assure you, Aidan, I'm not a bad person and I… I've been significantly humbled."

"Okay."

"Okay? That's it?"

"I don't know what you expect from me here, Meredith. We went over this two years ago."

"But not like this and I was hoping maybe you could say that you forgive me."

"What good would that do? I don't forgive you, but I am willing to give you a chance. Blake seems to think you're the best person for the job and I trust Blake."

"Aidan, you need to get over this if we're going to—"

"I am over it. Everyone makes mistakes. Let's move on, Meredith."

Meredith let out a wry chuckle. "You are so weirdly honest. It's…uncomfortable. I feel like I'm talking to Spock."

Blake belted out a laugh from where he sat in a chair across the room working on his laptop.

Aidan ignored Blake. "Do you think it's going to help your cause by insulting me?"

"No, I'm sorry. I promised myself I was going to get along with you somehow. If there's anything I can do to make the situation between us better—or even bearable, anything at all—just say the word. I don't want the past to get in the way of my work here and if you—"

Aidan interrupted, "It's fine. Besides, it would be impractical to hinder your work when we have the same goal."

"That's true."

"Fine."

Meredith and Blake spent the next two hours outlining her progress and plans for future publicity. Aidan paid attention and had to admit that he was impressed. Meredith really had managed to get their name out there. Their website, which Aidan had only been vaguely aware even existed, was stunning. Meredith was talented.

He also realized that maybe he had been a bit unrealistic about this whole process. Just because he didn't like the publicity stuff, didn't mean he could avoid it altogether. He could even see the rationale behind much of the effort. He commented on it.

Blake sounded excited. "Does this mean you'll come to the premiere?"

"No." Aidan didn't see the necessity. The benefits did not outweigh the pain the experience would cause him. "I don't see any reason why you need me there, Blake."

"Maybe because we worked incredibly hard on this film, Aidan, and you deserve to be acknowledged for both its greatness and success?"

Aidan grinned and responded in a sugary tone, "How sweet, Blake. Let's hug."

Blake chuckled. "Aidan, at least promise me you'll think about it?"

Aidan turned back to Meredith and asked another question. When the meeting finally concluded Meredith stood and reached for her coat. Aidan immediately spotted the lavender scarf curled inside. Janie's work was unmistakable.

And the sight of it caused a longing to see her so intense that it startled him.

Her one-word response to his text asking if they could talk spoke volumes: Sure.

Janie had to understand why he hadn't told her about Meredith. Aidan had never met anyone who seemed to get him like Janie did. If she didn't understand, things were probably hopeless for him where relationships were concerned.

He turned his focus back to Meredith. "Where did you get that scarf?"

"Isn't it lovely?" Meredith pulled a matching hat from the pocket of her jacket and arranged it on her head. "I bought both of these at the tourism office. I stopped there to speak with your sister about the best place for Kyle Wesley and his crew to stay here in Rankins, and to get some ideas about activities to arrange for them. The tourism office sells local crafts and artwork. Apparently some woman from right here in Rankins makes them. Emily showed me these sweaters she knits—incredible. I'm going to get ahold of her and see if she'll make me one."

Meredith started toward the door. "I'm staying at the Faraway Inn. I left my card with my cell number if you need me. I'll be here in the morning at seven to prep you guys before Kyle Wesley arrives and I—"

"Wait a second," Aidan said.

Meredith stopped and quirked one eyebrow in inquiry.

"Did you mean it when you said you would do something to make it up to me?"

Her eyes widened with surprise and she responded eagerly. "If I can, Aidan—yes, of course."

WHEN MEREDITH WENT to Emily for advice about how to entertain Kyle Wesley during his visit to Rankins, Emily ran with the opportunity to show off Rankins's many virtues. Emily and Meredith made a dynamic team, and Janie decided she wouldn't be surprised to see Kyle Wesley relocate to Rankins by the time they were through.

Kyle and part of his eighteen-person entourage embarked on a fishing trip with Bering's guide service, while the rest of the group enjoyed a hiking adventure. Over the next three days Emily organized a glacier-viewing excursion and an airplane ride over the valley and coastline in one of Cricket Blackburn's small planes, followed by a picnic bonfire on the town's waterfront. Birdwatching, wildlife-viewing and skeet-shooting were among the other popular offerings, and one evening the group was treated to an exclusive catered seafood dinner at the Faraway Inn prepared by the inn's talented chef, Javier.

By the third day, Janie couldn't help but feel sorry for Aidan. Between maintaining his bee studies, keeping up with Emily and Meredith's demands and entertaining Kyle, he seemed to be spreading himself pretty thin. She knew how much he disliked this kind of socializing, and in spite of her disappointment about their personal situation, she appreciated how he still managed to make time for her boys, which, she told herself, was what prompted her to do what she did.

Janie met him at the door that evening as he dropped off Reagan. He looked worn-out and Janie felt herself soften at the sight of his tousled hair and rumpled clothes, both more tousled and rumpled than normal.

"Hey, do you want to come in? Escape all the madness for a bit?"

He'd been gripping the door frame with one hand. Now he pushed away and gave her an eager look. "Yes. I was actually hoping you would ask."

Against her best efforts to remain casual, Janie felt her heart leap in her chest. "You were?"

"Blake wanted me to meet him and Kyle for a late dinner, but I told him I had plans. If you didn't invite me in I was going to go hide at Bering and Emily's."

"I happen to have an extra steak I could put on the grill, a spare baked potato in the oven and a fresh-baked cobbler if you want to firm up those plans?"

"Thank you." He blew out the words on a sigh of relief.

An hour later, Aidan leaned back in his chair and wiped his mouth with a napkin. "That was delicious. Thank you. Your food is… I don't know how to describe it. Emily had talked about your cooking but I didn't…and I never… Words just don't do it justice."

She laughed. "I'm glad you enjoy it. I like to cook. How are things going?"

He nodded. "Fine, I think. Blake tells me they are anyway. Blake wanted me to give everybody a tour of my lab and, you know, I'm not always certain about how I come across."

"I know."

He executed his lazy grin, but now Janie suspected exactly what that grin was hiding.

"It's called glossophobia, right? Your fear of public speaking."

His smile melted as his eyes met hers, and for the first time since she'd met him she saw something there she'd never seen before, an emotion she would have guessed he didn't even possess—fear.

"Don't worry, Aidan, you're really good at hiding it. You've obviously learned to live with this very well. I don't think I would have ever seen it if it wasn't for the interview."

He tipped his head in question.

"Your resistance to interviews was my first clue—after I got over taking that so personally." They exchanged grins. "There's also the list of off-limits topics, your avoidance of the film premiere and the fact that you're not exactly what I would call chatty in a crowd. When Jacinda asked you to speak in her class, I saw something then, too. I didn't realize what, at the time. But then I was watching footage of your guest spots on *Here's the Dirt* and I saw you—"

"You saw me?"

"You didn't know the camera was running, but you were rehearsing your answers. I…it's the same thing Reagan does before he speaks in front of people. He does great if he knows the questions and what he's going to say, if he practices and memorizes his answers—just like you do. He doesn't have your degree of fear, but… You are really, really good, Aidan. I don't think anyone else will ever figure it out. But for some reason I did. It just popped into my head and… I knew."

His gaze felt so intense Janie wanted to look away, but she didn't.

Finally, he tapped his fingers on the tabletop for a few seconds and attempted a smile, but

Janie could see the pain in his eyes. "Which is funny, really, that you're the one who figured it out because I've never been as comfortable with another person as I am with you—except maybe my mom and Emily. But that's different."

Janie didn't want to ask how it was different. She had to keep this friendly, platonic. She could be his friend, but if he was to say something— the right thing—she didn't know how she would be strong enough to resist. But she had to; she'd already had a taste of what kind of damage getting involved with him could do.

"Does Blake know?"

"No, nobody really knows. Blake knows that I don't like public speaking and that I avoid it as much as possible, but we've never discussed it as my having a phobia per se. I just annoy the hell out of him by avoiding situations where I may have to speak. Like you said, I'm okay if I can prepare, practice. And I know it's irrational so I try as much as possible to tackle it, face it head-on, but sometimes, especially when it's sprung on me, it's…it can be a struggle."

"Now I understand why you don't like the publicity surrounding your work and why you don't want to attend the premiere, but, Aidan, wouldn't you like to see your film displayed like that? In New York? Couldn't you go and—"

Aidan frowned. "I've thought about it, believe

me, but it wouldn't work. I would tell Blake that I don't want to speak, but inevitably he would put me on the spot. He does that—he likes to be in the limelight and so he doesn't believe that I don't. He thinks I'm shy." Aidan added a chuckle.

Janie grinned. She definitely wouldn't describe him as shy.

He was quiet for a long moment. Finally he took a deep breath and asked, "Do you think I'm a coward?"

"A coward? Are you kidding me? No, of course not. A man who studies an insect that could literally kill him is no coward. A man who does what you do, who faces the dangers every day that you face out in the jungle or the dessert or the ocean, or wherever you happen to be, is not a coward."

His lips twitched like they did when he was searching for words. "That's different—I'm not afraid of bees or ants or snakes or jellyfish or whatever other danger I might face in the field. I mean, not in this debilitating way. I weigh the risks, prepare myself, minimize my chances of injury and do what I have to do. If a problem can be solved I will solve it. But this…for some reason, Janie, this problem, I can't seem to solve."

Janie saw the anguish in his eyes, mixed with maybe some embarrassment, and a flood of emotions crashed over her—so many emotions…

She nearly laughed out loud as she thought about how she'd been assuring herself that she'd only fallen for him a little. She was so far past a little, she didn't know how she would ever recover.

"I had a terrible stutter when I was young. Speech therapy and my mom's patience helped me, obviously, overcome that. But as I'm sure you can imagine, in addition to my other…eccentricities, I was teased unmercifully. I learned how to handle the rest, but I have never quite completely overcome my fear of public speaking."

She remained quiet, hoping he'd share more of his experiences.

Aidan's phone buzzed on the table between them. Janie saw Meredith's number pop up on the screen. He picked it up, read a text and rubbed a hand over his jaw. He looked at her and something in his tired eyes made her heart flutter. He sighed. "Bad timing. I…uh, I need to go. I need to see Meredith about something. I wouldn't go right now if it wasn't really important."

"I understand," she said even as she felt a sharp stab of disappointment.

He stood, and stared out the window for a few seconds before meeting her gaze again. He shifted from one foot to the other. "So… I need to explain about Meredith."

"Aidan, no—you don't. That is your business.

I'm sure you had your reasons for not telling me and—"

"Not the reasons you're probably thinking. Kyle and his gang are leaving on Friday, and there are some things we need to talk about—and something I'd like to show you. Can we get together this weekend?"

"Aidan, I can't. I'm leaving for the weekend, too, for Shay's bridal-shower spa getaway. Friday is the boys' last day of school and..." Janie suddenly felt like canceling.

He pushed a hand through his hair and Janie had to fight the urge to reach up and smooth it back in place. "That's right. Emily's going, too. When will you be back?"

"Sunday morning."

He nodded. "Sunday evening then? Is that too soon? Will you need more time to spend with the kids before I steal you away for a few hours?"

"Are you kidding me? Give me fifteen minutes and I'll be ready for another weekend getaway."

THE NEXT MORNING a knock on Janie's door made Gabe and Finn squeal and run toward the entryway. They loved company, usually it meant they were about to be showered with attention from their grandmother or someone else equally enamored with their tiny identical selves. Janie walked over and swung open the door and found herself face-to-face with the last person she would have expected to show up at her home.

CHAPTER SEVENTEEN

GARETH WONDERED HOW he could have been so stupid.

He'd panicked—plain and simple. Fifth period PE and he had forgotten his gym shoes in his locker. He'd gone back to get them, and in a way it was lucky for him he had because he'd spotted Harmon Vetcher's dad in the office flirting with the secretary, Ms. Givens. A wave of nauseating fear froze him in his tracks for a few seconds. No... Not today, he prayed, even as he knew what was happening because there was only one reason that Marv Vetcher would be loitering around in the office.

Marv Vetcher was a police officer as well as Harmon's dad. Ever since those tenth graders had been caught with pot and some other drugs of a still unconfirmed but wildly rumored variety last year, the police had been called in to do random locker checks.

Gareth thought for a moment, gulping in a couple deep breaths. He hurried to his locker, his hand shaking as he dialed his combination. He cursed under his breath when he realized he'd done it wrong, he started over and felt a pop of relief as the lock opened.

He grabbed the paper bag and looked down at what he was wearing. No place to hide anything in his shorts and T-shirt. Forcing himself to think, he reached out to his sweatshirt hanging on the peg and felt inside the pocket. Yes, the key was still there. His fingers curled around the metal and he removed the key from the pocket. He looked down at his feet and then quickly changed into his gym shoes.

He could run faster in those.

MEREDITH MONTOYO HELD out a hand to Janie, her white smile gleaming against her lovely mocha-colored skin. An ungracious thought flashed through Janie's mind before she could stop it. What was wrong with her? Why was she so determined to dislike this woman? This gorgeous, younger woman who had managed to win the most intelligent, interesting, complex and... kind man she'd ever met. Of course she wasn't jealous. Ha.

"Janie? Hi, I hope it's okay that I stopped by?"

"Um, sure, Meredith, come in. Is there something I can help you with?"

Meredith walked in wearing an expensive-looking pantsuit and drenched with the scent of even more expensive-smelling perfume. At least she was wearing sensible shoes. MacGyver jogged toward her, his tail wagging excitedly. Meredith kneeled and buried her face in his sheepdog fur.

She kissed him on the top of the head. "Look at you, mister. You're a beauty, aren't you? You make me miss my Bellini."

Meredith, a dog person? Huh…

Janie invited her into the living room. Meredith patted Gabe's head with a stiff hand as she walked by, leaving both the twins staring uncomprehendingly at the perceived brush-off. Janie snickered and hoped Meredith didn't notice—clearly her human clan was used to more deferential treatment.

"Please, have a seat. Can I get you something? Coffee, water, juice box?"

"No, thank you. I'm fine. You have a lovely home—*very* charming." MacGyver sat on her feet while Meredith scratched his ears.

Janie followed her gaze around the toy-scattered floor, the coffee table containing two open picture books and three snack cups full of dry cereal and goldfish crackers. A pile of her knitting was oozing out of a basket on the floor beside her recliner—it appeared that Crosby had been napping in the soft yarn again. Meredith sat on the worn sofa next to a wadded-up blanket and a giraffe pillow buddy.

"Thank you, I'm really into that toy-store/day-care décor that is trendy right now." She motioned at the spilled cereal on the table in front of her. "I'm almost thinking more Cheerios, though, what do you think?"

Meredith's mouth fell open and then she surprised Janie by laughing—a genuine sound filled with joy.

"I'm sorry. I'm so used to being polite these days that sometimes I forget to be…real." Meredith gestured around. "Honestly, all of this stuff screams family and children and I love that. It reminds me of my parents' home growing up."

Janie ran a hand through her hair. "No, it's fine. Joking about the mess is my way of coping."

Meredith reached out to pet Crosby, who'd jumped up beside her on the sofa. Meredith didn't bat an eye when Crosby crawled onto her lap and curled into a contented ball while she scratched his cheeks.

She pointed toward Janie's basket of knitting. "That yarn is gorgeous—are you making a sweater?"

"Yes…it's for Violet—my niece."

Meredith eyed it appreciatively. "Very pretty. How long have you been knitting?"

Janie thought this might be one of the oddest experiences she'd ever had. She had no idea what this woman was doing in her home and now they were going to chat about knitting?

"Years. I learned from a friend of my grand-mother's when I was about ten."

"Wow. So you could probably knit pretty much anything, right? I'm guessing you made this blanket? Are these your favorite colors?" She asked the questions rapid-fire, running a hand over the throw on the back of the sofa that Janie had knitted in shades of green and blue.

"Pretty much, and yes, I do like green."

"Awesome. I understand from talking with Laurel at the *Rankins Press* that you wrote a human interest piece on Aidan?"

Janie reeled from the subject change won-dering where this could possibly be going. Was Aidan using Meredith to discuss the aspects of the article that he didn't like? She'd only turned in the piece yesterday. She didn't even know if Laurel had had a chance to look it over yet, much less Aidan.

"Um, yes, that's correct." Finn crawled onto Janie's lap and eyed Meredith suspiciously.

"Good for you. Do you like working at the *Rankins Press*?"

Janie shook her head. "Thank you, but I didn't really have anything to do with securing the interview. That's Laurel's thing. And yes, I do like my job—it pays the bills and I write a column that I enjoy."

"I've seen your column—it's fabulous. Aidan doesn't do interviews, though, you must know that. So, if you got one—he must really trust you."

Trust? Janie thought about the circumstances surrounding the interview. She certainly wasn't going to tell Meredith about their complicated beginnings and Aidan's attempt to assuage his guilt. Or about how she had begun to believe in the preceding weeks that she had, in fact, been gaining his trust, that he had begun to confide in her. Until Meredith had shown up in the flesh and enlightened her.

"He agreed to the article because his sister asked him to do it. As you know, Emily is the president of the tourism bureau and she was essential in securing these articles in the first place. She and Laurel are both forces to be reckoned with. I didn't have anything to do with his decision—trust me."

Meredith's lips curved up into a half smile and her perfect, delicately arched eyebrows traveled even farther north. "Believe me, Janie, I know Aidan pretty well. And he wouldn't agree to an interview with anyone—not even Emily—if he didn't have trust and confidence in them. Or something else…"

What was this woman fishing for? "I'm not sure what you mean?" Finn scrambled to the floor and hustled toward Gabe, who was dragging a bucket full of plastic food into the room.

Gabe shoved a wooden spoon into the container and began to stir.

"Stew, stew," Finn jabbered.

Meredith smiled in their direction and then pushed a lock of silky black hair behind her ear.

"I thought maybe you and Aidan were…together? Because the last interview he let anyone conduct was mine, and that was because he was trying to win me over. But I was pretending to be someone I wasn't because I was obsessed with my job."

Janie felt her hackles rising. "Well, you can rest assured that Aidan is not trying to win me over. He agreed to the article because Emily asked him to do it. And we are not engaged to be married or engaged in any other capacity for that matter. Now, what is it that I can help you with?"

A look of surprise danced across Meredith's features. But if she thought she was going to intimidate Janie into admitting something she had another think coming.

Meredith winced. "Listen, Janie, you don't

have anything to worry about where Aidan and I are concerned. I am not interested—"

Janie's cell phone vibrated. She picked it up and saw Aidan's number on the screen. "I'm sorry, I have to take this."

Meredith nodded. Janie stood and traveled into the kitchen.

"Hello?"

"Janie, hey, it's Aidan. This is going to sound really weird but I'm on my way home from breakfast with Blake and Kyle and I just saw Gareth come out of my lab."

"Gareth…what? Where is he now?"

"I don't know. I was across the street. He didn't see me, but he came out my door in a hurry and took off running. Shouldn't he be in school?"

Janie felt a rush of unease as she tried to make sense of this odd story. "Yes, um…"

The call waiting beeped on her phone. She looked at the display and her hands began to shake. "Can I call you back in a minute? The school is calling."

Janie clicked over to hear the news that Gareth had disappeared from school. She hung up and returned to her guest.

"I'm sorry, Meredith, but I really have to run. There's kind of an emergency…"

"Sure." Meredith stood and gathered her bag.

She smiled at Janie, but was it her imagination that she looked disappointed?

"Meredith, please forgive me if I sound rude, but is there a reason you stopped by? Is there something that you needed?"

"Yes… But, um, it's not important. I mean—it can wait. But…thank you. I hope you get this emergency handled."

Janie walked her to the door. She called her mom to see if she could come over and sit with the twins. Twenty minutes later she jogged into the school and skidded to a halt when she saw Gareth through the window of the main office. He was slouched on a chair outside the principal's door, head bowed and staring at his lap. Relief rushed through her. She thought she should be angry, but instead she wanted to cry. What in the world was going on with her child?

A punch of grief stole her breath. These were the moments when she missed Cal the most—these confusing, indecipherable teenage boy moments that she felt a dad would be so much better at handling.

Janie stepped into the office and Gareth either didn't hear her approach or chose not to acknowledge that he heard her.

She spoke his name quietly. "Gareth?"

He raised his head and the flash of anguish she

saw on his face nearly did her in. She kneeled in front of him.

"Honey, what happened?"

"Nothing." His voice sounded flat and deep. When had his voice become so deep?

"Gareth, the school called and said you took off—left campus with a bag of some sort right before locker check."

His eyes glinted with something hard—something she didn't want to see. Anger, she thought, and wondered if it was directed at her.

"Mom, please just take me home, okay? You can give me my punishment there. I don't want to talk about it here."

She stared down at the ground for a few seconds and tried to get a grip on her emotions. Finally, she patted his knee and stood.

She blew out a breath. "Wait here. I'm going to go talk to Principal Dundee."

The principal's door was open. The secretary waved her in and Janie felt a surge of emotion when she walked into his office. Mr. Dundee reminded Janie of one of those life-size floppy puppets with a slightly too-large head topped with a mop of perpetually disheveled dark brown hair and a seemingly permanent half smile.

"Janie, thank you for getting here so quickly. Please, have a seat."

"Of course," she said quietly and lowered herself onto the hard surface of a chair across from him. She listened to the principal describe this "disturbing event" that had transpired—Gareth leaving school in the middle of the day with a mysterious package he'd taken from his locker.

Yes, he, Ms. Givens and Officer Vetcher had all seen him. No, Gareth wouldn't reveal why he'd taken off or what he'd taken from his locker. His behavior could only be considered suspicious. In conjunction with the fact that he'd left the grounds during school hours meant that he was in serious trouble.

Punishment would be meted out after an investigation into what he'd been hiding in his locker was conducted. Could Janie please do the right thing and try to find out what Gareth was concealing? The school counselor who came from Glacier City two days out of the week would be there tomorrow. Mr. Dundee recommended that Gareth have a session with her. Meanwhile, he would investigate the incident from his end.

After the meeting concluded, Janie managed to collect Gareth and walk to the parking lot. Silence filled the car as she drove them home.

Aidan's pickup was parked in the driveway.

Gareth shot her a horror-filled look. "What is Aidan doing here?"

Interesting, Janie thought—this reaction. She'd called Aidan from the school and he'd told her he'd meet her here—of course, Gareth didn't know this.

She kept her answer ambiguous. "I guess we'll find out."

Gareth got out of the car and she watched him trudge into the house. She didn't tell him to go to his room because she knew he would. He was such a good kid. Or so she believed. What didn't she know? She couldn't seem to move.

Aidan opened the door and climbed into the passenger seat that Gareth had vacated.

"What did the school say? What did Gareth say? Why did he leave campus?"

Janie shook her head. She felt like she had no choice but to share this with Aidan—after all, Gareth had apparently broken into his lab, his home. She prayed he wasn't stealing, or worse. Regardless, Gareth was in huge trouble but it was so much bigger than that. What had she done wrong? She reminded herself it didn't matter, this was no time to speculate about her ineffective parenting.

She turned to look at Aidan and his gray eyes were searching her face and filled with such naked concern that Janie wanted to launch herself into his lap. He reached over and took her hand and she let him because his touch was comforting, and made her feel so much less…alone. A part of her said she should handle this on her own, but another part—the bigger, terrified part of her—wanted help... Aidan's help.

"There was a locker check scheduled at school. There were some kids last year who were caught running a little drug ring and since then they have really cracked down... Anyway, they are always a surprise for the students, but somehow Gareth allegedly got wind of it. He was seen taking something out of his locker and leaving the school in his gym clothes. He skipped two periods and showed up back at school in time for last period. I have no idea..."

"So he probably hid whatever he took from his locker inside my lab."

Janie nodded as her brain spun with possibilities—drugs, a gun, a knife, dynamite, pornography, devil-worshipping paraphernalia...

She tried not to cry. "I don't... I don't understand what's happening."

Janie's phone buzzed. She glanced at the display, intending to ignore the call, but it was from Tag. He'd probably heard about Gareth. She picked up, listened for a moment and then spoke a few words before clicking off. She closed her eyes and tapped the phone on her forehead a few times.

Aidan was staring at her. "What is it?"

"That was Tag. Because he's a paramedic he knows everything that goes on within a two-hundred-mile radius of Rankins—emergency-wise. The police want to talk to Gareth. But thankfully Officer Adams, the detective on duty, is about halfway to Glacier City right now, so we have a few hours. I need to talk to Gareth before they get here."

"The police? That seems extreme."

"Everyone is paranoid about drugs. I can understand."

Aidan nodded and Janie was suddenly slammed with the full force of what Gareth might be facing. "Aidan, I can't—"

Aidan let go of her hand and ran it up her arm to her shoulder. He squeezed gently. "I'll find it—whatever it is, Janie. I'll find it. And we'll deal with it."

Those words sounded so very sweet and she wanted to let the notion ease her anxiety. But she wouldn't—she couldn't let him get in the middle of this. Gareth was her child. The boys were her responsibility.

"Aidan, I can't let you do that. What if it is drugs? You'll have to give them to the police and I don't know—"

His hand snaked around the back of her neck and he nudged her face toward his so he could look into her eyes, which she knew were wide with fear.

"Janie, let's not jump to conclusions. I've been

spending quite a bit of time with Gareth. I think he has some issues, yes, but I don't think he's doing drugs. Let's take this one step at a time. We need to identify what we're dealing with here and then we'll figure out how to proceed, okay?"

She bobbed her head as she watched Aidan get out of the car. She sat and stared at her house for a long time and tried to decide what to do.

GARETH FLOPPED DOWN on his bed and stared up at the ceiling. He wished he could get something from his stash—just a photo or a handkerchief or his dad's watch…something. But he knew he couldn't risk it right now. His mom would be coming in any second. She was already freaking out, he could tell. He had no idea what she would do if she got a look at the stuff that he'd taken from her right now.

Gareth had stumbled on the box of his dad's stuff months ago. He'd been in the den just trying to remember his dad. He'd tried to open the cabinet door but it was locked, probably to keep the twins out. He'd found the key, opened the cabinet and discovered the box of his dad's belongings. Gareth assumed his mom had put the stuff there for safekeeping. There were cards, letters, photos, notebooks that his dad had written some of his seemingly endless lists in, his razor, his watch and a favorite pen...which had eventually led to his own letters...

At first he'd only taken a couple of photos—photos that he couldn't remember ever seeing before. He'd wanted to be able to look at them whenever he wanted. And little by little he'd been drawn back to that cabinet, to that box that held these small pieces of his dad. Gradually he had amassed a stockpile of items that he could remove and examine and touch, and feel closer to his dad for a little while.

The blank look on his mom's face on the trip home had scared Gareth. It reminded him of the way she'd looked after his dad had died. Before the twins had been born and she'd gone off the deep end—when she'd been merely sad and not totally messed up. His mom had recovered pretty well. She still wasn't the totally happy, fun mom she'd been before his dad died, but thankfully she was way better—she was closer than he could remember since Aidan had come into their lives.

Gareth wanted to be, too. That had been the point of this letter thing.

He never should have taken the letters to school. He might have been okay if he'd kept them in his backpack, out of sight. But this morning he'd taken out the bundle because his backpack was superfull and he hadn't wanted to smash them, which was stupid because they were going to get burned up anyway.

If it hadn't been for the locker check everything would have been fine. He had no idea how he was going to talk his way out of this one. Principal Dundee and Officer Vetcher knew that he'd taken something out of his locker, but Gareth felt confident it was now well hidden. No one would even think to look there...

He'd overheard Principal Dundee say something about smoking—maybe he'd go with that. How much trouble would he get into if he said he'd been smoking? Although in light of Grandpa Everett's death from lung cancer he might have a tough time convincing his mom of that one.

Crosby jumped up on the bed next to him. Gareth waited. Crosby knew the drill; he kneaded his claws on the comforter before circling repeatedly and finally curling up next to Gareth's back. Gareth turned his face into his pillow and cried.

AIDAN WAS IMPRESSED with Gareth's cleverness. An hour of searching and he hadn't found anything yet. Yet he felt certain that whatever Gareth had taken from his locker was here in his lab somewhere.

Aidan stood in the middle of the room and allowed his methodical brain to study every possible hiding space. He looked up. The building was old and the pipes were exposed—thick insulation covered them—but Aidan realized that at the location where they intersected there was plenty of space to hide something. But it was at least twelve feet up, how could he have…?

Aidan smiled because he knew how he would have done it—a nice, easy lob up toward that spot and voilà, the bag would be out of sight. But to get it down—even to check if it was there—he was going to need a ladder. He pulled out his phone and called Bering.

Less than an hour later Bering dropped off the ladder. Minutes after that Aidan had the brown paper bag in his hands. He resisted the urge to take a look inside. He called Janie and told her he was on his way.

CHAPTER EIGHTEEN

AIDAN CAME IN and placed the brown paper bag on the table in the breakfast nook. Janie stared at the crumpled bundle and wondered how drastically the contents of a simple grocery sack could change their lives.

"Do you want me to look?"

Janie wanted to say yes—she thought about how he'd said that word *we* earlier. But they weren't a *we*, could never be a *we*, but maybe in this case…

"I do. But what if it's something horrible, Aidan? What if it's something illegal? Then you're stuck in the middle of—"

"Something?" Aidan interrupted. "Stop overthinking this. I want to help."

She wouldn't have thought it possible to find even a touch of levity in this situation, but his comment made her smile. "Okay."

He stepped over to the table and unfolded the top of the bag. He peered inside, reached in and removed a stack of papers.

"Paper?" Janie said, baffled. Had Gareth been

cheating? She couldn't imagine how cheating would warrant his going AWOL in the middle of a school day.

"It looks like a letter of some kind." Aidan brought the thick sheaf closer for her to inspect. "And some matches."

"What kind of letter? A confession letter? Is he cheating in school? Oh, please…not a suicide note."

"No." Aidan calmly shuffled through the papers. "It looks like a stack of letters he's written to his dad—and a photo."

Aidan handed her a narrow photo strip—the kind you take in those booths where the camera snaps several shots in quick succession while you pose differently for each one. She recognized the images immediately.

She remembered the day very well. Six years ago she and Cal and the boys had traveled to Glacier City for a weekend of fun. They'd seen a movie, attended a street fair and craft market and had a blast. They'd all taken turns in the photo booth until they'd exhausted pretty much every combination of people and goofy faces they could imagine. This particular strip was of Cal and Gareth; the top image showed Gareth squeezing Cal's cheeks while they both made fish faces at the camera lens.

"What…?" Janie whispered and sank down

onto a chair. Aidan placed the stack of letters in front of her. She silently began to read. After several minutes she looked up at Aidan, who had taken a seat across from her at the table.

"I have no idea what this means. These are letters he's written to his dad over the last…" Janie shuffled through the stack. "The first one is dated more than a year ago. There are increasingly more as time has gone on—several in the last few months. He talks about the things they used to do together and how much he misses him. I feel like I'm invading his privacy by reading them but I want to understand what this means."

Aidan reached out and took hold of her hand. "Go talk to him and find out."

Janie nibbled on her cheek and thought about how to handle the situation.

Aidan gestured at the letters. "He doesn't know you have these, so I would go in there and see if he will tell you what he hid. If he tells you that, then maybe he'll want to talk about what he was doing and why."

That made sense. "Okay, do you…? Is there any way you could…?"

"I'm staying, Janie. I know Gareth doesn't trust me one hundred percent yet, but I think he might be starting to like me—or at least respect me a little. I won't get in the middle, but I will be here for you—for both of you—however I can. We will figure this out."

There was that word again. Janie blinked back tears even as she allowed herself to take comfort in the idea of being a *we*. Then she went to talk to her son—all the way down the hall, which suddenly seemed to have expanded to a length of at least three miles. She inhaled a deep breath and tapped softly on Gareth's bedroom door. She waited a moment, turned the knob and for some reason felt a flash of relief that the door wasn't locked.

"Hey." She crossed the room to sit on the edge of his bed. Crosby stood and meowed, pacing back and forth in front of Gareth, like a feline sentry on guard duty.

"Hey."

He shifted his body until he was sitting up and leaning against a stack of pillows. It reminded Janie of the times he'd been sick as a little boy and she'd bring him soup, or medicine, or a glass of juice, and he'd manage to sit up so she could take his temperature. How she wished this situation could be as simple as the flu...

"So, do you want to explain?"

"Mom, I'm so sorry. It's not what it looks like."

"Maybe you could help me out by explaining what it is then? So I can quit speculating. What were you hiding, Gareth?"

Gareth didn't answer, just stroked Crosby's fluffy coat. The cat's purr seemed as loud as a helicopter in the silence of the room.

"Principal Dundee thinks you may have been smoking? Apparently, your friend Anthony got caught smoking a few months back? I can't believe you'd be dumb enough to smoke at school, but—"

"Mom, I don't smoke. I haven't been smoking."

Janie felt another rush of relief, even though no evidence of smoking had been found. He did have matches and Anthony was a friend of Gareth's and today was the first she'd heard about this smoking incident.

"That's good. So, what did you take out of your locker?"

"Letters."

She was grateful for this piece of honesty. She hoped Aidan was right and this meant he wanted to talk—or at least would talk.

"What kind of letters?"

Gareth looked at her but his face was unreadable. She hated it that she didn't know her own son well enough to have an idea of what he might be thinking.

"Gareth, you're going to have to tell me. The police are going to be here to talk to you in a couple hours and I think things will go easier if I understand what's going on."

"The police?" He squeaked out the words in a high-pitched tone of anxiety.

Now she had his attention. "Yes, Gareth, in light of the drug situation at the school last year, Principal Dundee can't ignore this. You taking off like that might be probable cause for the police to question you, and me, to search our house, my car." She shrugged. "I don't know what all they can do—"

His brown eyes were filled with terror. "Mom, I swear. They're just letters. I write letters to Dad."

"Oh." A tsunami of relief hit her, but was immediately followed by another concern. "What kinds of letters? Are you angry with him for dying and leaving us?"

Gareth rolled his eyes. "Mom, I've been over that part of it for a long time. It wasn't his fault. He didn't leave us on purpose. I was never really angry with him anyway. I was angry at the circumstances."

"Okay, so…?"

"Remember that first counselor we saw in Glacier City? But she had a baby and had to quit so we started seeing Dr. Quartz?"

Janie nodded. "Yes, of course—Dr. Tibbets." They had all loved Dr. Tibbets. Dr. Quartz, on the other hand, she had some doubts about. Dr. Quartz had advised her to sit back and let the grieving process run its course. She suspected that she should have found some middle ground between the two doctors as the process truly seemed to be different for everyone.

"Yeah, well, she suggested that I write to Dad because I told her how I wished I would have said certain things to him before he died. But she said I could still tell him those things and it might make me feel better, so a while back I decided to try it. I've been writing letters to Dad."

Gareth scratched Crosby's ears—the cat had resettled on his lap and seemed to be casting dirty looks in Janie's direction presumably for upsetting Gareth and/or his naptime. Probably a combination of both.

"I've written him to tell him all of the things I loved about him, all of the things I miss, the things I wish I would have said and done—even some things I don't miss. Dr. Tibbets said I could do that, too."

So many emotions were crowding inside of her—sadness, relief, love, guilt, despair—she felt weak. And she was so tired. She wanted to lie down and close her eyes and sleep and hope that tomorrow would be a better day. Unfortunately, she'd done enough of that over the last few years, along with plenty of "hoping" things would get better on their own and "accepting" whatever that might mean. She needed to get a grip. She needed to face this—they needed to face this.

She took a deep breath.

"That sounds wonderful, honey. Do you want to tell me anything you wrote?"

He shook his head. "No, I already told Dad."

"Okay." Janie debated about whether to ask, but knew she had to because the police would. "Gareth, why did you leave the school with the letters?"

Gareth squeezed his eyes shut. "Locker check."

"Locker check?" What was she missing here? "But why—"

"I took the letters and a picture of me and Dad to school. I planned on burning the letters after school when I went over to Uncle Bering's."

That explained the matches. So, good, more evidence for the not smoking.

"But, I had to do something with them so they didn't get discovered during the locker check." He explained about how he'd left his gym shoes in his locker and went to retrieve them before class. On his way he'd spotted Marv Vetcher and known that locker checks were imminent.

"Why didn't you put the letters in your back-pack?"

"For one thing I had my gym clothes on and my backpack was in the locker room. I had no place to put them and I knew if I headed to gym with all those papers, Mr. Lott would ask me what was so important that I was late for gym class and make me hand them over. He would read them to the class—he seems to like embarrassing students."

Janie agreed this last part was likely true. Mr. Lott was a self-important, overly muscled, former small-town jock who seemed personally offended by anyone who didn't take physical education as seriously as he did.

"There isn't anyplace you could have hidden them in your locker? Inside a book? Anything?"

"Mom, they were checking for drugs. Don't you think that they know all the places to look? And besides, Marv Vetcher was the one doing the checks. What do you think would happen if he found those letters?"

That explained a lot. Janie knew very well that Marv Vetcher wouldn't hesitate to somehow leak the information to Harmon and Riley.

She felt a burning rage that things had reached this point with Harmon and Riley. Aidan was right. Something needed to be done. She was done feeling guilty and beating herself up because her sons had problems. From now on she was going to start solving these problems—and letting the boys solve them, too.

Janie nodded and took a minute to absorb everything he'd said. This all seemed plausible. Even more important, she believed him. Was she being naive? She needed to run the scenario by someone more objective than herself. Normally that would be Bering or Shay or her mom, but Aidan was already here. The mere thought of him waiting for her in the kitchen made her feel better, stronger. *We*, she thought, even as she told herself she shouldn't get used to the word—to the feeling. But she was going to go ahead and relish it right now.

One thing was still bothering her, though.

"So, you said you were going to burn the letters anyway at Uncle Bering's today after school? *Why* would you do that?"

Gareth looked down at his lap for a few long seconds, his fingers entwined in Crosby's thick fur. Then he looked back at Janie. "I wrote my last letter to Dad. I've said everything I need to say. And I think I can't just keep saying the same things over and over again because it makes me feel stuck. Obviously I can't send them anywhere, so I decided to burn them—you know, like in one final farewell? Say goodbye to Dad and just…let him go, I guess. I mean not all of him, but…"

"I understand, Gareth, and I think it was a good plan." It made sense to her. "What about the photo? Were you going to burn that?"

Something flickered across his face—it was there and gone so quickly that she might have missed it, except… She may not know her son as well as she'd like these days, but she knew a flash of fear when she saw one.

"How do you know about the picture?"

"Aidan saw you coming out of his place, Gareth. He found the letters."

Gareth stared at her with big eyes.

"He didn't read them."

"I'm not worried about that, Mom. Aidan's dad died when he was little, too. He understands. What I'm worried about is the police. If Harmon's dad sees them, then Harmon will know…"

Janie felt another stab of anger directed at Marv Vetcher and the monster child he had sired. "We're going to wait and see what the police have to say, but I have no intention of handing them over unless it's absolutely necessary. And I promise you, Gareth—they won't go to Marv Vetcher."

Gareth exhaled a huge sigh of relief. "I wasn't going to burn the photo, Mom. It was just to look at. Sometimes I can't remember Dad's face as well as I used to, so I, uh, I carry his picture. It was tucked inside the letters so I hid it, too."

Dr. Quartz had said not to push Gareth through the stages of grief, but it sounded like he was trying to push himself. Something told Janie that maybe that wasn't a bad thing, that maybe it was actually a really courageous thing.

JANIE RETURNED TO the kitchen to find Aidan sitting at her table. He'd made a pot of coffee so she poured herself a cup and took a seat across from him. Janie explained what Gareth had told her.

Aidan asked a few questions, but mostly he listened.

"So, I guess we'll see how it all plays out with the police."

Aidan ran a thumb over his chin. "I can't imagine they would pursue this after you explain the situation."

Janie allowed herself to take confidence in his words.

"Thank you so much, Aidan. I don't know what would have happened if you hadn't seen him coming out of your place."

"I'm glad I was there, too. Your boys have become really important to me..."

"They feel the same—obviously."

"What about you? How do you feel?"

"What?" She barely got the word out because her pounding heart seemed to be smothering her voice.

He leaned forward. "Things have been so crazy…we haven't had a chance to talk again about what happened between us the day I got stung. I know we said we'd talk on Sunday, but I don't want to wait."

Janie wished she could play dumb. She really didn't want to talk about that humiliating afternoon where she'd acted like a desperate housewife and Aidan had nearly died and the lovely Meredith had appeared and forced Janie to come to her senses.

She tried to give him an easy out. "Aidan, it's okay. I understand."

"You do?"

"Yes—you don't have to explain. It was just a moment—that day. I got caught up in it, too. But…" She swallowed down a sudden, unexpected lump of emotion. "Since that time I have come to fully realize how different our lives are."

Aidan slowly smoothed a finger over one brow. "A moment?"

"Yes, it was nice. It was a great kiss, and a nice afternoon—until you got stung and almost died. But then Meredith and Blake breezed through the door and they both represent these parts of your life that I don't know anything about—"

"Janie." Her name came out with a sigh of exasperation. "That afternoon was so much more than a moment for me. These last weeks, the time I've spent with you—I have never been happier. I've never felt like this with another human being in my life. I've never been able to truly be myself with anyone before and I'd like to explore the possibility of a relationship—"

She cut him off. "No."

He looked genuinely shocked and Janie was surprised by how much it hurt her to say the word—even though she knew it was the right thing to do.

"Aidan, I can't. First of all, my boys are everything to me and the risk is too great—"

"But I love your boys."

She smiled and tried desperately to keep her turbulent emotions at bay. "I know and I am so very grateful for that. What you've done for them in the time you've been here... I doubt I'll ever be able to repay you for that. But what would happen if it didn't work out between us?"

"Why wouldn't it work out?"

"Well, there's the communication thing."

His gaze went flat. "I'm aware, Janie, and I'm trying. With you I've have communicated, confided in, more than I ever have with anyone—ever."

Janie squeezed her eyes shut and tried not to enjoy that statement too much. She opened her eyes and faced him—this—head-on. "But, it's not enough for me, Aidan. There's so much about you I don't know—so much that is off-limits. Think about it, your own sister didn't know you were engaged. That doesn't bode very well for me or for any woman you decide to let into your life. I wrote an article about you and practically had to scrape the bottom of your shoes for tidbits to write about.

"You didn't tell me you were allergic to bees, you never mentioned your fear of public speaking, you didn't tell me about the boxing, or about your engagement. I had to figure all this out on my own and…you're probably used to being alone and so not having to factor in somebody else's thoughts and feelings. It's about sharing."

His gray eyes latched on to hers and she could see he was searching for words.

"Why didn't you tell me you were engaged?"

"Honestly? It didn't seem relevant."

"That's the thing with you, Aidan. You pick and choose relevance and risk and what you're going to reveal about yourself based on criteria completely different than mine. With me, what you see is what you get. What you said about me to Emily that day is true—I'm not worldly or sophisticated. I am, in fact, just a simple girl."

Aidan scoffed. "Janie, if you truly believe that, then you don't know yourself nearly as well as you think you do."

He stood up and Janie could see the hurt on his

face, radiating off of every plane of his body. But Janie was absolutely certain his pain couldn't possibly be a match for hers.

CHAPTER NINETEEN

THE VFW HALL opened at 8:00 a.m. so the students could get their booths set up in time for the science expo to begin at ten. Lunch would be at noon and demonstrations were scheduled to begin at one thirty and would last until four. The longest time frame ever, Ms. Treyborn had mentioned at least a million times, because so many students were participating this year.

Gareth had helped Elena and Reagan lug in all of the stuff for their projects and they were on their way outside to meet their mom when Harmon intercepted them in the hallway.

Harmon stepped close and Gareth could smell his disgusting breath that for some reason always reeked of pickles.

"Hey, Everett—everyone is dying to know what you had in your locker. And why you ran away from school like a scared little girl."

Gareth knew better than to react to Harmon's statement even as his heart started to hammer wildly in his chest. "What are you talking about, Harmon?"

"Rumor has it you took something out of your locker and left school with it. What was it?"

"None of your business. Now get out of the way. We have things to do."

"Was it a gun? Maybe you were planning one of those school shootings, huh? You're loony enough to do that. Or was it drugs—you've been hanging out with that geeky scientist guy who's been running around town. He looks like he could be into drugs. I've heard the police are investigating."

Riley laughed maniacally at the obvious reference to Harmon's dad.

Gareth rolled his eyes and said sarcastically, "Gosh, we'd love to stick around and chat about your brilliant criminal theories, Harmon, but my brother has a contest to win."

Harmon's snake eyes narrowed at Gareth. "If your brother wins this contest he's dead meat and he knows it." Harmon turned on Reagan. "Don't you—you eggheaded little wimp?"

Elena barked out a laugh. "Eggheaded? You do realize you just called him a smart person, right? Which is the opposite of you, moron."

Harmon sneered at Elena. "You know the only thing saving you from getting the crap beat out of you, too, Elena? The goodness of my heart and the fact that I know you secretly like me."

"You know that face looking back at you in

the mirror when you practice your tough-guy routine, Harmon? You better enjoy it because that's the only human being on the planet who is ever going to look at you without wanting to puke."

Harmon's face twisted into a snarl. "You little…"

"Egghead? I know and thank you. I can't wait to see your pathetic little project. Oh, wait—let me guess… Your daddy did it for you? You do realize he won't be up there with you waving his badge around when you do your demonstration, right? No one will care who your dad is when you're up there, Harmon."

Harmon's eyes narrowed menacingly. "At least my dad wasn't stupid enough to drive his log loader over a cliff."

Gareth balled his fists, tension cramming every inch of his body. Even though he knew Harmon was trying to bait him, it was difficult to let that insult pass.

Elena looked like she wanted to take out Harmon herself. "Let's go, you guys. Harmon probably needs to get busy measuring the vinegar and baking soda for the little volcano he made."

Harmon's nostrils flared as he glared at Elena. Gareth wondered if he was going to attack at that moment. Harmon's eyes flitted from Gareth to Reagan and back again. "Just remember that whatever happens today, I warned you, Everett."

Gareth didn't know whether that parting remark was directed at him or Reagan, but he didn't figure at this point that it much mattered.

JANIE WAS IMPRESSED by how many kids were participating. Not as many as had shown up at the meeting, but way more than she would have guessed would follow through.

Reagan had put countless hours into his project, and Janie knew he was ready. Family and friends had shown up to support him—her mom, Aunt Margaret and Uncle Ben, Bering and Emily, her cousins Tag and Hannah. Shay had come with Jonah, and Laurel was covering the event for the newspaper.

Aidan slipped into the hall and took a seat beside her, and Janie felt a rush of affection so intense she had to squeeze her hands together to keep from reaching out and touching him. She wouldn't have believed it was possible to feel more respect and admiration for this man than she already did, because in spite of what had transpired between them, Aidan had set that aside and put Reagan first.

The middle school students went first and one by one they presented their projects on the stage that had been assembled for the event. It was clear that the students had worked hard.

Finally it was Reagan's turn and Janie's pulse picked up speed as he wheeled out the large table displaying his project. A bundle of nerves churned inside of her until Aidan reached out and took her hand. The level of calmness he somehow managed to convey had her thinking she might be able to get through the next few minutes without passing out.

Silence filled the room as Reagan stood before the audience. He looked out over the crowd until, it appeared to Janie, that he found Aidan. Finally he grinned and began to speak. But Janie felt her heart sink as she realized his voice was not carrying throughout the room. She shifted, ready to alert someone that the microphone wasn't working. Suddenly the lights went out, too.

The audience began to murmur and she heard a few inquiries from the front near the stage.

She whispered, "Oh, no…" and started to stand. Aidan squeezed her hand to keep her from moving. The lights came on, the sound returned, and Reagan's voice boomed loud and clear. "Electricity," he announced. "It's so easy to take it for granted—until it's gone, right?"

Appreciative laughter began to resound as the audience realized this had been part of his demonstration. Janie had no idea her son had inherited her acting ability. She snuck a peek at Aidan and wondered if she looked as proud as he did. Her attention quickly returned to Reagan as he continued to speak.

"Many people believe Benjamin Franklin invented electricity when he proved with a kite, a key and a storm that lightning is essentially electricity. An important discovery, yes, and Franklin went on to experiment with electricity in other impressive ways along with Nikola Tesla, Thomas Edison and other great scientists throughout the world. But human beings have been aware of the existence of electrical charges since at least 600 BC, when the ancient Greeks experimented with what we now know as static electricity. And the Romans..." Reagan went on to condense thousands of years of history, touching on some of the high points and revelations. "In the year 1800, an Italian physicist by the name of Alessandro Volta is credited with creating the first electric battery he called a voltaic pile..." Reagan briefly outlined Volta's method and the improvements to batteries since that time.

"Now, in my demonstration I'm going to show the power of electricity using a common twelve-volt battery." He pointed at a shelf under the table. "This is a battery I borrowed from my uncle's pickup. I will explain as the demonstration proceeds the use of transformers, reducers, inverters and switches..." He continued his narration.

The display table had been partitioned into four parts, while a large round metal ball sitting on a pedestal—resembling a large shiny mushroom—stood alone on the far right side. Reagan flipped a switch and the first section came to life; lights flashed on an electric train as it began to roll along the tracks in a figure-eight pattern. The train's whistle sounded a loud tweet as it ended its journey by smoothly disappearing under the slightly raised platform under the second section.

A miniature shiny blue pickup, complete with working headlights and taillights, took up the journey from here, winding its way up an elevated, lighted incline. The pickup's horn sounded as it nosed against the wall of section three, where a connection was made to an intricate machine constructed of chains and gears. A loud rhythmic click began as a long arm descended and lifted a metal ball out of the back of the pickup. It rose, swiveled and carried the ball up to the top of the fourth section.

Here an elaborate set of elevated tracks had been constructed to resemble a roller-coaster thrill ride. The arm gently dropped the ball into a roller-coaster car, which began a zigzag ride down the tracks, setting off a series of flashing lights along the way.

When the car reached the bottom, it triggered a switch for the grand finale. An audible hum from an electric motor began to whir. As Reagan explained static electricity he picked up a Barbie and placed the doll on top of the ball. Slowly the doll's hair floated up to form a golden halo around her head. Reagan reached out and laid his hand on the ball. A collective gasp went through the audience as the static electricity caused Reagan's hair to stand on end as well.

The crowd went wild. He received the only standing ovation of the day. Reagan looked elated. Janie was ecstatic, too, but for a different reason. Reagan seemed like a different kid— no, not a different kid, a more mature version of himself. He was still confident yet he showed the funny and downright charming kid he could also be.

There was a short intermission before the awards ceremony. The generous and always gracious VFW crew served homemade cookies along with coffee, tea and soft drinks. The crowd was abuzz with talk of the children's hard work and phenomenal efforts. Many people congratulated her, and Reagan beamed as he was bombarded with congratulations, questions and comments.

A short while later, when they announced Reagan's name as the middle school champion, she turned and smiled at Aidan. He enfolded her in his arms and she wanted to cry—in a good way. She would have never doubted Reagan's ability to win the competition, but it was the *way* he won that filled her soul with joy.

Aidan had managed to make such a significant difference in both boys' lives in only a couple of months.

Later, she watched as Aidan and Gareth joked around about something and she realized that her older son was improving, too. Because really, the incident at school had turned out to be a positive one—not the fact that Gareth had yet to face punishment, but his overall intentions behind the letters.

He seemed to be tackling his issues and she couldn't help but think that the fearless way Aidan lived his life had something to do with it.

GARETH HOWEVER DID not quite share his mom's level of enthusiasm. He was extremely proud of his brother, of course. But as he watched Reagan wooing the crowd, the teachers, parents and judges, all the while he knew Reagan was screwed, which meant he was, too.

Harmon had warned him not to win this competition. And for whatever reason, Harmon seemed even crazier these days than he normally was. Gareth knew Harmon's dad was really critical of him and put a lot of pressure on him to be the best at football, to be the fastest, the smartest, and for some reason he had hammered him about this science-project thing. In turn Harmon's solution had been to threaten Reagan.

To Gareth, Harmon had lost five hundred dollars' worth of prize money and the prestige of winning the science expo. Gareth felt certain Harmon would interpret this as being humiliated in front of the entire school. He wasn't sure if he could protect Reagan this time, but he would try.

In spite of this, he was so freaking proud of his little brother. When the winner had been announced, he'd stood and clapped with the rest of the crowd, and whistled louder than he ever had in his life.

JANIE WAS HAVING another bad mom moment. Should she be leaving town when she wasn't sure what was going to happen with Gareth? She had explained the situation to Principal Dundee and since Gareth was a good kid and had never had any behavioral issues, he seemed reluctant to pursue the situation. Although, he'd told her that the police were still investigating and he wasn't sure what the outcome of their inquiry would be.

But ultimately they were only letters—how serious could things get?

Shay was her best friend, she was Shay's maid of honor and Emily had gone to a lot of trouble to set them up in luxury accommodations at one of the swankiest hotels and spas in Alaska for Shay's bridal-shower weekend. Plus, she wasn't going to lie, a weekend away with her best friends sounded like a dream.

"What do you think, Mom?" she asked Claire.

"I don't understand why you're even hesitating, Janie. We will be fine—the boys love staying with me. We have plans to make popcorn on the stovetop the old-fashioned way and watch movies tomorrow night. I'm going to bake a pie to celebrate Reagan's victory. Your Aunt Margaret and I are taking Violet and the twins to toddler swim on Saturday while Aidan takes Gareth and Reagan bee hunting, after which they are all playing basketball at Bering's. See? All kinds of plans—none of which require your participation."

Janie said dryly, "Gee thanks, Mom. That makes me feel *way* better."

Claire smiled. "Janie, you haven't spent a night away from your children for two years—not since you went with Bering to fetch Emily off of the cruise ship. And I wouldn't exactly call that a vacation. You're due and I'm excited for you—for all of you girls. You all work so hard."

Claire scooped up Finn and twirled with him in her arms. He squealed and giggled and Janie decided that her mom's speech had made her feel better. And in that moment she felt sure a weekend getaway was exactly what she needed. Tomorrow was the last day of school for Gareth and Reagan. The last day was always easy and Reagan would have a great time enjoying his science expo win. Gareth would be happy simply because it was the start of summer vacation. Her mom could pick the boys up from school and the fun would commence for all of them.

GARETH SHOULD HAVE predicted that Harmon would come for Reagan sooner rather than later. Their mom had left that morning so Grandma would be picking them up from school. Gareth had told Reagan to meet him in the locker room so he could get everything out of his gym locker, including the basketball he kept there.

Harmon and Riley came through the door as Gareth was stuffing the basketball in his duffel bag. Uncharacteristically, Harmon didn't say a word. He looked at Riley. Riley turned and shoved a broomstick through the handles on the doors so they couldn't be opened.

Gareth knew in that moment that he was going

to have to fight them both, and it wouldn't be pretty. And because of the "investigation" Harmon's dad had started, his punishment would probably be so much worse.

Reagan stared straight ahead, not making eye contact. Gareth could see his little brother shutting down and felt a blast of disappointment course through him. Gareth tried to put aside his dismay and mentally prepare himself for battle.

"So, we're going to do some eating today, *Little* Everett. Because I warned you. I told you—you would regret it if you came to the science expo and showed off like you do. But you didn't listen, did you? That five hundred dollars should be mine and you're going to give it to me. But first…"

Harmon took something out of his pocket. He peeled open a foil-wrapped bundle to reveal what appeared to be a wad of gray, red and purplish slimed-over fur. It looked like a chewed-up mouse. It smelled dead and rotten. Gareth nearly gagged.

"My dog puked this up yesterday. I thought it would be the perfect thing for you to take a bite of, Mr. Brainiac Show-off."

Gareth made a face. He knew Harmon was crazy, but this seemed over-the-top even for him. "You're sick, Vetcher. Come on, Reagan, let's go."

Suddenly Harmon's hand shot out and grabbed

Reagan by the back of the head, holding him tight by his hair. Harmon kicked his legs and Reagan went down on his knees.

"Let him go, Vetcher, you sick freak."

Harmon yanked on Reagan's hair. "Open your mouth, you wimpy little nerd."

Red-hot anger burst into flames inside of Gareth and he suddenly didn't care if he ended up in jail or wherever, because he was going to stop Harmon once and for all. He knew Riley would be on him as soon as he moved, so he was going to have to be fast.

But before he could even execute a move, Reagan somehow escaped and was standing in front of Harmon bouncing on the balls of his feet like Aidan had showed them.

"You little worm, that hurt." Harmon rubbed one arm before attempting to grab Reagan again.

Reagan sidestepped to his left. "Let us go, Harmon."

Harmon charged but Reagan easily dodged him again and repeated, "Let us go, Harmon."

"Not a chance, maggot." Harmon rushed Reagan, swinging a wild right-handed punch.

Reagan stepped inside and punched Harmon hard in the jaw. Harmon stumbled back a few steps and muttered, "What the h— I'm going to mess you up now, Everett."

Harmon came at Reagan again, and Reagan

punched him—three times, fast, a jab to the cheek followed by an uppercut to the jaw, and then a blow to Harmon's gut. And that was it. Harmon let out a wheeze and fell to his knees. He tried to suck in a breath and Gareth knew Reagan had hit him square in the solar plexus, exactly like Aidan had taught them.

"Are we done here, Harmon? Are you finished?" Reagan's voice sounded eerily calm and Gareth would be scared himself if Reagan wasn't his brother. Riley looked terrified.

Harmon brought one foot up under his knee like he was going to lunge at Reagan. "You are dead meat—you know that?"

Reagan shook his head. "Nope. No, I'm not. You're not going to touch me and from now on you're going to leave me alone. In fact, you're never going to touch or speak to me, or Gareth, or Elena ever again. You got that? Now, you better repeat it so I know you understand."

"You little psycho. You can't tell me—"

As Harmon lunged, Reagan punched him again, the blow landing solidly on his jaw. Harmon slumped sideways on his heels, losing his balance and grazing his forehead on the corner of the cement wall beside him as he went down.

"I can tell you whatever I want and the difference between you and me is that I can and will back it up. Now, say it."

Harmon pushed himself to a sitting position and leaned back against the wall. Blood leaked from a cut above his eye where he'd hit his head.

"You've got three seconds to say it, Harmon."

Harmon turned his head and spit. "Say what?"

"Tell me you understand."

"I don't—"

Reagan stepped forward, bringing his fists up again in his perfect flyweight stance. Gareth almost laughed, a combination of pride and relief and happiness coursing through him.

Harmon flinched, tripping over the words as he tried to get them out. "No, no. Fine, fine, I got it. I will leave you alone—and Gareth and Elena."

Reagan nodded once before turning to Riley. "Are you next, Shriver, or do you want to open those doors for us?"

CHAPTER TWENTY

On Saturday at approximately seven in the morning, Aidan was getting his equipment together for a day in the field. Aidan had enjoyed his visit with Kyle Wesley, although he was relieved he and his group had departed. Aidan couldn't imagine being surrounded by that many people all the time. He'd had enough of socializing to last him a while. Blake thought things had gone well and Meredith seemed satisfied with Aidan's participation.

This morning, he'd planned breakfast with Bering, Gareth and Reagan at the Cozy Caribou, and afterward they were all going out to look for bees. Bering had taken the weekend off to watch Violet so Emily, Janie, Shay and the rest of the bachelorette party could spend the weekend at the spa. Claire was taking Violet swimming so Bering offered to show Aidan a couple high meadows that had recently come into bloom with wildflowers.

Aidan picked up some clothing that Blake had left scattered around the place and threw the items on top of his suitcase, which lay open in one corner. He'd only been here a week but had already left his mark. As soon as Wesley had departed, he and Meredith had headed to Glacier City to do an interview via satellite. Aidan had to admit that Meredith seemed to be earning her paycheck.

Aidan hadn't been surprised when Blake had called to let him know they had decided to stay the weekend in Glacier City and return to Rankins on Sunday.

A knock sounded at the door and Aidan assumed it would be Bering. He opened the door and was surprised to find two police officers standing in front of him. Aidan recognized the ruddy-skinned, beefy face of Marv Vetcher and immediately felt defensive.

The other cop had reddish-brown hair, freckles and eyes that were an arrestingly pale shade of blue. He asked, "Dr. Aidan Hollings?"

"Yes."

"I'm Officer Adams and this is Officer Vetcher. We're from the Rankins Police Department. Can we come in for a few minutes?"

"No, sorry, I'm on my way out."

"We have some questions for you, Dr. Hollings."

"Can I ask what about?"

Vetcher crossed his arms confidently over his

chest and widened his stance, like he was trying to take up as much space as possible. Aidan assumed it was his attempt at intimidation.

Adams said, "We're here about the Gareth Everett case."

Aidan thought, *Case?* And the complex mechanism that was his brain began to hum.

"We've got a search warrant, Dr. Hollings. We'd, uh, like to come in and search your place here."

"A search warrant? On what grounds? What are you looking for?"

"We're not at liberty to say but I can tell you that Gareth Everett was seen running out of here last week—on the same day he went truant from school. Anything you'd like to tell us about that?"

Vetcher raised his brows like he already knew what they'd find.

An electronic buzz emanated from somewhere on Officer Adams's uniform. He plucked a phone off of his belt and glanced at the screen. He held up a finger as he stepped away to take the call.

Vetcher took a step closer to Aidan and lowered his voice. "I know what you did to my son."

"What?"

"I know that you're responsible for my son getting beat up yesterday, the last day of school. Harmon told me about how the Everett boys cornered him and Riley in the locker room. I know you've been teaching those boys some kind of ninja moves or something. And he used those moves on my son."

Aidan felt a level of pride and satisfaction that he'd never quite felt before. The boys hadn't told him. Aidan barely managed to keep the smile off of his face, but that became easier as Vetcher began to speak again.

"You aren't going to get away with this, Hollings. And neither are those Everett boys. I'm going to teach you all a lesson. As a matter of fact, I suspect that older boy may have been in the throes of a drug-induced rage. What else could he have had in his locker the other day that he needed to take off with and hide? That would also explain how he overpowered my boy and Riley Shriver. And that got me wondering where he may have gotten those drugs. I have it on good authority that you flew here directly from South America, and everyone knows that's the drug capital of the world."

Was this guy serious? His ignorance would be amusing if he wasn't so utterly and disturbingly sincere.

"I'M NOT HAVING my nails painted blue. It will look as if my fingers were slammed in the windowsill."

Saturday afternoon and Janie had already had a hot stone massage, a European facial with a papaya enzyme and a long soak in the mineral hot springs. She was positive she'd never experienced a weekend as relaxing as this one was shaping up to be. She'd slept for nine hours straight the night before on a bed she was pretty sure had been constructed out of angel feathers and unicorn fur. She was hoping for a repeat performance tonight.

Hannah giggled. "But, Janie, the blue will match your dress and pop when you're getting your groove on tonight."

Janie gazed up at her through her lashes. "My groove?"

"Yeah, you know." Hannah snapped her fingers and busted out some kind of impossible-looking dance move. Janie was impressed, but there wasn't much that involved athletic ability that Hannah wasn't good at; she used to be a professional skier.

Hannah turned toward her cousin and younger sisters and asked, "What do you think, you guys? The blue, right?"

Their cousin Adele had joined them for the weekend's events. They hadn't even known Adele existed until she'd come to Rankins the year before and revealed herself to be the long-lost daughter of their Uncle Eli. Emily had also surprised them all by flying in Shay and Hannah's youngest sisters, Hazel and Iris, for the weekend. Hazel, Iris and their brother Seth were triplets and the youngest siblings in that branch of the family.

Hazel said, "Blue."

Iris agreed.

Adele shook her head. "Sorry, guys, I agree with Janie. I like the pink. Have to admit though, given I've spent my life waiting tables, conservative nails are a part of my job."

Janie grinned at Adele, and then shrugged a shoulder at her younger cousins. "Sorry, girls, wisdom wins out on this one." She smiled at the nail technician. "I will take this lovely shade of pink."

"Good choice—very safe."

"Aka boring," Hannah said out the side of her mouth.

Janie thought about the fashionable and exotic-looking Meredith. Meredith—Aidan's ex. Young, hip, fashionable Meredith who probably wouldn't be caught dead wearing pink nail polish…

Well, that was too bad—Janie wasn't about to change who she was for anybody.

AIDAN HAD THE presence of mind to ask for an attorney. A quick call to Jonah and the lawyer informed him that under no circumstances should he allow the police inside. Jonah asked to speak with Officer Adams. Officer Adams moved away and spoke briefly into the phone, before walking back and handing it to Aidan again.

He put the phone to his ear. "Jonah? What's going on?"

"I'm not sure. This is weird. Unfortunately, Aidan, they have a search warrant—you have to let them in. But stall until I get there so I can take a look at it. I'll be there in about two minutes, I'm getting in my car right now."

Jonah lived in town with his grandfather, Caleb, in a large home on the waterfront, which also housed the law office of Cedar & Cedar that they shared.

"I appreciate this, Jonah. I don't have anything to hide."

Aidan glanced up and met Marv Vetcher's smug glare.

He listened as Jonah continued to do some stalling himself, reassuring Aidan that he'd help him however he could and instructed him not to say anything further to the police.

"Got it, but, Jonah, is there any way I can request that a certain officer not be involved in the search?"

JANIE SILENTLY VOWED that she would never again criticize Piper's nosiness or her penchant for gossip. And even if that wasn't possible, she would forever be grateful for her in this specific case.

The women were eating breakfast on Sunday morning before they met Tag at the little town of Mariana's airport for the return flight to Rankins.

Hannah looked up from her phone. "Janie, did you know that Gareth got into a fight with Harmon Vetcher?"

Janie lowered the bite of crab-and-cheese omelet she'd been about to shovel into her mouth. "What?"

"Yeah, Piper texted me that on Friday—the last day of school, Gareth apparently got into a fight with Harmon? Reagan and Riley Shriver were there, too. Piper knows because Harmon's dad has been spreading the story around town. The grapevine in Rankins is working overtime."

Janie tried to process this information. They would have already departed for this weekend trip when all of this went down. Neither Gareth nor Reagan had mentioned the incident when she'd spoken to them on the phone this weekend. Her mom hadn't said anything, which probably meant that the boys hadn't told her, either. She wondered if Aidan knew.

Hannah's phone chimed again. "Piper says that Marv Vetcher wants to file assault charges."

Assault? Janie tipped her head down and placed

a hand across her forehead. This was exactly the kind of thing she had been afraid of. That Aidan's problem solving would cause more problems. *Trust me,* Aidan had said. *I know what I'm doing...* He'd promised her that she wouldn't regret this.

The bottom line was that Gareth had hurt someone and he could be in very serious trouble. And it was all Aidan's fault. No, it wasn't all Aidan's fault. She had put her stamp of approval on the boxing lessons. Janie felt a surge of anger and disappointment and tried to keep the feelings directed mainly at herself, but she couldn't help but cast some blame at Aidan, too.

But she should have known better than to put the fate of her children in someone else's hands. She never should have let any of that deceptively harmless, heartbreakingly dangerous...*we* seep into her life. She'd let go and her worst fears had come true.

Shay reached over and patted her hand. "I'll call Jonah. Janie, I'm sure nothing will come of it. Marv Vetcher is a jerk and he's raising that kid of his to be the same. If Gareth did something to him there's no doubt in my mind that he deserved it."

"IT'S NOT MINE." Aidan shook his head. "Jonah, seriously it's not mine."

Aidan sat across from Jonah in the Rankins

police station. His jail cell looked like something from an old Western movie; thick iron bars with a lock secured by an oversize metal key and a green army cot in the corner. There were exactly two cells and, thankfully, Officer Adams, who seemed like a decent human being, had put the drunk driver who had been arrested the evening before in the neighboring cell. At least Aidan had only had to listen to the guy snoring all night.

"I believe you, Aidan. I do. But I stayed with Vetcher every second of the search. If he planted the stuff, he didn't do it yesterday."

Aidan tried to think the situation through.

"I don't even want to say this, but do you think it's possible that it could be Gareth's?"

Aidan didn't want to believe it was Gareth's. He didn't believe it was Gareth's. The only thing that Aidan could think of was that somehow Vetcher had broken in and put the small plastic bag of heroin in his place.

"How long before you can get me out of here?"

"Gramps is trying to get ahold of Judge Bingley. No one seems to know where he is and he refuses to carry a cell phone. But we're working on it, Aidan. Hang in there."

BY THE TIME they touched down in Rankins Janie's imagination was working overtime. Because in spite of the fact that Harmon probably did deserve whatever Gareth had dished out, his actions had landed him in trouble with the police—more trouble. How difficult could Marv Vetcher make this situation? The truancy episode hadn't even been resolved yet. And here she'd been so happy about the improvement she'd seen in Gareth…

Bering met them at the tiny airport. Janie didn't find it odd that her brother would show up to greet his wife—until he walked straight to her instead.

"Janie, I don't know how to say this, so I'm just going to—Aidan is in jail and the police are looking for Gareth."

"What do you mean 'looking for Gareth?'"

"Gareth is missing."

CHAPTER TWENTY-ONE

THERE'S SOMETHING ABOUT motherhood that brings out the superhero in women, because how else could Janie have managed to hold it together? Her thirteen-year-old son was missing and the police wanted to question her eleven-year-old. Gareth had allegedly assaulted another boy using the skills that Aidan had taught him, and now Aidan—the man that she had entrusted her boys with for untold hours over the last two months—was in jail on drug charges.

But...drugs? That was ridiculous. Aidan didn't do drugs. She just...knew it. Then again, she didn't think Gareth could possibly be doing drugs, either. But why else would he have disappeared? He had hidden the letters to his dad in Aidan's place, but it appeared that maybe he had hidden more than letters.

Janie didn't want to believe it, yet she didn't want to be that mother who refused to see what was right in front of her face. Aidan had pointed out the existence of *that* unfortunate trait already, and she'd received the message loud and clear. Or she thought she had…

Officially, the police wanted to question Gareth because Marv Vetcher claimed that Gareth had assaulted Harmon. Riley Shriver and Reagan were both supposed to have witnessed the incident, but neither of them had been questioned yet. Jonah knew the police would wait until Janie returned to Rankins to approach Reagan because he was underage. And, according to Jonah, Marv had also alluded to the possibility that the drugs belonged to Gareth.

Her first priority was to find Gareth.

She sat at her mom's kitchen table with Bering while they made a list of possible places he could be. Tag was already out searching with a couple of his paramedic buddies.

"All of my cabins have guests in them right now, but he could be out at the cabin on the bluff." That was the cabin Bering reserved for his personal use, and for the use of his family.

"It feels too obvious." Janie drummed her fingers on the oak tabletop.

Bering ran an impatient hand over his jaw. "That's what I'm thinking, too. The problem, which is also a blessing, with Gareth is that he already knows so much about wilderness survival. If he took off into the bush…" His voice trailed off, and then he looked Janie squarely in the eye. "Janie, it could conceivably be a while before we find him."

"Bering, don't say things like that." Emily had been busy putting together some food for Bering and Janie so they could head out to search.

But Janie had already thought of that. "No, he's right, Emily. We can't underestimate Gareth—he might not have Reagan's IQ, but when it comes to surviving in the outdoors he takes after his Uncle Bering."

Emily asked, "Have you asked Reagan? He's so honest, maybe—"

"Which is exactly why Gareth wouldn't tell him," Janie said.

"Cricket has already volunteered his plane if we need it to search. And if we don't find Gareth by tomorrow I think we should send him and Tag both up in the air."

Janie agreed.

Bering's phone chimed. He picked it up and read the text. "That's Jonah. Aidan is out of jail. They are going to start searching some of the places where the boys have been out bee hunting with Aidan."

JONAH DROVE AIDAN to his place so he could change his clothes and collect a few supplies. He desperately wanted a shower after his time spent in jail, trying not to wonder about the smelly mattress and the stained green blanket he'd had to use. But he knew he couldn't spare the time.

He wanted to see Janie—to try and explain, to apologize. But he knew that she would only be focused on finding Gareth right now, and so was he.

Blake walked in while he was stuffing items in his pack. His face twisted with confusion as he looked around. "What the hell happened in here? It looks like I've been living here by myself for the last two months."

"The police searched the place."

"The police? What for?"

"Drugs."

"Drugs?"

"Yep, I just got out of jail, where I spent the night incarcerated on suspicion of drug possession."

Blake's jaw dropped and his eyes went wide. "Uh-oh..."

Aidan stared at Blake. "Blake?"

"Aidan, oh, man, I am so sorry. I have papers for the opium. Duke O'Neil gave me a sample to show you to see if you could perform a source identification. He's having a hard time with this batch—he's thinking maybe the drug producers are trying to throw the authorities off by adding other markers. Anyway, I can't believe I forgot to give it to you." Blake walked over and retrieved a duffel bag that lay on its side on the floor. He scrounged around and pulled out an envelope. "Here's the paperwork."

Aidan quickly explained to Jonah that he'd done volunteer work in the past for an antidrug organization that analyzed seized drugs in order to identify which region the drug had come from. The information could be helpful to law enforcement in determining the chain of delivery.

Blake handed the envelope to Jonah. Jonah perused the paperwork, his face slowly blooming with a grin. "I can't wait to see the look on Vetcher's face."

"Why isn't the sample in an official package?"

Blake winced. "My fault—I was in a hurry. Duke had just received the sample, but he wanted to keep part of it to match against another, so I split it up and didn't take the time…" He shrugged a shoulder. "It's such a small amount, I figured if I got questioned the paperwork would be enough."

Aidan agreed with Jonah that it would indeed be sweet to tell Vetcher his drug charges were bogus. But that raised another question. The drugs didn't belong to Gareth, so why had he taken off? And why had Vetcher wanted to search his place if he hadn't known the drugs would be there?

HER MOM HAD last seen Gareth early Sunday morning, she told Janie. She'd made the kids a breakfast of pancakes and sausages. Gareth had eaten with his usual astounding teenager's appetite. Soon after, the police had shown up asking to speak to Gareth. Claire had immediately phoned Jonah, who had told her not to let them in or to allow them to see Gareth.

After the police departed, she'd explained the situation to Gareth, and Claire related that he'd taken the news well and hadn't seemed overly upset. Of course, she was beating herself up for that assumption now. She should have known better than to try and guess at Gareth's emotional state. When she'd finished getting the twins dressed, Claire had sought out Gareth and Reagan to go over their plans for the day.

She hadn't been able to find Gareth and immediately asked Reagan if he knew where Gareth had gone. Reagan hadn't known nor had he seen him leave. Claire had waited awhile, thinking he would show up, but soon accepted the fact that Gareth had left.

At that point Claire had called Bering.

Right now, Janie forced herself to think like Gareth. Her mom's house was only a half mile from her own. If he was running from something that he felt was extremely serious, Bering was right to think that his instincts would propel him to take off into the wilderness. His biggest problem would be transportation. Janie figured Gareth would head for home to get some supplies first—especially since he knew no one was there. Janie would be willing to bet that when they got there his bike would be gone. And then he'd...

"Bering, did you check and see if any of your ATVs are missing? Or even a boat? My guess would be he'd take off on a four-wheeler—that would give him more options."

"Yeah, I checked. That was one of the first things I did when Mom called this morning. Then Emily and I loaded up Violet and came straight here, but..." Bering looked thoughtful for a moment before emitting a groan of frustration. He tapped his fist on the table. "He was probably at our place already watching and waiting for us to leave."

"Exactly," Janie said. She stood and moved into the kitchen. She took a travel mug out of her mom's cupboard and filled it with coffee. She turned back toward Bering. "Let's go."

GARETH STEERED THE four-wheeler down the trail toward the river. By now his absence would have been noticed. Grandma would be worried, and probably Uncle Bering and Emily. He wasn't sure what time his mom was due back but hopefully not before he finished. He would be done with this part of his mission soon.

He was fine with taking the rap for "assaulting" Harmon. He was already in trouble anyway, but there was no way Marv Vetcher was going to get ahold of his letters.

AIDAN DIDN'T REACH the same conclusion as Janie. He had a different perspective of the two boys. He'd witnessed their camaraderie, their brotherly bickering and their love for one another on a different level. Aidan went straight to Reagan, who was now safely ensconced at his house with his grandmother and little brothers. He asked Claire if he could speak to Reagan and she readily agreed.

Aidan found him sitting on his bed in his and Gareth's bedroom, a notebook open in front of him. Aidan decided his best approach with Reagan would be the most direct one.

"So, Reagan, what do you think? Where would Gareth go?"

Reagan glanced down and Aidan could tell he was battling over how to answer the question.

"Hey, I get that you don't want to betray your brother. But we can't help him unless we find him."

Reagan met his eyes but remained silent.

Aidan changed his tactic. "Were you there when Gareth beat up Harmon?"

Something flickered in Reagan's eyes. "What do you mean?"

"Reagan, I don't know what you've been told, but Gareth isn't only in trouble for leaving school and possibly having drugs. The police also want to question him about assaulting Harmon."

Reagan gaped at Aidan. "But Gareth didn't touch him!"

Aidan knew what Reagan was going to say even before the words came out of his mouth.

"I did. Just like you taught us, Aidan. It was awesome. And I didn't start it, either—also like you told us. I waited for him to touch me first. Harmon cornered us in the locker room. He grabbed me by my hair and was going to make me eat dog vomit."

Reagan relayed the entire story. Aidan listened and the relief he felt caused beads of sweat to break out on his forehead. Of course he'd hoped that Reagan wouldn't have to use the skills he'd taught him, but he was perfectly okay that he had. Because the most important result was that the balance of power had finally shifted.

"I'm so proud of you, Reagan. Why didn't you guys tell me?"

"Gareth thought it would be better if we didn't

drag you into it. We felt pretty certain that Harmon wouldn't say anything because he got beat up."

Aidan told Reagan about Marv's story.

Reagan smiled. "He told his dad it was Gareth, because he was embarrassed to say it was me."

Aidan agreed this was probably the case. "We need to find Gareth, Reagan. We need to clear all this up. Do you want to help me?"

"Yes, and I want to talk to the police. Gareth doesn't need to protect me anymore."

Aidan could not imagine feeling more pride for another human being than he did in that moment. A knot of emotion gathered in his chest. He reached out to grip Reagan's shoulder and Reagan launched himself into Aidan's arms.

Aidan held him tight as Regan said, "Thank you, Aidan. Thank you for everything."

After a moment, Reagan pulled away and reached over to pick up a framed photo from the nightstand. He turned the frame so Aidan could see the photo of the boys with their dad. They were sitting together on top of a huge rock that jutted up out of a river smiling for the camera.

"This was our favorite spot. We loved to ride four-wheelers to this place. Captain's Rock— that's what we named it."

"It looks like a beautiful place, Reagan."

Reagan grinned. "It is, but that's not why I'm telling you, Aidan. This is the place where we spread our dad's ashes. Gareth took the letters and this is where he went. I know it."

JANIE AND BERING found Gareth's bicycle behind an outbuilding on Bering's property as Janie had predicted they would. A quick check revealed that one of Bering's four-wheelers was missing. The tracks led toward the mountains, but once he hit the ATV path that Bering and his guides used to access some of the wilderness areas, the tracks would mingle with the countless others already there. Two of Bering's guides had used the trail that day, so discerning which direction he'd gone would be difficult.

Janie tried desperately to keep her panic at bay. She stood facing the vast expanse of forest and wild country that abutted Bering's property and realized that she'd never felt so small and insignificant in her entire life.

She couldn't seem to stifle the sob welling within her as she looked at her brother. "He could literally be anywhere. Bering, what are we going to do?"

"THIS WOULD BE faster on four-wheelers," Reagan explained as he instructed Aidan to slow down to make an upcoming turn. "But this will get us there. We'll have to hike to the river from the road and it's steep and brushy."

Aidan pulled the pickup over and he and Reagan climbed out. He grabbed his day pack, checked to make sure he had water, bear spray and an EpiPen. Reagan slipped his own pack onto his shoulders.

There didn't appear to Aidan to be much of a trail, but Reagan took off through the brush like he knew exactly where he was headed. Not for the first time he marveled at the intelligence, resilience and self-sufficiency these boys possessed. He reassured himself that Gareth was using all of these traits now.

GARETH WAS SITTING on a tall rock that jutted from the edge of the riverbank. A sense of urgency had overtaken him when he'd found out the police wanted to talk to him about Harmon in addition to his taking off from school, and now drugs had been found in Aidan's place? Marv Vetcher had probably put them there. He was crazy and there was no way Gareth would allow him to see these letters. They were his private words to his dad and if that meant he would be in extra trouble for destruction of evidence or whatever—fine. He'd take it.

He'd also gladly take the heat for Reagan drilling his stupid son, too, but not before he told everyone what Harmon had tried to do first.

Gareth had finished burning the last letter and

sat thinking about his dad when his eye caught movement emerging from the brush. His first thought was a moose, but another flash of brown fur and a yearling grizzly cub emerged from the brush. Adrenaline shot through his bloodstream and his pulse began to pound because he knew the mom couldn't be far away.

He looked around, thinking quickly, like his dad and Uncle Bering had always taught him. He was a good fifteen feet above the ground and maybe forty yards away from the bear, although he knew his perch offered no protection from a grizzly. They were crazy fast and could jump and do incredible stuff. He glanced behind him, judging the distance to his ATV—at least twenty yards. And by the time he got there, started it up… It was no good; he knew the grizzly could be on him before he even reached the four-wheeler. He was going to have to be as still as possible and hope they moved on.

The huge sow emerged from the brush with her nose tilted high in the air. Gareth's heart nearly stopped as he realized the extent of his danger. Gareth wasn't sure how much time passed, he was barely breathing. His legs were falling asleep now and his toes hurt from crouching for so long on the rock. Thank goodness the breeze was in his favor, but if she kept coming this way…

That's when he heard the sound of voices over his shoulder. He turned his head very slowly, saw his brother and Aidan emerge onto the four-wheeler trail. Brush and the rock prevented them from seeing the bear—and vice versa. Except the bear heard, or smelled, them first, and she stood on her hind legs.

The sow dropped and charged like a brown lightning bolt in Reagan and Aidan's direction. Gareth had no choice. He jumped to his feet and screamed, "Bear, Reagan, bear!" He threw his backpack at the bear and she slowed her charge for a millisecond, before changing her direction to the most immediate threat—Gareth and his rock.

His canister of bear spray was ready and his last thought before his perch somehow flew out from under his feet and the world went black was that his dad would be proud because he'd saved his little brother.

AIDAN HAD KNOWN terror in his life. An angry baboon was terrifying. Fire ants were horrifying and the pain from the sting of a jellyfish had scared him so badly he'd thought he was going to die. But the sight of the bear charging full-tilt toward him and Reagan on the riverbank made all of his previous wildlife encounters seem like child's play.

His bear spray was at the ready in his hand. He popped the safety valve off the top, all the while moving around Reagan so the child would be positioned behind him. Suddenly the bear shifted directions and charged toward the large rock where Gareth stood.

As Aidan shouted and sprinted toward Gareth his brain registered the cloud of mist erupting from the rock. Suddenly the bear seemed to catapult backward. After somersaulting a few times, she came to rest on her feet and shook like a giant dog. She growled and pawed at her face, flopping her head one way and then the other. Her cub watched, pacing nervously. She finally moved rapidly away into the brush, the cub following.

Aidan realized that Gareth must have sprayed the bear. The relief he felt was almost overwhelming, until he noticed that Gareth was nowhere to be seen.

"Gareth?" Aidan yelled.

"He fell off the rock," Reagan said. "He was spraying the bear when his feet somehow slipped out from under him." Reagan ran around him toward the rock and Aidan followed.

They found Gareth crumpled on the ground at the base of the rock. Blood oozed from a small cut on the side of his head, where a large lump was forming. He was conscious—barely.

"Gareth, you're going to be fine, buddy. Stay with us, okay?"

Reagan grabbed his hand. "Gareth, you kicked that bear's butt. She's gone and we'll get you out of here."

Aidan debated about what to do. He knew you weren't supposed to move trauma victims but he also knew it could be a long time before help arrived. He handed his phone to Reagan before scooping Gareth up in his arms. "As soon as we have a signal, call your mom and tell her to meet us at the hospital."

CHAPTER TWENTY-TWO

JANIE HELD HER breath all the way to the hospital—or at least it seemed like that. Bering parked and without speaking they exited his pickup and ran to the emergency room door. They walked quickly down the hall until they saw Aidan standing near the nurses' station.

He hurried toward them. "Janie, he's going to be fine. The doctor says it's a mild concussion. Nothing broken."

Janie was profoundly grateful. She reached out a hand, placing it on the wall beside her. "Where is he?"

Aidan pointed at the adjacent door.

Janie rushed in and found Gareth propped up in bed with a white bandage on his forehead. Reagan sat in a chair by his side. They were both smiling.

"Hi, Mom," Gareth said.

So many words, so many thoughts, flashed through her brain, but Janie found that she couldn't speak even one of them. She stood silently and let her eyes take in the precious scene of her two oldest boys—whole and strong and mostly healthy. She cupped a hand over her mouth as hot tears clouded her eyes.

Then she walked over and hugged them both.

THEY KEPT GARETH overnight for observation. Janie insisted on staying with him even though he informed her that it wasn't necessary. The next morning Claire picked them up and drove them home, where she learned the whole story of the fight from Gareth and Reagan. Reagan had been the one to punch Harmon, but clearly he had been defending himself.

Officer Adams paid them a visit later that day to question Gareth and Reagan about the "assault." He spoke to Janie privately and revealed that he had also questioned Riley Shriver; he had corroborated Gareth and Reagan's account of the events. Officer Adams was troubled by the details of Harmon's bullying and told Janie he was going to recommend counseling for Harmon—and speak to his commanding officer about doing so for Marv as well. Officer Adams didn't seem intimidated by Marv Vetcher in the least and Janie felt a renewed confidence in Rankins's police force.

Janie had learned from Shay the night before that the drug matter had been cleared up as well. There would be no charges against Aidan and the specimen had been returned to Blake. Aidan still planned to do an analysis. She was so grateful to Jonah for advocating on her boys' behalf, in addition to helping Aidan.

Aidan. Janie could only imagine what he was thinking. She hadn't seen him yet, aside from the brief exchange in the hallway outside Gareth's room the night before. Janie was afraid he'd finally had enough of them all…

Later that afternoon while the twins were napping Janie peeked in their room to find Gareth, Reagan, MacGyver and Crosby all asleep on their bedroom floor. The tender sight warmed her heart and she considered joining them, when she heard a soft knock on the front door.

She found Meredith on her porch, a file folder in her hands and what looked like a laptop case slung over one shoulder.

"Janie, hi, can I come in?"

"Yes, of course." So much had happened recently that Janie had nearly forgotten her prior visit last week. Had it only been a few days?

Janie led her toward the living room.

"Mmm, smells good in here. Cinnamon?"

"And nutmeg. I just took an oatmeal cake out of the oven. Can I get you a slice?"

Meredith smiled. "Thanks, maybe in a minute."

They sat on the sofa and Janie waited politely for Meredith to get to the point.

"Before I show you what I've been working on, I want to say that you seem like such a nice person. Aidan deserves to have someone like you."

"Meredith, Aidan and I aren't—"

Meredith interrupted her with a grin. "Yes, you are. Or you will be." She pointed at Janie's knitting basket. "Is that an ugly Christmas sweater you're working on?"

It was. Janie had started it for Aidan. The pattern featured flowers and a bee wearing a Santa hat. Janie adored it already and no matter what happened between her and Aidan she planned to send it to him—wherever he happened to be when she finished it. But how would Meredith know about her ugly sweaters?

Meredith opened her laptop and fired it up. "Do you think you could do one with a Chiweenie on it?"

"I'm sorry—a ch-what?"

Meredith fiddled with her phone and then handed it to Janie. The screen held a photo of an adorable brown dog. "A Chiweenie—this is my Chihuahua-dachshund mix, Bellini. I'd love to place the first special order."

Meredith turned her laptop screen toward Janie.

The top of the screen read Jane E. Knits & Designs. Above that in smaller letters the following words stretched across the screen: knits, ugly sweaters, designs, order, special orders, about me, faq.

Meredith clicked on the knits icon. A photo of Meredith wearing one of her sweaters popped onto the screen. There were also photos of baby Violet and the twins, Gareth, Reagan, Shay, Jonah, Emily, Bering and even Blake—all wearing garments that she'd made.

"Meredith, what is this?"

"It's your website. Aidan had me do it. Now, keep in mind there was only so much I could do without your knowledge and approval. So, this can all be changed. But you get the gist of it, right?"

Janie stared at the screen. "No one is going to buy this stuff. They can make their own and besides…these prices—no way."

"Ah, that's where you're wrong. I don't want to make my own, Janie, but I want one. And this is the price I'd be willing to pay. Trust me, this is part of my job. I did my research."

"How did you get the stuff?"

"Aidan did that part."

Janie peered closely at the photos and recognized some items as those that Emily had put up for sale at the tourism office. There were also garments that she had made over the years that she kept in the closet in her sewing room. Her mom must have given them to Aidan.

Janie stared in disbelief. "People are buying these?"

Meredith grinned and clicked on something else on her computer. She pointed. "This is what has sold..." She clicked on something else. "And these are all the inquiries you've received about special orders."

Meredith turned toward her and said, "Janie, I know you probably don't want to hear this from me and I don't blame you. But I do want you to know that I didn't come here hoping to win Aidan back. He's not right for me and vice versa, and we're not... I'm in love with Blake, but the big oaf won't even notice me.

"One thing I have learned from my mistakes is that happiness in life is about doing what you love. I'm sure you enjoy your job at the *Rankins Press*, but you do it because it pays the bills, right? Whereas you love knitting. That's obvious. And I'm guessing it's never occurred to you that you could make a living with your passion. But it occurred to Aidan and he's done his best to help you make it a reality. Now, all you have to do is what you do best—knit."

A current of excitement ran through her even as she wondered if it was really possible. She didn't know anything about business or websites. She said so.

"I've agreed to hang out in town for a bit longer, to help you if you want help. I can stay as long as it takes. I do need to be back in New York in a couple of weeks before the premiere of *Seeds*, but other than that I can work from here."

Janie's eyes darted around. "Um, I need to..."

Meredith tipped her head toward the door. "Go. Babies are...sleeping?"

"Yes, actually, my entire family is sleeping. We had a busy weekend. But if they wake up before I get back, don't worry because Gareth and Reagan can hold down the fort."

AIDAN WASN'T HOME. Why was it, Janie wondered, that in the movies people were always where they were supposed to be when someone went to find them, but not so much in real life?

Janie stood outside Aidan's building and tried to guess where he might be. She was staring down at her cell phone trying to decide whether to call him when Blake appeared at her side.

"Janie, hi, are you looking for Aidan?"

"Blake...yes, I am."

"He's playing basketball at the community center."

"Thank you." She turned to go.

"Hey, Janie."

She spun back around.

"I wanted to thank you."

She shook her head. "For what?"

"For getting Aidan to do the interview, for talking him into going to the premiere—he's agreed to take a more active role in promotion and he told me that it's because of you."

"Blake—"

"I wish he would have fallen in love years ago—it's greatly improved his personality." He topped that comment off with one of his belly laughs.

Janie didn't know what to say. Aidan hadn't shared this decision with her, but then again, they hadn't had a chance to talk, either.

In love with her? Blake couldn't be right about that…could he? At this point she was just hoping Aidan would forgive her.

She took note of Blake's mischievous grin, which reminded her an awful lot of Meredith's. She wouldn't even be standing here looking for Aidan if it wasn't for Meredith.

"Um, Blake? Do you… The Faraway Inn has an amazing seafood buffet."

"Yeah, I've heard about it. I'll have to check it out before I leave."

"The owner happens to be my best friend. I could get you the best table. Maybe you should see if Meredith would like to join you for dinner?"

Janie watched as his lips curled up into a grin. "You think so?"

"I know so. Saturday six thirty work for you?"

"Um, yeah."

"Well, you better call and confirm with Meredith before she makes other plans. I have it on good authority that several men in town are intent on asking her out."

Janie witnessed the scowl transform his brow as he removed the phone from his pocket. She didn't stick around to see how the conversation went.

Janie could see the basketball game breaking up as she pulled into the parking lot of the community center. She got out of her car before she lost her nerve even though she had no idea what to say... She headed toward the court. Aidan met her gaze, holding a basketball under one arm as he came to meet her.

He stopped in front of her, looking troubled and sweaty and gorgeous. "Hey," he said. "How is Gareth?" And sweet...

"Good. He's going to be fine. Aidan, I just ran in to Blake and he said you are going to the premiere?"

He nodded. "I am. I figured if I preach about taking risks and facing fears head-on to your eleven- and thirteen-year-olds I should at least put it to practice in my own life. Your boys have been great role models for me."

She smiled.

"Janie, I'm so sorry. You were right. You've been right all along. I do need to learn to mind my own business and quit trying to fix things. None of this mess you had to go through with Gareth and Reagan would have happened if I hadn't gotten so involved in your life. You asked me to stay out and I didn't listen."

Janie stared at the man who had turned her life upside down at the exact time she had needed it to be upended—and then proceeded to make it right again in so many ways. The man she had fallen in love with despite her best intentions to guard her heart. And now he was apologizing to her and she didn't know whether to laugh or cry.

"I really thought I was doing the right thing."

"Aidan, no. I'm not right. You shouldn't be apologizing to me for saving us."

"What are you talking about?"

"I'm talking about you teaching my boys how to help themselves. About you giving them confidence and courage and showing them the meaning of bravery. I came here to apologize to you."

"To me?"

Janie gestured around her at nothing and everything at the same time. "Aidan, it is true that none of that stuff would have happened if it weren't for you. But do you realize that since you arrived in Rankins you've had a lacerated hand and a near-deadly bee sting, you've been thrown in jail, harassed by the police and nearly attacked by a bear? And all of this caused, in varying degrees, by me and my boys?"

Aidan flashed her a quick grin before his brows dipped down in consternation. "I wanted every one of those experiences, Janie. I like… adventure. I like taking risks. But that's the problem—I can see that now. I mean, I understand the dangers, but I do weigh the pros and cons differently than most people… I'm not doing a good job of explaining this.

"But I realize now that when other people are involved I need to be more…thoughtful. I'm trying to do that now—at least to undo some of the things I've put in motion."

"Then you're not going to be too happy about the fact that Meredith paid me a visit."

Aidan let out a groan as he glanced skyward. "I told her to scrap that whole plan."

"I'm so glad she didn't listen. I didn't even know how much I wanted that, Aidan, until I saw the website. But you did. You knew…"

His face brightened. "You like it?"

"Aidan, it's my dream. But I didn't even realize it was my dream until I saw it right in front of me. You may stick your nose into my business uninvited, but clearly my business needs your nose."

"What are you saying?"

She repeated his words back to him with a teasing smile on her lips. "I'm saying that never taking risks isn't living."

"Janie—"

"Aidan, seriously—hiding and hoping things will change all the while telling myself things are fine doesn't get me anywhere. In fact, as difficult as it is to admit, I think the boys and I have been slowly heading backward. I see that now. Everything you've done for my boys—for me— has made our lives so much better. Have things gotten a little messy in the process? Yes, but it's been a wonderful adventure and a learning experience and the end result is so very worth it. That old saying might be true that sometimes things have to get worse before they get better."

Aidan closed his eyes for several long seconds. "Janie, I don't know. I don't think it would be fair for you to have to put up with my reckless behavior…"

"Reckless?" She repeated the word with a laugh. "Being proactive isn't reckless. You're courageous and strong and I love that. Does it scare me a little? Yes, but I need that in my life. We—the boys and I—need that in our life."

She could see him waffling so she reached out and batted the ball out of his hands. She bounced it a couple times. "I tell you what—I'll play you for it."

"For what?"

"For a date."

"A date?"

"Yep, we have to start somewhere, right? If I win I'd like a date. If you win, you can ask me for whatever you want."

Aidan's mouth tilted up at one corner. "Whatever I want?"

"Within reason, obviously, I'm not a genie in a bottle."

He nodded. "Okay, what are we going to play?"

"How about bee?"

"Bee?"

"Yeah, you know how people play 'horse'? We'll play 'bee.'" Janie referred to the childhood game where the object was to make baskets that the opposing player would most likely miss, earning a letter for each basket. Turns were taken, the winner declared when he or she had successfully spelled out the entire word.

"Janie, I'm not sure this is fair. You can't…"

"What? Beat you?"

"Well, basketball is kinda my thing."

She grinned, and then lied. "I know. I've seen

you play. But honestly, Aidan, you're not as good as you think you are."

He tipped his head and eyed her speculatively and Janie imagined he was trying to work out what she was up to. But she also knew he couldn't resist a challenge.

Finally he shrugged and moved toward the court. "We'll see about that. Let's do this. You go first."

Aidan might have the fancy moves, but Janie had years of playing scrap-ball with her brother, her cousins and her boys. She planned to use all of her best tricks.

After warming up and practicing a few shots, she stood well past the free-throw line and turned her back to the basket. She held the ball with one hand and stood on one foot. "You ready?"

"I'm ready."

"Watch closely because you have to do everything I do or the shot doesn't count."

"I might know how to play this game, Janie."

"Just warning you…" She shot the ball over her right shoulder and could tell by the sound that she'd made the basket.

"Yes-ss," she hissed.

Aidan narrowed his eyes at her. "Impressive."

"Thank you." Janie jogged over and retrieved the ball. She tossed it to him. "Your turn."

Aidan positioned himself exactly like Janie had been. He held the ball in one hand.

Aidan stared deliberately at her as he took his shot. Janie found herself holding a breath as the ball arced toward the basket and...missed.

Janie let out a happy yelp. "That's a big fat *B* for me."

Her next shot was a complicated layup. Aidan matched her step for step and easily made the shot.

On her next turn Janie took it up a notch. She stepped to the three-point line and shot one-handed. She missed.

Aidan shot a triumphant smirk in her direction. "My turn."

Aidan stood off to one side of the basket, bounced the ball three times, then pivoted off his left foot and executed a graceful hook shot.

"Is that the best you've got?" Janie remarked. She took her position and made the basket.

Aidan grinned. And on it went until, after seven more shots, they were solidly tied with *B-E*.

It was Aidan's turn.

"Let's see here," he said as he spun the ball on the finger of one hand. He switched it to the other side, dribbled the ball between his legs and behind his back.

Janie rolled her eyes and said in her best unimpressed teenager tone, "Whatever."

But then he stopped and stepped slowly to the free-throw line. His face transformed with a serious expression. He met her eyes and held them as he shot the ball. It dropped through the net with a quiet swish.

Janie felt her heart soar because she knew he was giving her the opportunity to win the game, which meant he wanted a date. But that wasn't what she wanted—not exactly. And, she decided, now was as good a time as any to start taking some of her own risks.

She stepped up to the line, kept her eyes on his and shot the ball well to the left of the basket, purposely missing the shot. She grinned at him as the ball rolled off the court.

"Well, that spells *bee* for you—you win. Good game, though, right? I told you I had some moves."

"You certainly did—and do." His voice sounded flat but something about his tone and his stance made her pulse pound fast and hard.

"I beat you, but I know you lost on purpose. That isn't fair because *I* was going to lose on purpose."

"I guess you should have been a little more clever about it then, huh?"

"Apparently."

She tried to sound brave. "So, what do you want to ask from me? Anything you want."

"Mmm… Anything I want, huh?" His voice held an unmistakable challenge and Janie found herself holding a breath. "In that case…" He took a few steps toward her. "I want you—" he came even closer "—to come to the premier of *Seeds* with me. I will be so much less nervous if you are by my side—"

"Aidan, of course—" she interrupted, beaming brightly at him.

"I'm not finished. You really need to learn to let people finish their thoughts," he said, grinning.

"Oh, sorry." She pinched her lips together dramatically.

"For the rest of my life. I love you, Janie. I love you and I love your boys. Will you marry me?"

Joy, she thought, such a tiny word for such a huge emotion.

"I love you, too. But is that all you want from me? Because these requests are way too easy. After all, you just won a hard-fought game of bee here…"

His smile widened. "That's true. I did." He took a step toward her and Janie's excitement soared. "I wouldn't mind a few more kids."

Her heart seemed to skip a beat. "Aidan, yes, I would love to go to your film premiere, and marry you, and have more children. But…are you sure you want to do this? It's quite a risk and I can't guarantee your safety."

He tipped his head so his lips were nearly touching hers. "According to my calculations this is a case where the reward is most definitely worth the risk."

* * * * *

LARGER-PRINT BOOKS!

**GET 2 FREE
LARGER-PRINT NOVELS
PLUS 2 FREE
MYSTERY GIFTS**

Love Inspired®

Larger-print novels are now available...

YES! Please send me 2 FREE LARGER-PRINT Love Inspired® novels and my 2 FREE mystery gifts (gifts are worth about $10). After receiving them, if I don't wish to receive any more books, I can return the shipping statement marked "cancel." If I don't cancel, I will receive 6 brand-new novels every month and be billed just $5.49 per book in the U.S. or $5.99 per book in Canada. That's a savings of at least 19% off the cover price. It's quite a bargain! Shipping and handling is just 50¢ per book in the U.S. and 75¢ per book in Canada.* I understand that accepting the 2 free books and gifts places me under no obligation to buy anything. I can always return a shipment and cancel at any time. Even if I never buy another book, the two free books and gifts are mine to keep forever.

122/322 IDN GH6D

Name   (PLEASE PRINT)

Address   Apt. #

City   State/Prov.   Zip/Postal Code

Signature (if under 18, a parent or guardian must sign)

Mail to the **Reader Service:**
IN U.S.A.: P.O. Box 1867, Buffalo, NY 14240-1867
IN CANADA: P.O. Box 609, Fort Erie, Ontario L2A 5X3

**Are you a current subscriber to Love Inspired® books
and want to receive the larger-print edition?
Call 1-800-873-8635 or visit www.ReaderService.com.**

* Terms and prices subject to change without notice. Prices do not include applicable taxes. Sales tax applicable in N.Y. Canadian residents will be charged applicable taxes. Offer not valid in Quebec. This offer is limited to one order per household. Not valid to current subscribers to Love Inspired Larger-Print books. All orders subject to credit approval. Credit or debit balances in a customer's account(s) may be offset by any other outstanding balance owed by or to the customer. Please allow 4 to 6 weeks for delivery. Offer available while quantities last.

Your Privacy—The Reader Service is committed to protecting your privacy. Our Privacy Policy is available online at www.ReaderService.com or upon request from the Reader Service.

We make a portion of our mailing list available to reputable third parties that offer products we believe may interest you. If you prefer that we not exchange your name with third parties, or if you wish to clarify or modify your communication preferences, please visit us at www.ReaderService.com/consumerschoice or write to us at Reader Service Preference Service, P.O. Box 9062, Buffalo, NY 14240-9062. Include your complete name and address.

LARGER-PRINT BOOKS!

GET 2 FREE LARGER-PRINT NOVELS PLUS 2 FREE MYSTERY GIFTS

Love Inspired®
SUSPENSE
RIVETING INSPIRATIONAL ROMANCE

Larger-print novels are now available...

YES! Please send me 2 FREE LARGER-PRINT Love Inspired® Suspense novels and my 2 FREE mystery gifts (gifts are worth about $10). After receiving them, if I don't wish to receive any more books, I can return the shipping statement marked "cancel." If I don't cancel, I will receive 4 brand-new novels every month and be billed just $5.49 per book in the U.S. or $5.99 per book in Canada. That's a savings of at least 19% off the cover price. It's quite a bargain! Shipping and handling is just 50¢ per book in the U.S. and 75¢ per book in Canada.* I understand that accepting the 2 free books and gifts places me under no obligation to buy anything. I can always return a shipment and cancel at any time. Even if I never buy another book, the two free books and gifts are mine to keep forever.

110/310 IDN GH6P

Name	(PLEASE PRINT)
Address	Apt. #
City	State/Prov.	Zip/Postal Code

Signature (if under 18, a parent or guardian must sign)

Mail to the **Reader Service:**
IN U.S.A.: P.O. Box 1867, Buffalo, NY 14240-1867
IN CANADA: P.O. Box 609, Fort Erie, Ontario L2A 5X3

Are you a current subscriber to Love Inspired® Suspense books and want to receive the larger-print edition?
Call 1-800-873-8635 or visit www.ReaderService.com.

* Terms and prices subject to change without notice. Prices do not include applicable taxes. Sales tax applicable in N.Y. Canadian residents will be charged applicable taxes. Offer not valid in Quebec. This offer is limited to one order per household. Not valid for current subscribers to Love Inspired Suspense larger-print books. All orders subject to credit approval. Credit or debit balances in a customer's account(s) may be offset by any other outstanding balance owed by or to the customer. Please allow 4 to 6 weeks for delivery. Offer available while quantities last.

Your Privacy—The Reader Service is committed to protecting your privacy. Our Privacy Policy is available online at www.ReaderService.com or upon request from the Reader Service.

We make a portion of our mailing list available to reputable third parties that offer products we believe may interest you. If you prefer that we not exchange your name with third parties, or if you wish to clarify or modify your communication preferences, please visit us at www.ReaderService.com/consumerchoice or write to us at Reader Service Preference Service, P.O. Box 9062, Buffalo, NY 14240-9062. Include your complete name and address.

LISLP15

YES! Please send me **The Montana Mavericks Collection** in Larger Print. This collection begins with 3 FREE books and 2 FREE gifts (gifts valued at approx. $20.00 retail) in the first shipment, along with the other first 4 books from the collection! If I do not cancel, I will receive 8 monthly shipments until I have the entire 51-book Montana Mavericks collection. I will receive 2 or 3 FREE books in each shipment and I will pay just $4.99 US/ $5.89 CDN for each of the other four books in each shipment, plus $2.99 for shipping and handling per shipment.*If I decide to keep the entire collection, I'll have paid for only 32 books, because 19 books are FREE! I understand that accepting the 3 free books and gifts places me under no obligation to buy anything. I can always return a shipment and cancel at any time. My free books and gifts are mine to keep no matter what I decide.

263 HCN 2404   463 HCN 2404

Name _____ (PLEASE PRINT)

Address _____ Apt. # _____

City _____ State/Prov. _____ Zip/Postal Code _____

Signature (if under 18, a parent or guardian must sign)

Mail to the **Reader Service**:

IN U.S.A.: P.O. Box 1867, Buffalo, NY 14240-1867
IN CANADA: P.O. Box 609, Fort Erie, Ontario L2A 5X3

* Terms and prices subject to change without notice. Prices do not include applicable taxes. Sales tax applicable in N.Y. Canadian residents will be charged applicable taxes. This offer is limited to one order per household. All orders subject to approval. Credit or debit balances in a customer's account(s) may be offset by any other outstanding balance owed by or to the customer. Please allow 4 to 6 weeks for delivery. Offer available while quantities last. Offer not available to Quebec residents.

Your Privacy—The Reader Service is committed to protecting your privacy. Our Privacy Policy is available online at www.ReaderService.com or upon request from the Reader Service.

We make a portion of our mailing list available to reputable third parties that offer products we believe may interest you. If you prefer that we not exchange your name with third parties, or if you wish to clarify or modify your communication preferences, please visit us at www.ReaderService.com/consumerschoice or write to us at Reader Service Preference Service, P.O. Box 9062, Buffalo, NY 14269. Include your complete name and address.

MMLPBPA15

READERSERVICE.COM

Manage your account online!

- Review your order history
- Manage your payments
- Update your address

We've designed the Reader Service website just for you.

Enjoy all the features!

- Discover new series available to you, and read excerpts from any series.
- Respond to mailings and special monthly offers.
- Connect with favorite authors at the blog.
- Browse the Bonus Bucks catalog and online-only exculsives.
- Share your feedback.

Visit us at:
ReaderService.com

RS15